REDEMPTION

THE REVELATION SERIES

BOOK THREE

RANDI COOLEY WILSON

Published by Secret Garden Productions, LLC
First Edition edited by Kris Kendall at Final-Edits
Second Edition edited by Liz Ferry
Cover Design by Bravebird Publishing
Cover Photo by ©Melkor3D
Book Formatting by Indie Formatting Services – Jeff Senter

Redemption (The Revelation Series, Book 3)/ Randi Cooley Wilson
Printed in the United States of America
Second Edition January 2016
ISBN-13: 978-1499156942
ISBN-10: 1499156944

ALSO BY RANDI COOLEY WILSON

THE REVELATION SERIES

REVELATION

RESTRAINT

REDEMPTION

REVOLUTION

RESTORATION

THE ROYAL PROTECTOR ACADEMY

VERNAL

AEQUUS

NOX

For Sara,

*Because true love does exist, and when you
find it, it will move your soul like nothing else.
Thank you for all your love and support,
always.*

"So hand in hand they passed, the loveliest pair that ever since in love's embraces met— Adam, the goodliest man of men since born his sons; the fairest of her daughters Eve."

—John Milton, Paradise Lost

1 Left Behind

On the morning the darkness first descended, it settled into every fiber of my existence. Emptiness materialized deep within my veins, wrapping itself around each organ, starting with my heart, then my lungs, and finally, it crept its way into my soul.

The vacant days are consumed by loneliness, and the nights by endless grief. Darkness pushes me further and further into desolation. I feel as though I'm treading water, and at any moment, my body will just give up, forcing me to sink into the murky river.

I'm drowning, because in spite of everything, I still belong to Asher. Each and every heartbeat is his. Every single one of my breaths is for him. Though I'm the one who was left behind, I know in the deepest corners of my heart that my protector is hurting too.

Sitting on the window bench in my room, I inhale a shaky breath while using the back of my hands to wipe away the escaped tears. *Crap. I didn't think I had any left to shed.*

As my fingers brush over the surface of my cheeks, I'm reminded of the lifelessness my skin now suffers from, due to the strain in our blood bond. It used to be filled with heat and desire. Now, it's cold and unfeeling, enveloped in an invisible armor, preventing life and warmth from penetrating it.

My gaze lifts to the dreary clouds, my only connection to my gargoyle. Large hazel eyes reflect back at me in the windowpane. Mocking me. Filled with sorrow. Without thought, I rub my chest, trying to relieve the emptiness his absence has caused. I keep my focus trained upward, toward the heavens.

"I miss you, Ash," I whisper into the empty room, and remind myself of the last word he said to me before disappearing into the rain-filled sky: "*Forever.*"

The rest of my sentinels—the London clan, his family— found me sitting on the wet grass, in the cold rain, soaked and weeping. My body was rocking back and forth in an attempt to comfort itself, while my mind slipped into a catatonic state. The only sound that fell from my lips was his name, spoken softly, over and over again.

Every day, I go over in great detail the last moments we shared on the rocky cliff. I attempt to discover a clue or inkling of something, anything, I could have said or done that would have changed his mind. Made him stay with me. I could have fought for us. The energy wasted, I always come up empty-handed. My eyes close and I inhale while memories flood me, then float away, a daily occurrence.

"I've got you, Eves. You're safe. We're all here, cutie." Callan's voice was the first I heard before Asher's younger brother lifted me into his protective arms.

His words weren't comforting. He was mistaken. They weren't all there. Asher was gone. Vanished into the inky heavens.

"Where the fuck is he?" Keegan's angry tone cut through the downpour.

"I don't know," Abby answered.

Her expression filled with worry as her gaze locked onto mine. I stopped repeating his name long enough to utter that he'd left.

Following Asher's disappearance, he reached out to Michael with instructions for the clan. The only piece of their conversation the archangel would share with me was that Asher was safe and under the watchful eyes of the council. Then he informed me I would be returning to Massachusetts the next day, under the protection of the London clan.

That was all.

No, *I'm sorry.* Or, *I'll see you soon.* Michael said nothing to indicate my dark prince would return.

I squeeze my eyes tighter as the words Lord Falk, leader of the Royal Gargoyle Council of Protectors, said drift through me. *"Mr. St. Michael, it has been brought to the council's attention that you are in violation of our laws. You have been accused of having infringed upon the oath you swore to uphold with regard to your loyalty to both the human race and your charge, Eve Collins. What say you?"*

3

The accusation was thrown out during the tribunal held at Domus Gurgulio Castle in County Kerry, Ireland.

After Asher made it clear the ruling body didn't have any solid evidence to support the charge, the council, of which he's a member, decreed he is no longer appointed my protector while they continue to investigate the allegation of misconduct.

Due to lack of evidence, they weren't formally able to charge him with violating his protector oath, a sentence that carries a punishment of eternal stone petrifaction. For that, I'm grateful. Knowing he's somewhere breathing in the world eases the pain, a little.

I glance over at my bed with longing. It would be so easy to crawl back into it like those first few days. After removing me from the rainstorm, the clan brought me back to their home in Wiltshire, England.

They placed me, fully clothed, in a warm bath and tried to coax me into eating and talking. I refused. Instead, I walked into Asher's room, grabbed the *Property of London* shirt he liked me to sleep in, changed into it, and curled up in the fetal position in the middle of his bed.

Surrounded by his scent of smoky wood and leather.

My anguish was overwhelming. I cried myself to sleep for days, never moving. What was the point? I felt empty inside. I spoke to no one. Failed attempts were made to get me out of bed, dressed, eating, and conversing.

McKenna, in a rare show of sympathy, stepped in and explained to the clan that I needed time and space to deal with the stress my separation from Asher was causing the blood bond.

Two days later, she stormed into the room with her mate, Keegan, the eldest St. Michael. At her orders, the handsome warrior snatched me out of bed and carried me into the shower while turning on the cold water. I shrieked in pain as the little prickles of water hit my skin, causing me to squirm in Keegan's drenched, powerful arms.

Once McKenna was satisfied I was clean and awake, she wrapped us each in a towel before Keegan brought me back into the room and gently placed my shivering body on the floor. Without words, he took his leave.

The beautiful blonde warrior just stood there with her hands on her perfect hips. Sapphire eyes watched my every breath. A few moments later, her cousin Abby walked in with fresh clothes and a plate of food.

Damn gargoyles ambushed me.

"I'm not going to let you do this to yourself. You're stronger than this, blood of Eden. Get your fucking ass in gear and pull yourself out of this shithole you're creating," McKenna spat at me with her lack of tact.

I ignored the harsh statement. It's typical McKenna.

Both gargoyles got me dressed and sat next to me on the floor in Asher's bedroom. McKenna threatened that I wasn't allowed to return to his scent-filled bed until I ate something.

Following an hour-long standoff, I did. Pleased with their successful efforts, they continued this torment every day. Either Keegan or Callan, Abby's mate, would grab me out of bed and douse me in cold water while the girls force-fed and dressed me.

After three weeks of depression, I'd had enough of their antics and feeling sorry for myself. McKenna was right. I needed to pull myself out of the shithole. Knowing I had about an hour before I was forced into an icy shower, I got up on my own, showered with warm water, dressed, and made my way downstairs to the kitchen.

When I entered, the London clan was eating breakfast with Fiona, the shape-shifting panther and manor's caretaker. I rolled my eyes at the strange sight.

Fiona always reminded me of Mrs. Potts from *Beauty and the Beast*. The short, plump shifter nervously fiddled with her gray hair, placing the loose strands back into her bun, while throwing me a maternal glance.

No one said anything. They all watched me with cautious and stunned expressions as I grabbed a coffee mug and scone, then sat down with them. Without a word, I nibbled on the pastry. Fiona ended her gaping and shuffled over to pour me some coffee. I managed to mutter a thank you. Once they decided I was mentally stable, everyone returned back to the table conversation.

Pleased with my presence, Keegan announced we were leaving that afternoon for Massachusetts. And we did. A few hours later, we boarded their private jet before arriving at La Gargouille Manor. The estate I've grown to love is located just outside the Kingsley College area, where I'm currently sitting, in my old room.

I inhale the rain-filled spring air floating in from the open window. My suite overlooks the wooded area behind the house. Unconsciously, my right hand moves to my neck, searching out the necklace Asher gave me. My fingertips brush over the delicate feather lying on its side.

The darkness creeps back in.

I choke back the sudden feeling of absolute despair. The memory of when Asher gave it to me hits me hard. At the image of him, my heart clenches. It's been so long since I've seen his indigo eyes, striking face, and sexy stubble-dusted jawline. I squeeze my eyes shut, holding onto the vision before it fades.

"It's beautiful, Asher." I breathe out.

"I asked your aunt to make it especially for you. It's an angel's wing, a symbol to remind you of the divine presence in your life. May I?" he asks. I nod as he brings the necklace around my neck, securing the clasp.

"I love it. Thank you." I turn to face Asher. "But I don't need a necklace to remind me that I have a divine presence in my life. I have you."

As the memory fades, emptiness fills me again. My eyes open with the painful reminder he's gone. Anger and frustration begin to build and run through my veins like poison. He left me behind. My hand tightens around the silver chain and I yank it hard. As the clasp breaks, the delicate piece of jewelry falls lifelessly in my hand.

I hate looking at it. All the trinket does is remind me of broken promises. I lift my arm to throw it out the window, but a smooth, seductive, masculine voice hits me in the gut, like a punch. His unexpected presence knocks the wind out of me.

My body refuses to turn toward him. It's rooted to the spot where I'm sitting, almost as if I'm being held down by a thousand weights. My heart rate picks up at the sound of his voice, and his familiar scent assaults me. *Shit.*

"Are you sure you want to toss away something that means so much to you?" the gargoyle queries from over my right shoulder.

My hand clasps the necklace in a tight clench. *Crap.* He's right. I detest him for being correct, but he is. *Damn him.* I allow my anger to boil so that when I do finally face him, I can release it.

The striking being I know so well moves to sit next to me on the bench. After a quiet moment, he shifts his eyes to the window's view. My breath hitches while I take in his facial features. *God, he's so good-looking.*

"What are you doing here?" I ask, my tone lined with loathing and resentment.

He turns to face me, bestowing a sexy smile while a set of beautiful eyes lock onto mine.

"It's nice to see they didn't have to sedate you on the plane after all," he chuckles quietly.

A short, strangled laugh escapes my throat. It's a foreign sound. "Seriously, why are you here?" I ask with a lackadaisical attitude.

The attractive gargoyle adjusts his body toward me.

"I'm your new protector, love," Gage answers, holding my gaze.

I study him for a moment, shocked, allowing his statement to sink in. "According to whom?" I release in an angry snarl.

Gage's lips tilt in a half smirk. "The Royal Gargoyle Council of Protectors, the Angelic Council, and the London clan," he responds without hesitation.

My eyes turn into slits as I stare into his sea-green gaze.

"That makes absolutely no sense. Who would be dumb enough to appoint you as my protector?" I seethe.

Gage hesitates for a moment before shifting his focus back to the window. "Asher."

8

My heart lurches and my stomach drops at the sound of his name. "This is some sort of sick joke," I whisper, choking on the words.

"Asher requested me during his tribunal. It was his condition following the council's ruling. I can assure you, it's not a joke, love," the good-looking bad boy explains, with nothing but honesty on his face.

I search my mind, trying to remember. Then, like a bad dream, I recall the exchange.

Gage observes me as realization dawns. I lift my gaze to his and exhale in an unfriendly manner. *Holy hell.*

I scoff. "I'm supposed to believe that all of a sudden, you've had a change of heart? Now you're protecting me from Deacon, Lucifer, and the dark army? Those whom weeks ago you were planning to hand me over to as a form of debt payment?"

The golden blond-haired man watches me, amused.

"There's no reason for you not to, daughter of Heaven. I took the oath and all." Gage pauses before continuing in a sensual tone. "Although, you shouldn't expect the same kind of *special treatment* that Asher gave you, love. That is, unless you want our relationship to be that way," he mocks, and I control my urge to smack the beautiful right off of him.

"Oh my God! Are we bonded?" I panic, worried that I'm no longer connected to Asher.

His face falls. "No. You and the dark prince are already blood bonded. With your bloodline, a second protector connection can't be linked."

I start chewing the inside of my cheek and clasp my necklace tighter. My mind goes into overdrive in an attempt to grasp what he's saying, and what all this means for my future.

Gage's large hand closes over the one I have gripping my last lifeline to Asher. "Relax, love. The St. Michaels are still your full-time protective clan. They don't trust me either." He smiles as if he's pleased about that. "I'll just be your main guard. You'll continue to live here, train with them, and be protected by all of us."

I stand abruptly, pulling myself out of Gage's reach.

"This is insane. I don't want you."

Gage stands calmly in response to my overreaction.

"This is your new reality, love. You might as well get used to it. I suggest you get a good night's sleep. I'll be here in the morning to collect you for classes. Spring break is over. It's time you get back to your life."

I watch Gage, watching me. After a moment, I have a completely irrational meltdown. Followed by an outrageous response. I grab my daggers from their sheaths and point the tips to his heart, while my eyes hold his angrily.

Gage doesn't flinch. He just stands there, unaffected, as my heart beats wildly, trying to process everything.

"Fuck," I draw out, fuming, and lower my weapons.

"Thank you for not stabbing me, love," he quips.

"CALLAN!" I shout and turn to run out of my room and down the stairs. "CALLAN!"

In an instant, both Callan and Keegan are at my side, their eyes glowing, weapons drawn, and black wings out. They're ready to fight off whatever danger I'm in as they scan me for injuries.

"What's wrong, Eve?" Keegan asks with a controlled concern all over his warrior face.

Both brothers are staring at me like I've lost my mind. Which, no doubt, I have. Before I can respond, Callan snaps his gaze behind me. At the sight of Gage, who followed me at a leisurely pace, the laid-back gargoyle stands straighter and pulls me behind him in a protective stance.

"What the hell are you doing, Gage?" Callan questions heatedly, lowering his weapon.

Gage shrugs in a bored manner. "She needed to know."

"We agreed to tell her together."

Callan and Keegan retract their wings.

I shift my focus between Keegan's and Callan's backs.

"It's true?" My voice is raw.

Callan sighs. "Yeah, cutie, it is." His tone is solemn as he turns to face me.

My annoyance level rises to an all-new high, and fury boils in my veins. I think I've moved on from the depression stage of grief to the anger. I need something or someone to take it out on. Gage is looking like a really good target at the moment.

I move from behind Callan so quickly that, for a moment, I think I might have picked up supernatural gargoyle speed from Asher.

"I thought you didn't pick sides, Gage?" I spit out with venom.

He stays calm, not taking the bait. "I don't, love. I'm free to do what I like. This," he points between him and me, "I like." *What the hell?*

"And when the higher bid comes from Deacon, to hand me over, what will you like then? Which side will you be on in that moment?" I challenge.

Gage shrugs. "It won't come to that." He holds my eye contact, nonverbally asking me to trust him. I don't. My world keeps getting turned upside down and I'm sick of it.

In response, I huff like an irate child and storm off. *Irrational? Maybe. In my defense, my mindset isn't exactly clear at the moment. I'm highly emotional.*

Once I'm outside the room, I stop and lean against the wall. Willing myself to calm down, I listen to them talking in low, intense voices.

"Why is it, again, you agreed to do this?" Callan asks Gage with disdain.

"I didn't have a choice. The prince of the gargoyle race appointed me with the council's blessing," Gage states matter-of-factly.

Keegan grunts. "A royal decree, blessed by the council, never obligated you before."

"It did this time. You forget I'm the only one who knows what it's like to lose a mate. She's angry with the dark prince for leaving. Her emotional state is fragile. When the bond is stressed from that kind of loss, it makes someone a bit . . . mentally unstable. I'm the only one of us capable of helping her through that volatility," Gage offers. His reply is lined with insouciance.

"They weren't fully mated and Asher didn't die." Keegan's tone is harsh.

"A bond stress and a bond break mentally and emotionally wounds the same," Gage replies coolly.

He would know since he lost his human mate, Camilla, to death at his father's hands.

A few moments later, a warm sweater is draped around my shoulders. I turn to see Abby standing next to me, offering a sad smile. Her beautiful long red locks set off her concerned crystal-blue eyes, which at the moment bore into me.

"His love for you is immeasurable. I swear to you he'll be back," she says.

My grunt forces her to lean in further.

"Gage is temporary. Asher is forever," she assures me.

All I can do is offer her a blank expression.

The tears won't even come anymore.

Now, like Asher, they're gone too.

2 New Protector

Exhausted after my training session, I return to my room and notice my necklace sitting on the bed, fixed. It's lying next to a handwritten note from Gage informing me he'll see me in the morning. I exhale roughly. Deep down, I'm grateful to him for taking the broken pieces and putting it back together. He's right. I really do love it.

I pick up the delicate piece of jewelry and run my fingers over it before returning it to my neck. At its placement, the ache in my chest builds again. I push the dejection down. Trying to fight it off is becoming a chore.

I'm drained from the darkness that constantly creeps up on me. It's making me weary and bad-tempered all the time. After showering, I shoot off a quick text to my Aunt

Elizabeth, confirming I'll see her next weekend, and plop down onto my bed.

Grabbing my laptop and textbooks, I decide to get organized since I'll be formally returning to my classes tomorrow after a two-month bereavement leave of absence.

I flinch at the sting caused by the memories of Aria's death. The vision of Deacon's sword going through her abdomen while she tried to protect me won't fade.

The pain is still raw.

My eyelids become heavy while reading my syllabuses. I close them for just a brief moment, relaxing before I slip into a deep sleep.

For the first time in weeks, my body is warm as two large hands cup either side of my face. The pad of a thumb traces my bottom lip. I must be dreaming because I would know the feel of him anywhere.

A muscular and familiar body presses me down into the mattress and I sigh in contentment. Every place I come into contact with him, my body hums with energy, igniting me.

"Open your eyes, siren." Asher's deep, masculine tone penetrates my dream state.

I want to comply with his request, but I'm afraid this is only a dream. At some point, I'll wake up and the darkness will return. Instead, I keep them closed, comforted by the sound of his voice.

"I'm here. Open those beautiful eyes and look at me, yeah?" he commands, using a seductive tenor.

My eyelids flutter open and lock onto an indigo gaze positioned above me. Watching me with a cautious intensity, my protector bites his lip in apprehension.

"Asher?" My voice is soft and unsure.

It's been so long since I've felt him.

"Are you expecting someone else, siren?" he teases, but his voice is tense.

Without hesitation, I jerk up and propel myself at him. The force triggers him to lean back on his heels as I climb onto his lap and cling to him like my life depends on it.

After a brief moment of surprise, his entire body relaxes and strong arms wrap around me, drawing me against him tightly. Relieved at my response, he rests his face in the crook of my neck, inhaling.

"Oh. My. God. Asher." I exhale an unsteady breath, basking in the comfort of his arms.

Asher groans against my neck and I feel his lips pull into his signature sexy smirk.

"It's so fucking hot when you say that." At the release of his favorite response, his breath tickles my skin and sets off a serious case of goosebumps.

It's in this moment that I know he's real, and my emotions spiral out of control. Tears I thought no longer existed escape my eyes, flowing freely down my cheeks.

"I thought I would never see you again," I choke out in a sob, and squeeze him harder.

After holding me for a minute, he leans his head back and lifts his hands to my face, brushing away the tears.

"I will always come for you," Asher vows, looking into my water-filled eyes.

I clutch him, afraid he'll disappear. "You left." I force the words out of my tight throat.

Asher holds my head in a firm grip while stroking my cheeks with his thumbs.

"I swore I would come back when I could," he reminds me in a gentle tone.

"I can't do this without you," I whisper, my hands fisting his white T-shirt.

Asher's face falls with pain as his forehead meets mine.

"I need you to be strong." His voice cracks with emotion. This separation is difficult for him too.

"Without you, the dark seeps in," I reply, panicked.

Asher takes my chin and lifts my head so he can study my gaze. "I promised you that when the skies turned black, I would reach you. I know you're miserable. Believe me. I feel it too. I risked coming to you tonight because I gave you my word that I would pull you from the darkness and always bring you home, yeah?"

"I remember," I speak softly, holding him tighter. Scared that at any minute, I'll wake up and he'll be gone.

"You're home. I made sure the clan brought you here, and on my honor, when I can, I'll push the darkness away forever. In the meantime, you have to trust me. I once told you that you're stronger than I thought you'd be. It's true. You have to reach inside and pull that girl out until I can return to you, and fuck . . . by the grace, siren, I will come back," he states firmly.

My eyes slide to the Celtic cross tattoo on his forearm, then back to his face. His masculine scent fills me, setting off all my senses.

"When?" I ask, my voice getting stronger now.

"As soon as the council clears me, you're my first destination. I'm protecting you the best way I know how to at the moment." Asher pleads for understanding with his eyes.

I nod at his promise, then close my eyes and accept his words. He's protecting me. When I reopen them, an intense gaze locks onto mine and his irises begin to glow with desire.

In one breath, Asher's mouth crashes to mine. The contact ignites a fire in my soul. Every stroke of his lips recharges me, putting all the broken pieces back together. The need I've been pushing aside for weeks rises to the surface, clawing to be released. His hands move to the back of my neck, forcing me closer.

I cling to him. My hands dig into his chest, tugging him to me. Asher discharges a deep, raw sound that vibrates through me and penetrates the nothingness that had taken hold of me.

With each tremor, the emptiness abandons its grasp, making me his again. Branding me.

Our kiss becomes harder and more demanding, and I whimper across his lips. Asher takes advantage of the opening and our tongues reunite in a feverish dance.

Warm hands slide down my back and lift my tank top just enough so they can feel the skin on my lower back. I savor the sensation of his caress and his lips against mine.

He pulls away just an inch to gaze into my eyes as we attempt to catch our breaths.

"Fuck. I miss you." He pants out, as my rapid breath fans his face.

"Me too, pretty boy," I say, running my hand along his jawline.

He grimaces. "I have to go, but I'll see you soon."

I move my head up and down slowly. "I love you."

My hands fist his shirt one last time.

"Forever." Asher plants one last gentle kiss on my lips.

I close my eyes, realizing this is our last moment together for a while, and soak him in.

"Wake up, siren," he orders across my lips with a solemn tone.

At his command, my eyes open with a start, and concentrate on the ceiling in my room.

My textbooks and laptop are in the same position as they were when I fell asleep. The light from the MacBook is the only illumination in the now-dark space.

I exhale and roll my face into my pillow, stifling a moan of disappointment that I'm alone, again. My cheek lands on a wet spot, where apparently, I was drooling on my pillow. *Gross.*

My fingers lift to my swollen lips and pull into a smile. Asher risked a dream walk to visit me. It was real. My body still hums with his energy. I feel lighter and whole again. With a renewed sense of peace, I'm ready to face tomorrow, because I know Asher will come back to me, and when he does, I'm going to kick his ass for sticking me with Gage. *Damn gargoyle protector.*

కొత

I release a heavy sigh at the sound of Gage's classic black Wiesmann Roadster pulling into the driveway. Spring semester at Kingsley College really isn't turning out how I'd envisioned it. Come to think of it, the fall semester wasn't much better.

I groan dramatically into my oatmeal, causing Callan to lift his eyebrows in interest.

"Something on your mind this morning, cutie?" he asks, amused.

I push my bowl forward. "Do I have to go?" My voice comes out as a quiet whine.

Callan tosses his banana peel into the trash and walks over to the kitchen island. Standing across from me, he leans his elbows on the granite so we're at eye level.

"You owe it to yourself to get your life back on track, Eves. I know it's hard, but you're not alone. We're all here for you," he says, his voice lined with affection.

"Not all of you," I whisper, and swallow the painful lump forming in my throat.

"When it's safe, Asher will be back for you." His sincere eyes hold mine.

"I know. But why Gage?" I question, unable to wipe the annoyed scowl from my face.

"That . . . is something I can't answer." Callan pauses reflectively for a moment. "I will tell you this: I know my brother, and I'm aware of how he feels about you and your safety. His reasons, whatever they are, are for your protection. Asher would never do anything that places you in more danger. It's obvious he thought Gage would protect you just as he would, and still is," he reaffirms.

Before I can respond, Gage swaggers in, looking all bad-boy gorgeous. He's wearing his signature black outfit, tailored pants, a V-neck shirt, and designer shoes. An unlit cigarette hangs from his perfect lips. *Crap. Why does my 'new reality' have to be so hot?*

"I went from brooding dark prince to walking sexy cancer stick," I mumble.

Callan laughs quietly and hands me a brown bag.

"What's this, Dad?" I smile, pleased with myself, returning my focus to him.

The guy I've come to think of as an older brother studies me before giving me a megawatt toothy grin. "You seem better this morning. It's nice to see. Welcome back, cutie." He winks and points at the bag. "That is full of baked goodies of the chocolate chip variety. To help you through your first day back."

My face softens at the gesture before my eyes land on his T-shirt. This one reads: *Be A Flirt and Lift Your Shirt.* I release a light laugh at its sentiment.

"Nice shirt," I muse, pointing at the scribble on it.

Callan looks down and returns his focus to me with a bright smirk. "My fans think so."

I scoff. "You have fans?"

"Hey, don't underestimate the power of my charm, cutie," Callan counters.

I hold up my hands in surrender. "Wouldn't dream of it, gargoyle."

"You ready to go, love?" Gage asks from behind me, interrupting our playful banter.

A long breath escapes from my lips. I turn around and face Gage. "As ready as I'll ever be," I reply sarcastically, and pick up my messenger bag.

Callan reaches for my elbow, stopping my movement.

"Eves, just remember the rest of the clan will be around the entire time. Regardless of what Gage says, you will never fully be left alone with him." The warning was stern and meant for Gage, not me.

I give Callan a genuine smile before dropping a chaste kiss on his cheek. "Thanks."

"Anytime, cutie." Callan winks at me before narrowing his eyes toward Gage. "She's to be returned in the same condition she leaves in," he informs, without room for argument.

"All right, temporary protector. Let's go," I say to Gage, before he and Callan get into it.

We walk out side by side to his sports car. Without a glance my way, he immediately walks around to the driver's side and gets in. I hop into the passenger seat, noticing the interior smells like Gage, cigarettes and spice.

"You don't open doors for women anymore?" I ask, since he's usually more chivalrous toward me and the ladies in general.

He shrugs. "I open doors for women who are friends, I'm dating, or sleeping with. You, love, are now an assignment."

"Charming," I mumble under my breath.

Without another word, he starts the car and pulls us away from the manor and towards Kingsley College. Once we're closer to campus, he finally decides to acknowledge me.

"How much longer until you refocus on the ascension?"

The question is fair but pisses me off nonetheless.

"I don't know, Gage. When does the ache of being left by the person you're bonded to end?" I pose, with sarcasm dripping from my lips.

Since we're not 'friends,' what business of his is it?

"It doesn't. You just move it to a different compartment in your heart until it's ready to be felt again," Gage answers with an even tone.

"You would know," I retort, and keep my gaze on the landscape rolling by.

He grunts. "I suppose I deserve that. So go ahead and take your anger out on me because Asher isn't here to absorb it. But just remember, love, your prince will return. Camilla won't."

He falls silent for the remainder of the ride with the exception of his nervous tapping on the steering wheel. *God, I'm an ass lately.*

A few moments later, Gage pulls into the coffee shop near the college. I turn my gaze to him.

"Why are we here?" I blink in confusion.

He smiles. "I need more caffeine and nicotine to deal with your mood swings. I'm guessing you could use a cup too before class."

Opening the driver's side door, he gets out and doesn't wait for me. Once I'm out of the car, my eyes scan the area. The last time I was here was with Asher, I was running from the barghest, a hellhound sent by Lucifer to confirm my existence and protection. I shudder at the memory.

Lost in my own head, I don't hear Gage approach with a lit cigarette hanging from his mouth.

"Café mocha?"

I turn to face him. "What?" I ask as he blows smoke next to my face. *Lovely.*

"Café mocha? It's what you ordered before. Would you like me to get you the same thing?" he questions, sucking in and blowing out the last of his habit.

"Yeah. Thanks," I offer weakly.

He flicks the remains of his nicotine stick in the trash then walks into the coffee shop. Leaving me outside, unprotected. *Awesome.*

"Some sentinel," I mumble under my breath and follow him into the café. "Forget something?" I ask in a light tone, stepping up next to him.

Gage turns and pulls his eyebrows together in contemplation. *Seriously?*

"Did you want whipped cream? I figured last time you didn't order it with, so I didn't this time." His answer is sincere and clueless.

"Um . . ." I'm taken aback. "No. I meant me. Did you forget me? Aren't you supposed to be keeping me safe?" I ask. "You just left me standing in the open, outside."

Gage studies me for a moment. "I don't babysit, love. If you're in danger then I'll help. You're a big girl, Eve, and I understand you have a limited amount of training and knowledge of what you're up against. It's time you spread those wings and fly, daughter of Heaven." His voice suggests he's bored with me. "It's on you to speak up if you need me."

My mouth falls open. *Is he for real?* "So that's it. If something attacks me, you'll come running to my rescue, but other than that, good luck, Eve?" I ask in astonishment.

Gage shrugs. "I'm a gargoyle. Not a nanny. That's Asher's thing with you," he chides.

"Wow, that's . . . new."

Usually the clan is on top of me every minute, with Asher bossing me around all the time. I'm not used to being treated . . . normal.

"Besides," he tilts his head to the front glass door, "Keegan is outside in the parking lot."

I chew on the inside of my cheek. "Oh, right."

The barista calls Gage's name and we pick up our beverages in comfortable silence before heading back to his car.

"Thanks for the coffee."

Gage gives me a seductive smirk. "You're welcome."

After a few minutes, he pulls us into the college lot, then shuts off the engine.

"If you don't want to babysit me, then why did you agree to take me on as an assignment?" I question, curious about his motives.

He shifts in his seat, staring out the window. After a few moments of silence, Gage sighs and puts another cigarette in his mouth. "Asher asked a favor. That's all I'll say about it." He gets out, walks around and sits on the hood to light up.

I follow him and lean against the car, while he blows the smoke between his lips on a large exhale.

"Fair enough. I won't ask anymore."

His glance slides to mine and he nods once in acceptance. "Time to get you to Philosophy 101."

Gage pushes off from the car and starts walking toward the building that houses my class, while I'm left to contemplate how the hell he knows my schedule. Like an obedient puppy, I follow behind.

Asher is incredibly good-looking, with his dark brown hair, blue eyes, perfect stubble-dusted jawline, tall muscular frame, and tattoos. So I'm used to the stares and sighs of appreciation from girls when I walk with him.

That said, nothing could have prepared me for Gage's rock star status. I swear, he melts girls' panties off just by walking past them. We've had to stop at least a dozen times on the way to my class for giggly, airheaded females so they can try to get into his pants.

The entire time, Gage is cool and confident, giving each one his focused attention and panty-dropping smile. No doubt a lot of these girls are going to dream about him tonight.

I roll my eyes internally, and by the fifth stop, I decide just to continue walking to my lecture. He lets me and doesn't follow.

Thank goodness Deacon is nowhere around. Unless that's what Gage wants—for me to trust him so Deacon can swoop in. At the unpleasant thought, my eyes dart around wildly, searching for signs of danger.

"Come on, blood of Eden, we're going to be late." McKenna's hostile voice filters through my thoughts.

I turn in surprise to face her. "Wait, you're in this lecture?"

She smirks. "You didn't think we'd let you hang out with the traitor alone, did you?"

"No. But. You? Philosophy?" I question, knowing how she hates to be challenged or asked questions. And let's be honest, isn't that the entire point of philosophy?

"It's a prerequisite, so let's go," she orders with a harsh tone and a flip of her blonde hair.

"Fine." I retort, and walk into the lecture hall with her in tow.

Randi Cooley Wilson

3 Land of the Leprechauns

Gage never showed up during my class. No surprise there. I'm wondering why he's even bothering at all. Then again, maybe I'm just so used to having Asher around whenever I need him that my relationship with Gage is normal and generally how it's supposed to work.

McKenna, on the other hand, has been breathing down my neck for the last hour. My gut tells me that she isn't going to let Deacon surprise her again, like he did in London. I'm pulled from my reverie when her cell phone goes off.

"Wait here, blood of Eden. If you move, I'll stab you," she demands, answering her cell.

"Wouldn't want that, would we?" I heave a sigh before turning away from her.

My gaze scans the campus, looking for Gage. Instead of the gargoyle, they land on someone watching me from behind the bench that sits under the oak tree. I keep my focus on the bizarre man and readjust my messenger bag on my shoulder. A sense of cold dread glides over me like a breeze, and my body releases a small shudder.

The stranger is extremely tall, maybe around seven feet. His deep, almost black, eyes contrast against his pale skin and raven hair. He's dressed in all black. Military boots, cargo pants, and a black-hooded, slim-fitting leather jacket that cuts off at the waist complete his ensemble.

Fingerless, black-gloved hands hold a large weapon, which looks like a samurai sword. It's so huge he's leaning on it as if it were a cane. *What the hell?*

The dark pools of his eyes call me, luring me to him. I watch with fascination as his lips turn sinister. With the flick of a wrist, he releases thousands of black snakes, angrily focused on me with their yellow eyes, slithering on the campus grass like a sea of black water. They're hissing as they race toward me at an incredibly fast pace.

Frozen, due to my unhealthy fear of the spineless creatures, my eyes go wide at the sight. The snakes slide over one another in an attempt to get to me faster. *Holy shit!* Finally, I get a hold of my horror and decide to turn back to McKenna, who I can still hear talking on her phone to Keegan as if nothing is happening.

Suddenly, large arms wrap around me in a tight grasp and I open my mouth to scream. The hand attached to the solid arm covers my mouth, forcing me to fight the hold in a panicked state. I don't have my daggers, and that was my first mistake this morning.

Gage's voice is at my ear. "Easy, love. What's wrong?" His tone is low and calm.

I squeeze my eyes shut, then open them. The snakes and strange man are both gone. *What the fuck?* My heartbeat is pounding in my ears, and I begin to tremble in Gage's arms.

He turns me around and holds my upper arms while he dips his chin to look into my terrified eyes and pale face. I swallow the bile crawling up my throat.

"What happened?" Gage's expression is marred by confusion at my fearful state.

"S-snakes," is all that I manage to get out.

His eyes scan the area, then land back on my face before he pinches his brows together. "You're going to have to help me out here, love. I don't see anything."

My heart is racing in my chest. I inhale, trying to form words. "A guy . . . in black . . . and thousands of snakes. Black with yellow eyes."

Not quite as articulate as I would have liked.

At the description, Gage examines the quad one more time, while my gaze flicks behind him, meeting McKenna's questioning glare. She's looking at me as if I've gone batshit crazy.

"I'm not sure what you saw, Eve, but there's nothing there. Not anything I can pick up on anyway." He looks over his shoulder at McKenna and she shakes her head back and forth, agreeing she sees nothing. "Are you positive you didn't, maybe, imagine something?" he asks.

"I know what I saw, Gage!" I bark.

He watches me, his features tight with disbelief. "Well, whatever it was, it isn't here now."

I just stand there as humiliation washes over me. *Crap. Maybe I did imagine it all.* I haven't slept well since Asher left, and it's possible that my mind is playing tricks on me.

I swallow the dread I was feeling a few minutes ago. "Yeah, okay," I give in, wishing that Asher were here, because he would believe me without question.

Gage just studies me. "Let's get out of here." He nods his head toward his car.

"I can't do that. It's my first day back," I reply weakly. "I have one more class."

"What do you think you're doing, traitor?" McKenna snips at Gage.

"Sure you can," he answers, ignoring McKenna and cupping my elbow, dragging me to his car.

"For fuck's sake," I hear McKenna seethe behind us.

This time, Gage opens the door for me and doesn't let go of my arm until I'm completely in the car and settled. My eyes follow Keegan and McKenna as they head toward the Escalade, no doubt to follow us.

Twenty minutes later, my heart rate has returned to a semi-normal level as Gage drives us into a wooded park near campus. I've never been here before, but a lot of students come here to hike, bike, run, and spend the day on the trails. He shuts the car off and just sits back in a comfortable manner, giving me the space and time I need to pull myself together.

It's actually pretty refreshing. Usually after one of my panic attacks, Asher's hovering with questions. Having some space is good. New. Energizing. After a little bit, Gage turns to me and ends my internal rant.

"Ready?" he asks.

"For what?"

He doesn't answer. Instead, he gets out of the car and heads to the trunk, pulling out two gym bags. Since he didn't prompt me to join him, I manage to drag myself out of the car and meet him before raising a curious eyebrow when he hands one of the duffel bags to me.

"Running gear," he says, tipping his chin toward the bag. "How long has it been since you last ran outside of the training room?"

I don't even recall, if I'm being honest.

"How do you know I run?"

Gage gives me a sly smirk. "I pay attention, love. You can change in the car. I'll change out here," he offers while reaching for the belt on his pants.

I avert my eyes, wondering what I've gotten myself into with Gage, and slide into the safety of the roadster to change. Once I'm dressed, I meet back up with him near the trunk.

It takes me a moment to center my thoughts because I've never actually seen Gage in anything other than black dress clothes. He's still in black but now it's running shorts and a tank that shows off his arm muscles, which are just beckoning me to run my fingertips over them. *Damn, he's hot. Focus, Eve.* I lift my eyes and meet his gaze. Unlike Asher, Gage doesn't acknowledge my gaping. My guess is it's because he's used to women throwing themselves at him.

"So you just carry my running gear in your car these days?" I tease.

He smirks. "I figured you might want to run on trails at some point. It doesn't help that the St. Michaels keep you locked up in that training room. No wonder you're seeing shit. You need fresh air and to run free, outside."

"Even though you just made me sound like a dog, I appreciate the sentiment," I retort.

He pulls his brows in confusion before releasing a light laugh. "Sorry. In no way did I mean to compare you to a dog. But, if you want, I can throw tennis balls and have you fetch them for me."

"Nah, I'm good today. Thanks though." I offer a small smile. I like this side of Gage.

"Fair enough. Let's hit the trail," he commands.

I stand rooted in my spot nervously. "Asher really doesn't like me being out in the open."

The statement is lame. I know it. Gage knows it. However, historically, it's been proven that my luck is crap when outdoors.

Gage stands in deep thought for a time. "You can't hide forever, love. You're no safer in the house than you are out here. Regardless of what your dark prince says, you need to start living again. Besides, you've got me. What could possibly happen?" he asks in an overconfident tone, motioning his hands down his fine-looking body.

I roll my eyes. "I don't know, Gage. What could happen? I mean, maybe this is what you want. Me, out in the woods, alone, so Deacon can get his hands on me," I state matter-of-factly.

His eyes connect with mine before he nods his head in understanding. "I get it. You don't trust me. But Asher seems to believe that I can keep you safe, and you have faith in him."

"Right. Okay then, let's go for a run." I turn toward the path, but Gage's quiet voice stops me, forcing me to spin back toward him.

"Why do you trust Asher so blindly and me not at all?" Gage asks almost inaudibly.

I pause for a moment, taken aback by the question. "He's never given me a reason not to trust him. You, on the other hand, are like a game of chess. There are no ulterior motives where he is concerned."

Gage smiles but it's forced. "That you know of."

"Your issues with Asher and his family, over Camilla, are not my affair."

"He has lied to you on multiple occasions, and yet, you just accept him at face value?"

"Asher has twisted the truth, but it's been done for my protection."

"So he tells you," Gage states coolly.

I sigh. "Yes, Asher has told me some untruths. I can assure you though, each one was done strategically and with thought only of my safety. I've never been thrown, on purpose, into harm's way with him. It's his life's mission to protect me. Do I blindly give him my loyalty and forgive his missteps? Yes. That's how unconditional love works, Gage. As someone who was once mated, I know you know this." I hold my stance.

Gage runs his fingers over his lip in contemplation. "Unconditional love? Are you saying that you're in love with him?"

I go rigid.

I need to watch what I say and to whom I say it.

"If that is the case, it isn't allowed. You're his charge. The prince is under oath. I would have thought you learned your lesson at the council trial," Gage points out.

"Asher hasn't broken his oath. I might feel that way for him, but he hasn't said he feels that way for me." I backpedal. *Crap. I have to remember not to trust Gage.*

He lets out a loud bark. "What do you really know about Asher St. Michael?"

"Everything I need to," I respond.

"Then you are more naïve than I originally thought."

"Are you suggesting I don't really love him?" I cross my arms and narrow my eyes.

"The bond makes you think you do, that you can't be without him. It's why you're suffering now. The mood swings, the crawling of your skin, and the constant ache from not having the energy hum. It's all part of the *bond*. Not *love*. What you have is infatuation and desire, perhaps even a crush. I'm not so sure you're in love with him, though." His statement is lined with incredulity.

At Gage's sentiment, my heart drops. "You know nothing of what I feel for Asher. Don't presume to. You're assigned to protect me, not school me in matters of the heart."

Gage's face softens. "It's not your fault, you know. A mate link is normally done after you fall in love. Then you're bonded. Michael and Asher took away your free will to make that decision. Ironic, since they're both fighting a war to allow mankind their free will. They've tied you to him and you don't even know that you're a prisoner, not a soul mate." His voice is gentle.

My anger rises with his insinuation. "I am not a hostage. I would bleed out for him, without thought. Even despite the connection, I know that without Asher, I'm nothing. It's easy for you to speak of love when you've built walls high enough around your heart that you forget what true love is. Sacrifice. Shelter. Loyalty. When that person becomes the only reason for your existence. Destiny or not, Asher is my forever. When I close my eyes, I see him and me at the end of this journey. Everything that I feel, it's all for him."

"You suffer this way for him, knowing that he can't give you a family? A mundane life?" Gage questions. "There will be no children. Asher is the prince of the gargoyle race, soon to be king if he fulfills his protector assignment. Do you think the gargoyle line will embrace a human queen, one that their king spat on their traditions and oaths to take? He's broken vows to his people, ones they will not easily forgive. Even for the daughter of Heaven." His intonation is mild, but firm.

"I don't know, Gage. I want him. Only him. Forever. Everything else is just details."

He scoffs. "Life is normally lived within the details. I will give you credit though, you are devoted and unwavering in your allegiance, and that, love, is the sign of a true mate."

"Asher has my steadfast loyalty and trust. Until he breaks it," I stand firm.

"Well, then, let's hope the dark prince never breaks it."

I lift my chin and push my shoulders back. "He won't."

"Love is blindness, that's for sure," Gage replies, moving past me toward the running trail.

I exhale my agitation and lift my eyes, catching McKenna's narrowed ones. Deciding to ignore her usual death glare, I spin to follow Gage on the footpath, but he's already too far in front of me to catch up.

Damn gargoyle speed.

Halfway through the run, my lungs are burning. Even though I've been conditioning daily, I'd forgotten how grueling actual trails are. If the muscle cramp in my side is any indication, I probably need to rest before continuing. I stop and bend over, taking in several deep breaths before standing upright. Gage is by my side in an instant.

"You okay? Need a break, or water?" he questions with an even breath.

"I'm fine. Let's keep going," I wheeze out in defiance.

"Eve, WAIT!" Keegan shouts from somewhere behind me as I take two steps forward.

Without warning, I'm falling. *What the hell?* My body is projecting at a fast pace toward lime-green earth. I let out a choked scream before slamming my eyes shut in preparation for the impact of my body against the ground.

Abruptly, my plummet is stopped. Two strong arms wrap around my waist in a firm hold. With hesitation, I open my eyes to see Gage's staring back at me in fright.

I release a grateful breath that it's him before I realize we're stuck in midair, his gray wings spread as they glide us toward the ground.

"I've got you, love," he says in a controlled voice.

I just swallow and nod. It's all I can do not to pee my pants. After Gage places us firmly on the ground, he stands taller and sets his hands on his hips.

"Did you not hear Keegan say, WAIT?" Gage asks.

"What the hell just happened?" I whisper-shout.

"Portal," he answers in a bored fashion.

I arch a brow at him. "Come again?"

"A portal. Gateway. An invisible entrance to another realm. It was on the trail. Only supernatural beings can see them, and you, human girl, ran right into it. Hence the plunge from the skies," the massive gargoyle explains while scanning the area.

Holy crap! My life really does keep getting crazier.

"Did you jump in after me?"

Gage's eyes meet mine. "Yes. I told you, I'm your new protector."

"Temporary," I correct.

"Semantics. I was doing my sentinel job, which is starting to prove to be a challenge. You know, love, you get yourself into more unrealistic jams than most humans," he accuses, slightly amused.

"Did Keegan and McKenna follow us?" I ask, refocusing the conversation.

"They were shut out of the portal before they could."

My eyes go wide. "I'm alone . . . with you?"

Gage smirks seductively. "It would seem that way. Stay here for a moment while I check things out." He moves to walk away before narrowing his eyes at me. "I mean it, Eve. Don't move until I get back." His tone is hard.

"Wait. You're just going to leave me here? What if I get attacked?" I screech.

"As I recall, you have daggers and are clearly not inept at using them. The faster I can do a sweep, the sooner I'll be back." The gargoyle shoots into the blue sky.

Leaving me standing in a field, unprotected—without my daggers. *Worst. Protector. Ever.*

"Crap," I throw out and take in our surroundings.

If it weren't for the unexpected nose-dive to my death two minutes ago, I would admit the land is lovely. It looks like a page right out of a storybook. As if we've landed in a miniature version of Ireland with moss, rocky cliffs and cobblestone paths. The grass is lime green, and the rolling hills are filled with clover, making deep valley patterns.

In the distance, there's a large rock wall with a gentle waterfall cascading down it, pooling at the bottom where wild horses are grazing. The sky is crystal blue, with not a cloud in it. Large mushrooms line the earth, buried among the tall blades of grass and moss carpets.

My eyes continue to roam, landing on a section of forest where I notice a small village of bonsai trees everywhere. Although, upon closer inspection, I notice these aren't ordinary bonsai trees. They look like tiny homes. The tree houses are connected with small bridges and ladders, creating a large woodland community.

Where the hell are we?

I move closer to the shrubbery settlement and discover that each dwelling is ornamented with minuscule doors and windows. The way the bark curves and shifts makes the vegetation look like tiny castles and cottages. There must be at least a hundred dwarfed trees.

I keep my eyes trained on the woodland village and exhale. "Please tell me we're not near goblins," I beg quietly. My recent run-in with a rather rude goblin, Godry, has me hating all small mythological creatures.

"It's actually far worse, love," Gage states from behind me, startling me.

I cover my heart and spin, narrowing my eyes at him. "Crap. You almost gave me a heart attack. Announce your approach next time."

He ignores my dramatics. "We're in the Land of the Leprechauns."

I just hold Gage's gaze for a moment before breaking into hysterical laughter. "I'm sorry, like rainbows, unicorns and pots of gold? Those leprechauns? Seriously, where are we?"

Gage schools his features. "Love, I would be careful with how I react in certain realms. Not everything is what it seems." His warning is stern.

"What it 'seems like' to me is that a Smurf mated with a box of Lucky Charms," I reply.

"Smurf?"

"Smurf. You know, the cartoon. Little blue creatures that live in mushrooms?"

"I'm not familiar. But little blue creatures living in mushrooms sounds more like you're on a bad acid trip than truth," Gage replies in a thorny manner.

I cross my arms rebelliously. "Oh. I see. Smurfs are totally not believable. Yet I am supposed to believe in gargoyles, fairies, angels, selkies, goblins, and now leprechauns?"

"You know, love, you have the attention span of a goblin. Has anyone mentioned that to you before? It's actually mind-blowing that you can't focus for more than five minutes."

My mouth falls open. "There's no need to insult me by comparing me to a goblin, Gage," I huff, as something sharp pricks my knee.

I drop my hand to the spot, where there is a microscopic gold knife embedded into my leg.

"Christ," Gage spits out. His wings snap out before he snatches me in his arms and harshly throws me down on the ground, covering me with his body as thousands of the toothpick-sized gold daggers begin flying at us, making tiny whooshing noises as they approach.

"Stay down, love. We're under attack," he warns while shielding me with his hard body.

"Under attack? What's in my knee that stings so badly?" I ask, gritting through the pain.

"They're pugiones being pitched at us by the leprechauns." Gage groans.

"Pugio? Like the dagger that killed Julius Caesar?"

"The very same."

"Why would leprechauns want to harm us? Aren't they magical and fart rainbows or something?" I question.

Gage grunts as the little beings continue their assault.

"These are assassin leprechauns. Part of the dark army. Christ, we're surrounded. Hold on. I'm going to flash us out of here. Don't let go," Gage orders.

Holy hell.

I am seriously never eating Lucky Charms again.

4 Death Wish

I land with a hard thud in ice-cold liquid and begin treading water in a panicked state. Forcing my head upward, I break the pond's surface. My lungs suck in air, replacing the cool liquid and causing my coughing to become violent.

Once I've gathered myself together, I look around and see Gage relaxing on a rock next to the water, watching me fight for each breath. He's casually wringing out the excess water from his tank top, which is now clinging to every muscle on his chest. *Asshat.*

I force myself to swim to the shoreline and pull my body out of the water before I collapse on the soft grass, out of breath.

"No need to assist me. I've got it," I say sarcastically through uneven pants.

"I can see you have it under control," he counters, giving me a sideways glance before taking off his shirt and twisting out the remainder of the water.

I crawl the last little bit onto the grass and roll onto my back while continuing to pull air into my lungs. "Why am I always getting wet around you?" I grind out through my tight jaw.

Gage moves so he is standing over me. "Do you really want me to answer that?"

I girlie growl at him—actually girlie growl.

"I'm really starting to hate you."

"Hate me or just semi-dislike me?" he asks, placing his soaked shirt back on. *Sad.*

"Is there a difference?"

"A large one."

Gage kneels down and examines my leg.

"What are you doing?"

My eyes follow every one of his movements with unease and curiosity. Little cold beads of water drip from his hair, landing on my skin.

"The pugio has poison in it. I have to get it out," he states calmly, and moves closer to my tingling leg.

"Poison?" I repeat. "What about you? They must have hit your wings like a thousand times?" I sit up, attempting to control the fear spreading through my body.

"It's only dangerous to those who have a soul." Gage focuses on my knee, holding it still.

"How do you get it out?"

My leg is now beginning to pulse painfully.

Gage's eyes meet mine. "I need you to trust me, love. Can you do that?"

Well, shit. This can't be good. I pause, chewing on the inside of my cheek.

"No. But it hurts like hell, so do what you need to," I concede.

He nods once. "I need to remove the knife, then suck the poison out."

"Suck? As in . . . mouth on wound and suck?"

"It's the only way to drag the poison out before it hits your bloodstream. Once it does, it will paralyze you." His sea-green gaze holds mine for what feels like forever.

Suddenly, my leg goes from a dull throb to a full-on burn. God, I wish Asher were here. Sighing my annoyance and fighting the urge to scream, I agree.

"Just do it," I order through my clenched teeth.

Shit! How could something so small cause so much goddamn pain?

Gage gives me a half-apologetic smile before wrapping my leg tightly in his arm, choke-hold style. Once my leg is secure, he yanks out the small weapon. It hurts like hell. I bite my lip, muffling a scream as my eyes water.

"Take a breath, love. Almost done," Gage encourages.

Through my ragged inhaling, I watch his every movement with an unhealthy fascination. Inch by inch his mouth moves closer to the wound. When his lips are within a breath of my knee, he blows lightly on the open cut, easing some of the discomfort. My stomach drops at the sensation. I release a soft sound of appreciation.

His eyes lift, watching me between his long, blond lashes while his breath soothes the sting. Slowly, his tongue darts out and runs over the small wound, first running it lengthwise, and then in circular motions. At the contact, I pant out a ragged breath.

"I'm going to suck it now, love."

The double meaning sends tremors up my spine.

Gage's mouth closes over the wound, and in a gentle motion, he begins to suck the lesion. The longer he does it, the less my leg burns. Finally, the pain is gone completely and I have feeling back in the limb. He licks the sensitive spot one last time and plants a soft kiss on it before lifting his head.

Seeing my comfort, Gage pulls back and smirks.

"All better?"

I nod. "Thank you," I whisper with a dry throat.

"With your healing abilities, you should be fine in a few minutes. Enough time for us to devise a way out of here," he says, sitting straight up and scanning the empty land.

"Do you need help?" I point to the last of the daggers on his arm as he plucks them off.

"Most of them fell out when we hit the water."

"Won't the poison in your system hurt you?" I question, a bit shaken.

He moves his head back and forth. "As I said, it only affects those with a soul. We should go before the leprechauns come back."

With Gage's assistance, I stand and meet his stare. "So, what's the plan? How do we get out of the Land of the Leprechauns and back to our realm?"

"Carefully and strategically. They're assassins, trained by Lucifer's army. So we need to be mindful and focused," Gage states. "The only other gateway I know of is on the south side of the realm. We're on the north, so it's a bit of a hike. You up for it?" He jerks his chin toward my knee.

"My leg feels better. I'm ready." The lie rolls off my tongue. It's still really sore.

"We need to get to higher ground, though. We'll never make it on foot. If I teleport us, the leprechauns will sense our continued presence in their realm and be able to determine our location," he explains.

"Why higher ground?" I ask, testing the pressure on my leg.

"Leprechauns are afraid of heights," he answers offhandedly, as if I should know this.

I sigh. "Of course they are."

I swear, nothing surprises me anymore.

"I told you before, things aren't always what they seem. You need to learn to understand realms, Eve. You have gifts. Use them," he scolds.

"I can't believe leprechauns are evil," I retort.

"I can't believe you don't know they are."

"Well, how would I know? I thought they produced rainbows and pots of gold," I argue.

"They create beautiful things to lure you into dark behavior like greed and stealing."

"I suppose when you spin it like that, it makes sense," I huff. "Pretty sure I'm never going to look at rainbows the same way again."

The side of Gage's mouth lifts. "We need to get moving. You up for flying with me?"

"Flying?"

Flying is something I've only done once with Asher, when he saved me from Deacon. Trepidation begins to run through my veins. This feels intimate. Something I should be doing with Asher, not Gage. It's unsettling.

"Don't tell me the daughter of Heaven is afraid of heights," Gage teases playfully.

I swallow. Hard. "No. Not of heights." *You . . . definitely.*

"All right, then come over here." He motions for me to move closer.

Pushing away my anxiety, I move toward the sexy gargoyle whose wings have expanded.

Gage drops his voice. "You okay, love?"

"Fine."

"Still don't trust me?" he asks in a quiet tone.

My eyes lift and lock onto his. "Working on it."

He reaches for both my hands. Once I'm in his grasp, Gage tugs me closer, so our chests are touching. Without releasing my gaze, he lifts our interlocked hands behind his neck and repositions mine so they're clasped together. Very slowly, he drops his arms, allowing his fingers to graze the skin on mine as his find their way to my waist, pulling me taut to him.

"Don't let go." The command is a soft murmur. "This is going to be a fast ride."

I nod my head and hold on tighter, closing my eyes. Gage moves even closer and leans into my ear. "Trust me," he requests and rapidly shoots us up into the air.

Seconds later, my running shoes touch down on soft grass, and I pop my eyes open. Relief floods through me. I step away from Gage to steady my body, grateful to be on solid ground.

He offers a hollow smile before tilting his head toward a path. "We have a small walk to get to the sacred pools. There we'll find the gateway back to the earth realm."

"Okay," I reply and follow along, my leg feeling less and less achy. "Why can't you just teleport us back?"

Gage faces forward, continuing to walk at a fast pace. "Certain realms allow supernatural powers over others. The Land of the Leprechauns is protected by the dark army. Therefore, anyone who's not associated with the demonic legion can't fully use their powers here. That rules out my teleportation gift. Wouldn't matter anyway. I can only use it within realms, not across dimensions."

"Why am I able to realm jump to the Kingdom of the Fae and Eternal Forest?" I press.

"Your bloodline permits you into the Fae Kingdom because it is protected by Heaven. As for the Eternal Forest, love, neither Heaven nor Hell guard it. It's Switzerland, if you will, neutral on all matters of religion, politics, and supernatural species. Which is why, I'm guessing, you needed to stone state with the dark prince to get there."

"I don't understand."

Gage stops and turns to me. "You and the dark prince possess light and dark bloodlines. Combined, you can enter any dimension or realm. Alone, you can only jump to realms that match your bloodline."

I ponder what he has said for a moment.

"How do you know about Asher's bloodline?"

Gage exhales roughly. "They must get off on keeping you in the dark."

"Enlighten me then," I suggest as we continue through dense woods.

"When we get back, I'll introduce you to a friend of mine. He'll be able to shed some light on Asher's bloodline. He'll be more informative than the St. Michaels have been."

I snort. "This information will be provided out of the goodness of your heart, right?"

"Believe it or not, Eve, my extension of these olive branches are my way of showing you I can be trusted. By the way, snorting is extremely ladylike," he adds.

"Why is it so important to you that I trust you?"

Gage stops walking, turns, and scans the area behind me. "I don't know. Maybe on some level, you remind me of Camilla. Or perhaps it's because I know how this world works, the cruelty of it. Regardless of what you think, or where my alliances lie, I believe in free will. I see what they're doing and I disagree with their methods. No one should be used as a pawn in someone else's war. If this realm has taught you nothing else today, take this away. Nothing and no one is ever what they seem."

"Does that include you?"

"Especially me."

"Then I'll watch my step."

Gage just studies me for a moment before motioning behind him. "We shouldn't stand here any longer. Let's keep moving. I'm sure the clan is having a coronary waiting for you."

We continue to walk along the woodland path in silence toward the sound of waterfalls. If this realm wasn't filled with angry little leprechauns that wanted me dead, I might actually be inclined to explore it. I guess even amid evil, there is beauty.

After a while, Gage and I come up to a large mountain. Cut in the middle of it are stunning waterfalls. The clear liquid cascades elegantly, off the glistening rocks. Sunlight filters through the center of the peak, beaming off the crystal water. The foothill's damp stones are covered with low trees and vegetation.

There are five waterfalls descending off the rock formation. At the bottom of each, a small pool of water collects. It's breathtaking the silent way the water falls, gently gathering into the waiting body of water.

"These are the sacred pools. Our gateway back to the earth realm," Gage explains.

"Sacred pools? I thought this kingdom is ruled by the dark army?"

"It's a stipulation of the peace treaty. Where there is dark, there must also be light. A balance. Even the malevolent realms must have a divine presence and vice versa."

"Sounds fair to me."

"You up for a swim?" Gage asks, nodding again to my sore knee. "It's the only way to get back."

"Yep, anything to return. How do we do this?"

Before Gage can answer me, there is a rustling in the trees. Without warning, thousands of tiny pugiones begin flying toward us.

"Shit," Gage snaps while unfurling his wings and folding me in them, protectively.

Even though I'm pressed against his heart, all I can hear is the whooshing of the tiny daggers, followed by soft grunts as each one strikes Gage.

In an instant, Gage teleports us to the top of the pools, and without warning, we're plunging toward one of the bodies of water. I close my eyes, praying that he knows which one is the portal.

Trusting in him.

The next moment, we both land on a hard surface. Gage flips so I fall on top of him as he takes the brunt of the impact. Grunting from the collision with the ground, he releases me. I manage to ungracefully roll off of him and sit up on the dirt running path.

"By the grace, blood of Eden!" *Guess we're back.*

I turn to McKenna's anxious face.

"Missed you too, cupcake," I throw out while attempting to stand.

McKenna narrows her eyes and then yanks me, none-too-gently, onto my feet. Keegan extends his hand to Gage, assisting him before scanning the gargoyle's body.

"Pugiones? The gateway was to the Land of the Leprechauns?" Keegan asks.

"That'd be the realm," Gage confirms, his face slightly pained.

"Let's get you back to the manor. We'll remove the daggers and get some salve on the wounds so you can begin to heal," Keegan suggests.

Keegan gives Gage an austere expression before turning to me. "Are you all right, Eve?"

My eyes move from Keegan to Gage.

"Fine. Just a little shaken up."

Gage nods to me with appreciation at my omission of the knee injury.

"Let's get you and the traitor to the manor before Abby texts me again," McKenna barks.

When we return, Callan is pacing by the door like a worried parent. As soon as I enter the house, Abby screeches into her cell phone.

"She's back. Yes, unharmed." She sighs in annoyance before ending her call and pinning me with a relieved stare.

Gage and Keegan move around us toward the kitchen, but my focus is on Abby. I watch her every movement, knowing that Asher was on the other side of her discussion.

"By the grace, cutie. You have a death wish," Callan admonishes as he embraces me.

"Were you speaking to Asher?" I ask Abby over Callan's shoulder.

Her eyes drop to her feet and she goes still. My heart plunges, knowing she was.

"Were you?" I ask again, forcing myself out of Callan's hug.

Abby's face morphs into an *I'm-sorry-but-I-can't-tell-you* expression.

"I'm going to go check on Gage." I try to move, but Abby's tiny voice stops me.

"Ash just wanted to know that you're okay," she whispers to my back.

"Then he should be here himself to witness that I am," I throw over my shoulder.

When I finally make my way into the kitchen, I notice Keegan pulling out the last of the small daggers from Gage's sagging wings.

There must be thousands of the tiny weapons in a bowl on the counter. I watch Keegan apply the balm to each bleeding pinprick. Gage doesn't even flinch, just fiddles with his unlit cigarette. *God, that has to hurt.*

"Are you okay?" I question, wincing at the scene.

"Yeah. There were just a lot of them. I'll be healed in no time." Gage offers a tight smile.

I clear my throat. "Thanks for coming in after me and um . . . protecting me."

"Next time, like Keegan did, I'll be sure to warn you BEFORE you step in and fall," Gage says.

"You knew the portal was there," Keegan accuses. "Why didn't you stop her?"

"She needs to learn to be more careful. On her own, without someone telling her every five minutes that she's in danger. How do you expect her to survive by herself if you all keep babying her?" Gage retorts. "The clan should have trained her properly on gateways."

"We're protecting her OUR way. You'd do well to remember the oath you recently took to do the same," Keegan snips, throwing the ointment jar on the counter and storming out.

"You knew I was about to step into it?" I cross my arms. "And you just let me fall?"

Gage throws his cigarette on the counter before giving me a pointed glance. "Eve, you need to discover these things on your own. How on earth are you going to stay alive if you are unaware of the supernatural dangers you're facing?"

"Screw you, Gage," I spit out, then turn to leave.

With lightning speed, Gage is in front of me, holding my upper arms. "Are you even taking the ascension seriously? From my standpoint, you are no better off than you were months ago. You're a liability to the St. Michaels. No wonder they keep failing at protecting you. You can't even protect yourself, love."

I shake out of Gage's grip. "You know nothing."

Gage takes a menacing step toward me. "I know this. There is a war on the horizon, between Heaven and Hell. You're the monkey in the middle. These are not cartoon characters. They are real supernatural beings with the power to destroy the world. It's time you face this, head on."

"I HAVE!" I shout.

He shakes his head. "No. You've been play-fighting and falling in love with someone you shouldn't be. There is real danger coming. If you don't want to end up like Camilla, I suggest you get your head on straight. Otherwise, that death wish that Callan seems to think you have won't be a wish at all."

"Is that a threat?" My voice is low and throaty.

"It's a warning," he assures before leaving the room.

Randi Cooley Wilson

5 Homecoming

The briny fresh air infiltrates my lungs. The ocean's scent allows me to finally breathe after what feels like weeks of suffocation. I inhale deeply and my eyelids flutter shut. My body soaks up the spring sunshine.

The crashing of waves into the shoreline lulls me into a peaceful calm. For a brief moment, I pretend that I'm normal and enjoying the earthly benefits of being alive.

Strong arms wrap tightly around my waist and tug me back to a warm, muscular chest. Asher lifts his hand and moves my hair to one side, over my shoulder, so he can have access to my neck. I tilt my head to the right, making it easy for his lips to gently brush the sensitive skin under my left ear before leaving a trail of soft kisses.

"Someday, when this is all over, I promise you'll have the peace you're craving. It will be just you and me, siren," he vows quietly.

I sigh in contentment. "That's all I want, Ash."

"I'll light the world on fire to make sure you get it."

I turn to face him and push up on my tiptoes. Leaning in, I give him a slow, molten kiss, pushing everything I feel for him into the gesture. I want to fill every space of his soul, the way he does mine.

It's like I'm trying to climb inside his heart and live there. I'm not sure how long we stay like this, in our own private, perfect moment, but I never want to leave.

Breathlessly, I pull away. My eyes find Asher's.

"What is it you want the most?"

Asher's intense gaze holds mine. "Redemption."

"Love?" Gage penetrates my reverie. "We're getting ready to dock."

My eyes snap open, yanking me from my daydream. I swallow the disappointment that it was only a dream when I notice we're about to reach the port in Vineyard Haven.

Crap. I miss Asher.

"You sure your aunt is going to be okay with me tagging along today?" Gage's voice is uncertain as he drags nicotine into his lungs from his cigarette.

"Are you kidding? She'll be thrilled to have the company. I think she's pretty lonely now that I'm living away," I respond.

"It's nice that you're still so close with her." His thumb rubs along his bottom lip.

"I missed her a lot when we were in England. I'm looking forward to just spending some quiet time at home and catching up."

I heave a sigh and fiddle with my necklace.

Gage is quiet for a moment, his face thoughtful as he watches me play nervously with the piece of jewelry. "Let's head down to the car so we can get off the boat as soon as we dock."

Once we're in the roadster, Gage drives onto the main road heading to Oak Bluffs. After a silent ride, each of us lost in our own head, we arrive at my aunt's white gingerbread cottage.

Her spring wildflowers are starting to bloom and climb the white picket fence, embracing the house lovingly called Gateway to Paradise.

"This is . . . quaint?" he muses.

I turn to Gage and let out a short laugh. "Are you asking me or telling me?"

"I'm not sure; it's very . . . beachy and gardenish."

"I'm sure my aunt will be thrilled with your assessment of our home," I taunt, as he pulls in behind her hybrid in the driveway.

We both exit the car just as my Aunt Elizabeth appears on the walkway ready to greet us. I run over to her and she yanks me into a firm hug.

"Welcome home, love bug," she says near my ear in a quiet voice. "My goodness, look at you. Your hair is longer and you look older," she points out with a slight sadness in her voice.

I grin and motion behind me. "Aunt Elizabeth, this is Gage, my *temporary* protector."

"Actually, I'm her *NEW* protector." He offers his hand to my aunt. "Pleasure, Elizabeth."

My aunt's hazel eyes look awkwardly between us, and she forces a smile. "Well, it's nice to meet you, Gage. Please come in. I've got some hot chocolate waiting."

The minute I step into the cozy living room, I see him. Gage stiffens next to me and stops in his tracks. My aunt turns and offers me an apologetic expression.

At his full height, the warrior looks even more intimidating, and while his jade gaze is warm when it meets mine, I become unnerved at his mere divine presence. Even after all our training sessions together, he still intimidates me.

The archangel stands to greet us. "Eve." He bows his head to me, reminding me that I need to follow protocol and greet him the same way. "Mr. Gallagher." His attention turns to Gage.

"Michael," Gage responds, less than enthused.

"What are you doing here?" I ask.

"He's here because the London clan doesn't trust you to be alone with me," Gage explains.

The archangel smiles at my aunt as she steps to his side.

"Actually, I invited him. I thought it would be nice if we all spent a little time together," she says in her insincere voice. *Weird.*

"Libby is correct. I was invited. Though Gage is accurate as well. The London clan doesn't entirely entrust your safety with Mr. Gallagher. After being called to the council meeting, they asked me to oversee your visit," he offers.

My focus shifts to Gage, who rolls his eyes. "I'm in need of some nicotine. Excuse my absence during your domestic reunion," he replies, stalking out the front door.

"I'm surprised that a warrior of Heaven doesn't have anything better to do than chaperone an eighteen-year-old college student." The jab causes my aunt to shoot me a disapproving glare.

"Eve, please exhibit manners and respect. I've raised you better than that," she scolds.

"Sorry," I mumble. *And I'm ten years old again.*

"Apology accepted. How about while we wait for Gage to return, we sit. I have some of your favorite snacks spread out. I can't wait to hear all about school." My aunt ushers us toward the couches. "So, tell me everything." She beams enthusiastically.

"It's only been a week, so there isn't much to tell." I sit on the couch across from them. After more prodding, I finally offer bits and pieces about my semester and classes.

"It's . . . different without Aria . . . and Asher." My voice cracks on the release of his name.

"I trust that your new protector is working out well?" the dark-blond-haired angel inquires.

"We're fine. Right, love?" Gage says, entering the living room, the scents of cigarette and spice following him. My eyes linger a bit too long.

I yank my focus from Gage back to my aunt. "It's not ideal, but the temporary situation is adequate." I use a formal voice.

Gage smirks at my assessment and flops down next to me on the couch, leaving enough space so that I can breathe comfortably. I snag a mug of dark cocoa before watching Michael and my aunt closely.

The warrior of Heaven is sitting close to her on the love seat. His muscular thigh is completely brushed up against hers and her face is in a state of constant bliss. *Ew. Maybe she isn't as lonely as I thought. Is that even allowed, a human and an angel?*

"The London clan told me about your visit to the Land of the Leprechauns recently. I am happy to see you returned in one piece and without permanent harm," Michael says.

My eyebrows shoot up. "I guess nothing is private anymore?" I murmur offhandedly.

"After London, I would have to agree, daughter of Heaven. Privacy is something that does not seem to exist between us, does it?" the archangel smirks with intent.

"I guess that's the price I pay for being touched by an archangel's spirit," I retort with a mocking tone.

Damn, my mood swings are back.

"How is your training going, love bug?" my aunt steps in, hoping to end our undertones.

"Fine, I guess." I shrug noncommittally.

"Eve still has a lot of work to do. However, Elizabeth, her skills are improving each day. Her mental control over her gifts is remarkable, and now that she is versed on portals, she's focusing on becoming more aware of her surroundings," Gage answers proudly.

"That is excellent news. I am glad to see you take training seriously," Michael interjects.

"As opposed to?" *Why does it feel like he's baiting me?*

"Eve, I do not wish to upset you. However, in my opinion, your time with Mr. St. Michael was not used efficiently. With Gage, it is my belief that your skills, overall, will improve, and you will be better equipped when the time comes. He understands the darker side of this better than you think. Then again, I also deduce that you are able to focus more with Gage than with Asher," the archangel challenges.

"Would your assessment of my relationship with Asher happen to be one of the reasons you and the council removed him as my protector?" I cleverly remark.

Real mature, Eve.

The nerve-racking warrior of Heaven moves to the edge of the couch, holding my gaze. "I had nothing to do with Asher's dismissal as your protector. That was a Royal Gargoyle Council decision. The Angelic Council does not get involved with supernatural tribunals."

"However, it's okay to be involved with every other aspect of my relationship with Asher?" I snap.

"That is enough, Eve," my aunt warns.

I'm still agitated. "Aunt Elizabeth, I was under the impression my homecoming was to see you and spend time with *you*. If Michael wants to antagonize me, then he can do it during normal training hours instead of under the pretenses of a visit home."

"Daughter of Heaven or not, I will not allow you to speak to Libby in that manner," Michael cautions, standing and stepping protectively in front of my shocked aunt.

I bark a laugh. "I'm sorry, who appointed you my parental guardian? I think I have a solid enough understanding of how your world works now. You taking me from my dead parents and handing me over to someone who pretended to be my blood relative does not merit a scolding from you on appropriate familial behavior."

"Love." Gage's voice is quiet, but firm.

The archangel just studies me and swallows, unsure of how to continue to address me.

"I need some air. If you'll excuse me." I jerk off the couch and head to my room.

When I reach the middle stair I hear my aunt's concerned voice. "Perhaps I should go and check on her?"

"Elizabeth, the stress on her protector bond with Asher is causing her to be highly emotional and slightly volatile. Let her cool off. Give her some room," Gage suggests.

"Perhaps Mr. Gallagher is accurate. Libby, let's give Eve a moment to collect her emotions. Perchance, would you like to join me on the beach for a walk?" Michael invites.

"Fresh air would be lovely." As soon as I hear my aunt's shaky voice, I'm crushed. I drop to the stair and inhale. *Shit. I need to get my temper under control. Damn gargoyle bond.*

"They're gone, love." Gage's voice drifts up the stairwell.

I look up to see him at the end of the staircase. He tilts his head toward the front door.

"Let's go do something fun and normal. Want to show me around the Vineyard?"

We just watch one another for a moment before I nod and make my way down the stairs. Once I hit the bottom step, Gage extends his hand to me. My eyes shift between it and his palpable stare. I'm unsure if I'm ready to take it.

Am I ready to allow Gage to be a part of my life?

I swallow hard while he patiently waits for me to decide. After what feels like an eternity, I take the last step and walk toward him slowly. I keep my focus on the rise and fall of his chest with each breath he takes.

Once close, I lift my gaze to his and whisper, "I can't."

He stares at me for a moment, lowering his empty hand. With an understanding nod, he gently opens the front door, holding it for me to walk through, and I do.

❧❧

Gage and I return a few hours later, after spending a really fun afternoon on Circuit Avenue, pretending to be tourists. We ended up walking around in the whimsical shops, grabbed ice cream at Mad Martha's, and he even allowed me to buy him a T-shirt at Soft as a Grape, although it had to be black.

It was perfectly normal and exactly what I needed.

"Eve, is that you?" my aunt questions from the kitchen as we enter the living room.

"Yeah, it's us." I shift my eyes to Gage.

He offers an encouraging wink.

My aunt enters the living room, playing with a light brown strand of her long hair that has escaped her ponytail. She's watching me like she wants to say something, but holds back.

"I'm just going to run out to the porch for a cigarette. I'll be back," Gage says, and leaves.

My aunt's gaze drops in disapproval. "He sure does smoke a lot," she mentions.

I exhale. I need to apologize. "I'm sorry about earlier. My temper lately is short."

"Thank you. And I'm truly sorry about the situation with Asher. I understand you care for him very deeply. But, Eve,

65

Michael and I are not the enemy. Yes, we've made mistakes, but everything he and I have done has been to protect you. Our decisions were never made lightly or in a malicious way. They've been determined with consideration and love for you," she cajoles.

"I get it. Everything just sets me off these days. I feel like I'm crawling in my own skin. It also doesn't help that everyone keeps lying to me. Except Gage, surprisingly," I admit.

"Untruths for protection reasons are different than everyday lies," she counters quietly.

"Not if you're the person on the receiving end," I throw back. "Anyway, Asher being gone is just making me a little unstable, so . . ." I look everywhere but at my aunt.

She opens her arms to me, and I accept the invitation. I can feel myself relax as she embraces me. "Come in the kitchen and tell me all about it. I know we discussed it on the phone, but it might help to get it off your chest in person. I realize it was hard to lose Aria, and then to have Asher disappear . . . I'm sure it was crushing."

"It was," I whisper, inhaling her scent.

She smells like the ocean and home.

"You can help me prepare dinner while we chat. I think the *I Believe in Gargoyles* apron Callan got you at Christmas is still here." She smiles.

"Great," I drag out and roll my eyes.

My aunt was right. After two hours of girl talk, I do feel a lot better—lighter—as the four of us sit down for dinner. The conversation flow is easy and, to be honest, pleasant. I'm just gathering the last of my things to catch the ferry back when I hear Gage and Michael in a heated discussion on the front porch.

"You aren't going to tell her?" Gage questions, anger lining his voice.

"Mr. Gallagher, I realize that you are somewhat lax when it comes to following oaths and protocol, but this is truly none of your concern, nor is it part of your assignment."

"If it has to do with Eve, then it is my concern. Temporary or not, I'm her protector."

"She is not to know. We are not ready to tell her. The London clan understands this."

"Don't you think she should decide what she's ready for?" Gage seethes.

I head out to the porch and see Gage standing tall, arms crossed, lit cigarette hanging from his fingertips. His expression is menacing.

"What's going on?" I ask warily and place my messenger bag on the Adirondack chair.

Gage just points a hard look at the archangel. "Either you tell her, or I will."

"Tell me what?" I ask, as my aunt joins us.

"Michael?" she inquires with a curious tone.

"It's all right, Libby. I have this under control," the divine warrior assures her.

"Tell her," Gage grits out of his tight jaw.

"No," Michael answers in an unwavering manner.

"Gage?" I ask, my voice barely audible.

His eyes move between Michael and my aunt. "Christ," he barks before he puts out his cigarette and rubs his face. "I was just making sure Michael informed you of the role he had in Asher's assignment removal," he lies.

I'm unsure how I know he's lying, but it's the first time he's done it, and it actually hurts.

Michael visibly relaxes. "I was reminding Mr. Gallagher that I had no part in the ruling."

It's silent for a moment while everyone inhales. I know Michael is lying. I'm sick of it.

"I've had it." I turn to the archangel. "Gage was right. You've taken away any and all free will I've had to make my own decisions. You might not have sent Asher away, but you certainly made it clear that we can't be together. After YOU bonded us, without my permission, by the way. So whatever this new secret is that you're not willing to share with me, I'm done. You can't keep making decisions for me."

Michael steps forward and begins to glow, I'm assuming in anger. "Do not accuse me of something I have not done. I am a soldier of Heaven. Your free will is yours."

My blood pressure rises and I begin to see red. "Really? Mine?" I release an emotionless laugh. "That has to be the funniest thing I've heard all evening."

Aunt Elizabeth moves to Michael's side and gently lifts both palms to me in an attempt to calm me. "Eve, honey, let's just take a step back and cool off."

I pin my stare onto Michael. "Am I free to love Asher? No. It's against the rules. Rules that were set without thought of me, just like a bonding that was done without my consent. I guess I should be grateful though, to have my family. Oh, no, that's not true either. My parents are dead and I was taken away, once again, without my permission. Let's not even mention the fact that at some point, you touched my bloodline and put me in the middle of a centuries-old war, then left me to fend for myself while you constantly question my training and how I'm dealing with an ascension, which I never asked for. Again, not allowing me to walk away from this destiny you've imposed. I would say you have ended all my free will."

I'm on the verge of tears, but I can't stop my mouth. It's as if a switch was thrown on and I can't turn it off. I feel Gage move closer, but he doesn't speak. Through my fog, I'm grateful he's giving me space to deal with this.

"Once you were created, it was decided that you were destined to restore order. Bring justice and balance to the world," Michael says without compassion. "That is your fate."

"Exactly. I have duties and responsibilities. My entire life has been planned out. Tell me, Michael, how did you pick me? Was it random? Did you just see my mother and father and say, hey you know what, that baby should be stripped of humanity and free will so that Heaven can ensure world domination?"

My aunt gasps. "Eve!"

For the first time, Michael's eyes flash with an unreadable emotion as he steps to me, causing Gage to move in a protective stance between us.

"I created you out of love, not duty and honor." The archangel shakes with rage.

"Is that what you call it these days?" I reply.

"STOP!" my aunt yells, startling me. She's never raised her voice before. "Just . . . please stop." Her gaze darts to the angel then me. "Michael and I created you . . . out of love for one another. You're ours," she whispers in a solemn voice.

"What?" I speak softly.

She pushes her shoulders back and stands taller as she addresses me. "I am your biological mother, Eve. And Michael . . . is your biological father. Katherine and Robert Collins were dear friends who agreed to watch over you."

My world tilts as I just stare at her. I must have stood there for a long time, silent and in shock, because I don't recall Gage turning and taking my face in his palms.

"Love?"

"I need Asher," I whimper and fist his shirt. "I need him now. I can't . . . I can't do this anymore . . . please get him. You have to get him and bring him here," I beg hysterically.

My aunt—no, my mother—moves toward me, eyes watering. "Eve, please, let us finish explaining." Her voice cracks and Gage moves us farther away from her reach.

I just stare at Gage, whose face is marred by sympathy.

"Take me home," I demand, barely audible.

Gage just nods. "If that's what you want, love."

My aunt moves toward me. "Please," she begs. "Allow us the opportunity to explain."

Michael grabs her waist from behind and folds her into his embrace as she breaks down.

Gage takes my hand in his. I stare at it while he squeezes and pulls me to him, extending his wings. Without a word, he shoots us up into the night sky.

Some homecoming.

6 Divination

My focus shifts from the picturesque view of Paris back to the roaring fireplace. Gage flicks the last of his cigarette into the fire, then moves fluidly from the hearth's warmth to the built-in bar in his loft.

I watch him as he pours two glasses of brandy. "Have you gotten a hold of Asher yet?" I ask in a voice I don't recognize.

"Not yet, love," he answers solemnly before walking to my wilted form on the couch. "He is in council meetings. They are not permitted to leave for any reason."

"It's probably for the best. I'd most likely castrate him," I laugh without humor.

"I won't deny that I'd enjoy watching that." He hands me a glass of the amber liquid.

"Thanks for getting me out of there so quickly."

He smirks sexily. "Going back to get my car and your bag was fun."

"You all knew, didn't you?" My voice is a mere whisper. *Even Asher? How could he?*

His lack of response is my answer. Without words, he takes a seat across from me, sipping in quiet contemplation.

"I don't know who to trust or what's real anymore." My eyes meet his. "Especially Asher, knowing how I craved a family . . ." my voice trails off.

God, Asher keeps lying.

"Sentiments I understand all too well, Eve." His expression becomes crestfallen.

I pull the blanket tighter around me in an attempt to console myself. Realization sinks in—this is why Gage is so closed off. He trusts no one, because everyone lies and betrays.

"I'm going to have to take you back to La Gargouille at some point. When they return, the clan will most likely come and break my door down in search of you. It's fifteenth century, irreplaceable. I'd hate to have to bill you for it," Gage says, with a wit I rarely get to see.

"Not tonight. I just can't," I plead.

How can I face a family that keeps things from me?

He watches me for a long time before getting up and heading to another room. I place the glass on the coffee table and catch his sly grin as he reappears, holding up a DVD case.

"What's that?"

"*The Smurfs*," he answers, then holds up another in his other hand. "And, I'm embarrassed to say, *The Smurfs 2*. I thought since I blew your mind with the leprechauns, you could blow mine with little blue beings who live in mushrooms."

At his gesture, the walls that have begun to form around my heart crack. "Do you have popcorn?"

"Of course."

"Goobers?"

"Do I look new here, love?"

"Yes."

Gage looks at me in confusion.

"Isn't that what you are? My new protector."

His eyes hold mine for a few moments, before a panty-dropping smirk crosses his lips.

"That is, without doubt, what I am, Eve."

I nod and stare at the only person I fully trust at the moment, before offering a smile.

After we get the snacks and set up the movie, we snuggle in on the couch. I blankly watch the screen while thoughts of the past few months run through my mind.

My life is so different, and right now, in this moment, out of everyone who has entered my life recently, I'm grateful that it's Gage who is here with me. There are no pretenses with him.

Inhaling, I move closer to him and curl up into his side, resting my head on his shoulder. His entire body goes rigid for a moment. I hold my breath, thinking he'll ask me to move. After a bit, he relaxes and sinks into the cuddle, wrapping his arm around me, protectively.

ॐॐ

"Seek the scrolls," a voice whispers softly. My eyes flutter open and adjust to the dim, buzzing, overhead fluorescent lights. Stacks of books come into focus as I lift my head off the hard surface I'm drooling on. I become conscious of the fact that I'm in the library on campus. *Crap.*

Groaning, I stretch my body and check my cell phone, realizing how late it is. I type off a quick apology text to Abby, since I was supposed to meet her downstairs ten minutes ago.

Once we returned to Massachusetts, Gage recommended the London clan back off a little. They're allowing me personal space after the newest bombshell was dropped. The St. Michaels claim they had no knowledge of my biological connection to my aunt and Michael. The jury is still out on whether I believe them or not.

Asher no-showed, but did call and text me upon our return, every five seconds. I didn't answer. I'm still hurt at the idea he knew they were my parents all along and never told me.

At the thought, I angrily begin to shove my books and iPad into my bag, when a familiar coldness floats over my skin. At the frigid caress, my body automatically goes on high alert.

It's late, and the library is empty and quiet. All I hear is the sound of my heavy breathing. I scan the floor for signs of danger and quickly make my way to the elevator.

As soon as I press the down button, the temperature in the room drops, so much so that my breath comes out in a cloud form. *Oh shit. Come on. Come on. Come on.* I will the elevator to move faster, and remind myself that Abby is downstairs waiting for me.

"Eve." My name hangs in the frosty air.

My eyes dart to the right, where the sound came from. Standing behind a stack of books is the same man I saw in the quad. Again, he's leaning on his samurai sword, his dark, lifeless eyes studying me.

Turning, I fully face the stranger. "Who are you?"

Brilliant, Eve, bait him.

His lips tilt up in a wicked grin. "Thoren." His voice echoes with disdain.

"What do you want?" I bristle, proud I sound stronger than I feel.

"You."

"You'll have to take a number," I come back in a smart tone.

"Lucky for you, my number was just called." The malice in his voice booms.

"Who sent you?"

He tilts toward me with his sinister eyes. "Lucifer."

The elevator dings and the doors open. I stand there for a moment longer, staring at Thoren, before a familiar male voice floats out from the open access.

"Miss Collins, I don't have all evening. Will you be joining me or staying on the fifth floor?" Professor Davidson inquires.

Just as fast as it dropped, the temperature returns to normal. Thoren has vanished. After a moment of shock, I release a breath and turn to the architecture lecturer, entering the elevator.

"Everything all right, Miss Collins?"

"Yes. Thank you," I manage through a shaky breath.

He fixes his bowtie, the way he did during class last semester, and nods once. "All right."

I lift my eyes and watch the numbers as we descend. *Why on earth is this taking so long? It's only five floors.* I need to calm the fuck down and get myself under control.

"If I may, you're very pale. Are you sure you're feeling well?"

"Yes. Thank you," I repeat on autopilot, and force a smile.

"At this late hour, the library tends to bring out the unease in people." His voice is gentle.

"I'm fine. Just late to meet my friend," I attempt to be pleasant.

"I see," he responds with a voice lined in disbelief.

There is awkward silence and tension in the small space, until we hit the third floor.

"I'm pleased to hear that it wasn't Lucifer's demon that set off your nervous energy, daughter of Heaven," the educator throws out in a casual tone, as if he's discussing the weather.

At the pointed statement, I turn my head and tilt it toward him. "Excuse me?"

"Thoren."

"H-How?"

"How do I know about Thoren, Miss Collins? You'll forgive my lack of decorum, however, I am aware that Mr. St. Michael is no longer your primary guardian. That, daughter of Heaven, is the reason upper-level demons, like Thoren, are hunting you. Regrettably for you, Mr. Gallagher and the rest of the London clan are not able to feel their presence."

My mouth is hanging open, yet I can't figure out how to shut it. The elevator dings, signifying that we've reached the main floor. The sound snaps me out of my stupor.

"Let's get you into my office. It's charmed for safety. There, I will happily attempt to answer any and all of the questions running around behind your beautiful eyes." His smile is warm.

I exhale roughly. "Um, I need to let Abby know. She's waiting outside for me."

"Very well. I'll simply need a few moments or so of your time this evening," he responds.

After convincing Abby that I'm not avoiding her, but need more time to finish my thesis, I follow Professor Davidson into his office. It looks typical of a college teacher's office. It's dark, with books strewn everywhere, and it's dusty. *He really needs to clean more.*

"May I offer you some tea, Miss Collins?" he asks, while placing an elegant silver tray on his antique mahogany desk. It's host to a white bone-china carafe, dainty teacups and saucers.

"No. Thank you," I respond and take a seat in an old worn leather chair across from the middle-aged gentleman.

Professor Davidson sits back in his own executive chair and tents his fingers under his chin. "Let me begin by formally introducing myself. My name is Dr. Henry Davidson. As you have already assessed, I'm a gargoyle. At the moment, my current assignment is the protection of Kingsley College."

"I see." *I don't really, but it seems a more appropriate response than get the fuck out.*

"I was assigned here when you decided to join the student body. The council realized the demonic legion and dark army could infiltrate the campus while looking for you, and that would place humans in danger. Hence the reason for my presence," he explains further.

"Are there other protectors here that I don't know about?"

"Yes."

"Do Asher and the St. Michaels know that you're here and who you are?"

"Prince Asher is aware, since he is on the council. Once he was assigned as your protector, and you accepted your academic spot at Kingsley, he ruled in favor of the college's protection."

Great, something else that Asher "left out" of previous conversations.

"Why didn't he say anything to me when we had your class together last semester?"

"That's for him to answer. I assume he didn't want you to be concerned with it."

"Which clan are you with?"

"That isn't important. What is, is that I am an elder, and with that comes a level of prestige and privacy. I realize you are unfamiliar with our ways. I'll ask you to be respectful of what I can, and can't, offer you in the way of information. The oaths are imposed for reasons."

"Right. Who could forget those pesky oaths?" I sigh. "Would you at least indulge me and answer how it's possible for you to sense Thoren, if the others can't?"

"Like the prince, I have a dark bloodline, hence my gift to sense higher-level demons. It's a rare attribute that very few gargoyles possess. My ability is the reason I was chosen to protect the college from the demonic legion and dark army," he answers calmly.

I ponder this. "Asher can also sense higher-level demons?" I ask quietly.

"Yes. Mr. St. Michael not only has the ability to manipulate darkness, but his bloodline also allows him to sense higher-level demons, such as Thoren."

"Doesn't he share the same family bloodline as Keegan and Callan?" I question.

"Asher has a stronger lineage than his brothers, which is why he is next in line to the throne and will eventually rule our people. Surely that has been mentioned to you?"

"It has." I let this information sink in for a moment. "I'm sorry, Professor, I don't understand. If Asher shares the same parentage as Keegan and Callan, how is his bloodline stronger? Does he have different parents?"

"Asher's line is stronger for the same reason that yours is directly connected to Heaven. It was altered. Just as you are the last descendent of Eve, Asher is a direct descendent of Adam, through Lilith, the first female demon."

I go still. Adam? Eve? Lilith? *I swear to all that is holy.*

"I can see further explanation is needed," the professor says, taken aback that I'm unaware of this information. He shifts in his chair. The leather creaks and groans under the weight.

"Please," I answer on a frustrated breath, knowing the shit's about to hit the proverbial fan.

"Are you familiar with divination, Miss Collins?"

"Prophecies? I suppose, some. What do they have to do with Asher and me?"

"At the order of an archangel, both your and Asher's bloodlines were touched, or altered, by Everley, the cherub angel of ancestry. Your bloodline is actually derived from Eve, Adam's second wife, and a light of Heaven. Asher's lineage is a result of being altered to include the bloodline of Lilith, Adam's first wife, and a demon of darkness. Your combined lines have been designed to fulfill the divination outlined in the scrolls. The prophecy states the souls of the daughter of light and the prince of dark shall join together. United as one, the two will, until the end of days, bring redemption to creation."

I just stare at the professor, wondering if he's lost his mind, or if this is truth. It's hard to tell. The gargoyle is quirky in that *I'm an intellect* way, but scattered in that lovable *doesn't have an email* way. He reminds me of a scholarly Indiana Jones. Perhaps he smoked too much in the sixties. That would explain the crazy-ass information he just dropped on me.

Truthfully, it's not all that outrageous, given I'm in love with a gargoyle, am being chased by the devil himself, and most recently found out that I'm the daughter of an archangel.

"Miss Collins, are you still with me?" His tone is less than amused.

"Sorry, I was absorbing your thoughts on the divination," I reply.

He releases a deep sigh, sensing I'm not focused. "When you visit with Sorceress Lunette, she will confirm the divination and show you the scrolls as proof."

"This information contradicts what I've been told," I challenge.

"I do believe that Priestess Arabella informed you that your future is not what is being presented as truth," he adds. *Crap. Again, it's all a lie.*

"I think . . . I'll take that cup of tea now, if you don't mind," I say through a dry throat.

"Of course." The professor stands stiffly, pours, then offers a teacup to me. He watches me closely as I allow the hot liquid to soothe my throat.

"If I'm following what you're suggesting correctly, then Heaven predesigned Asher and me so we'd have a soul connection? Knowing all along, at some point, we would meet, fall in love, and save the world?" I reason out loud.

"I wouldn't have put it so plainly, Miss—" I cut him off.

"The Royal Gargoyle Council of Protectors would never have granted me Asher's protection if the prophecy was true," I state in a firm tone, watching the professor.

"Miss Collins, the council does not know what is written in the scrolls. Garrick, our late king, only made it known that Asher's bloodline was of superior lineage, spinning it to the council that the darkness in him would be beneficial when he takes the throne. Asher will be the first king who is gifted enough to defend mankind against ALL demons. The success of his assignment to protect you is something he is required to fulfill in order to inherit the throne. It's a contingency set by the Royal Gargoyle Council of Protectors. That is all. The ruling body is unaware of your fates, or each of your parts in the divination of redemption," he states.

"And Michael?"

Slate-gray eyes hold mine. "The archangel was the one who gave the approval to the cherub to alter both of your bloodlines with light and dark. Therefore, I would assume the warrior of Heaven is aware of what is written within the prophecy."

We sit in silence for a brief time, while I absorb everything being said. Sadness looms over me when realization sets in that not only is Asher drawn to me by the blood bond as my protector, but also, if the divination is true, this was all a big plan. So that Heaven would succeed over Hell. We're the key, not just me. It's us, together. We were fated to fall in love.

"This is what Gage meant when he said I was a pawn," I state, emotionless.

"Pawn or not, Miss Collins, without darkness, there is no light. To that accord, without light, there would be no darkness. Everything must balance," the elder gargoyle instructs.

"Is that why Asher agreed to be my primary guardian? Has he been pretending all this time to feel for me so that we can fulfill the divination?" I question rhetorically.

"I'm sorry, Miss Collins. That is a question that only the prince can answer." His voice is low.

"Who else knows about the scrolls?"

"Aside from me, as the keeper of the scrolls, and Sorceress Lunette, as the guardian of the scrolls—Heaven, Prince Asher, Mr. Gallagher and now, you," he answers.

My hands are shaking, so I place the delicate teacup on the desk and stand abruptly. *I need out of this office.* I register a knock on the door before Gage walks in. He's eyeing both the professor and me suspiciously while he twirls an unlit cigarette in his hand in a casual manner.

"Everything okay, love?" he asks, on guard.

"How did you know I was in here?"

"Henry. It's nice to see you again. I assume you've downloaded Eve on the scrolls and the divination?" Gage ignores my question.

"I have. As you asked of me," Professor Davidson answers point-blank.

My eyes flip to Gage's. "You told him to tell me?"

"Once again, it is my opinion that you should have all the facts, love. Henry is the old friend I spoke of during our time in the Land of Leprechauns."

"Well, now I have them." My tone is lined with aggravation.

Gage holds my eyes for a moment, then nods once.

"I'll give you two a moment to catch up," I offer, looking between the two gargoyles.

"Abby is waiting for you outside. Stay with her," Gage orders. *Damn bossy gargoyles.*

I snatch my messenger bag up and head to the door, opening it to exit as I hear Professor Davidson's voice make its way through the dust specks in the dim beams of light in his workplace.

"Miss Collins . . . for the record, the divination never spoke of love. Only that the two souls would be entwined as one," he adds as if it's supposed to make a difference.

Without a look back, I walk through the door, needing to escape. Still not ready to face Abby, I head toward the back of the building. I know it's risky, but right now I need to digest everything that, once again, has been thrown in my freaking lap.

As soon as the cool night air hits me, I squeeze my eyes shut and take in a deep breath, attempting to hold back the tears. *Shit! Don't break down. Not here.*

Does Asher even love me or has this all been a game for him? Gage is right. I have no free will. Everything from birth and before has been decided for me, including love. It dawns on me that I'm not my own person.

I've been fooling myself into believing I have control over any of this. It's all a diversion and I'm the key. *When am I going to wake up from this nightmare?*

Everyone, every single person I know and cared for, has lied to me.

7 Forbidden Fruit

The smell of fresh grass encompasses me, swallowing me up like a wave. My eyes drift to the sky, immersed in its perfect shade of blue. Smiling to myself, I pretend, like I did when I was a child, that the sky is the ocean and I'm so far underneath it, no one will ever find me.

A passing airplane leaves behind a line of white billowing smoke, and I imagine it's a boat and the trailing vapor, waves that are too far away to ripple through me.

My eyes close, absorbing the warmth of the sunshine. Its yellow beams penetrate through the light green leaves as they sway gently in the spring breeze. It's in these small private moments that I'm able to appreciate the beauty that is life and the world. I can center myself and allow the outside forces of the universe to disappear. I just . . . exist.

A shadow falls over me, cutting off the warmth—an odd occurrence, since there are no clouds in the sky. My eyes pop open to see Callan looming over me, chomping on a red apple. He's chewing at it viciously, like a horse. *Ugh, gross.*

"You're blocking out the sun." I point toward the ball of fire.

Callan plops down next to me on the grass. The sound of his exaggerated crunching invades the quiet of nature. I study the child-like way the gargoyle is relaxing next to me, without a care in the world.

Looking down at me, he holds out the mangled fruit.

"Want a bite, cutie?"

I squint. "I don't know. Is it poisoned, or will it provide me with knowledge?"

He chuckles. "I think you might be taking this whole bloodline thing too seriously, Eves."

"That's a first. Most of you think I'm not taking it seriously enough," I quip.

Placing the core on the ground next to him, Callan scoots down and stretches out next to me before placing his hands behind his head.

"For the record, in the Garden of Eden, when Eve ate the forbidden fruit, it was never established that it was an apple. The fruit could have been anything. A pear, a banana, an orange . . . well, you get the point. Any one of those items she snacked on might have pissed off the big guy," he quibbles.

I roll my eyes. "Your point?"

"Sometimes, a myth is just a myth. If you want truth, you need to seek facts," he expands.

"Does that mean you don't believe in the divination?"
Please say no. Please.

He closes his eyes, soaking in the sun. "I believe that my brother loves you. End of story."

"I wish I had your conviction."

"You do. You just don't know it."

We sit in comfortable silence for a while, just watching the sky, before Callan speaks.

"Family dinner in an hour," he says, kissing my temple and standing.

"Okay," I draw out.

"Don't be late, because you don't want to miss out on Gage peeling potatoes." He wiggles his eyebrows at me.

I laugh. "I thought that was Keegan's punishment?"

The adorable protector shrugs. "It's good to shake things up a bit. Plus, Gage ate all the cookies I baked this afternoon. All. The. Cookies. He must be reprimanded accordingly."

I smile and shake my head at his silliness. "That, I have to see."

"It's not to be missed," he throws over his shoulder as he walks toward the house.

☙❧

Callan was right. This is the best scene ever. Even Keegan is sitting on a stool watching, amusement evident on his face.

Gage has on one of Callan's aprons. It reads *Can I Check to See If My Hot Dog Fits Your Bun*. The visual has sent me into a laughing fit twice. He's standing at the sink next to piles—and I mean piles—of potatoes. There have to be at least a thousand of the little brown spuds mounded up.

Gage looks over his shoulder at me, an unlit cigarette hanging. He looks miserable.

"Glad you're finding this humorous, love." He groans as the nicotine stick bounces.

"I am. I truly, truly am," I reply and continue to help a giggling Abby with the salad.

"Shut up and peel, traitor," McKenna spits out, which just makes it even funnier.

Callan approaches Abby from behind. "Do you really need that many potatoes, baby?" she asks.

"My girl might want hash browns in the morning," he says with a light tone, then drops a peck on her lips and squeezes her butt.

Their cuteness factor really is getting gross.

"This sucks," Gage throws out after only peeling five of the earthy vegetables.

I decide to walk over and give him a pep talk. "Nice apron."

His eyebrows lift as he leans in conspiratorially. "Callan said the ladies love the aprons. Is that true?"

I have to bite my bottom lip to prevent another laugh from escaping. "It certainly makes you look like something special, gargoyle. What that is? I'll need to give it some thought."

Gage tosses the peeler into the sink. "I need a cigarette," he grumbles, and walks out the French doors onto the patio while the laughter follows him.

❧

"Babe, dinner was so good," Abby compliments, squeezing Callan's hand with pride.

The small gesture hits me hard. *No matter how angry I am, I miss Asher.* I excuse myself, and retreat to the peaceful solitude of the library. I spread out my labs, which I need to work on if I'm going to pass my classes this semester. It feels good to focus on college for a bit, normal. After a few hours, I'm spent, and just finishing when Gage walks in.

"Hey."

"Need any help, love?" he questions and points to the clutter of papers.

I just stare at him. "You know, I don't even know if you've been to college or not. It just dawned on me that other than Camilla, I really don't know anything about you."

Gage sits down on the floor and pauses for a moment. His thigh brushes mine while he runs his thumb over his lower lip in thought.

A sexy, panty-dropping smirk crosses his mouth. "My favorite color is black. I have a thing for fast cars, in black. And I love coffee . . . black."

I roll my eyes, which causes him to laugh lightly. *Dear God, he should do that all day, every day.*

"I enjoy listening to Arctic Monkeys and Metallica. If I could be any animal in the world, I'd be a lion like my clan mark," he announces.

"And school?" I push.

"I graduated from the École des Beaux-Arts, the most prestigious art school in Paris."

My eyes go wide. "Holy shit, Gage. That's impressive."

He returns my response with an empty smile, void of all emotion. The wall's back.

"I know the guys own Katana and other businesses. What about you?" I ask, wanting to know more about him. "Do you work or anything?"

"I own architectural firms and several art studios," he shares absentmindedly.

My eyes hold his. "Really?"

"I was assigned to Camilla as her protector when she attended art school." His eyes flick out the windows in a far-off gaze. "It's why I also attended. She was enrolled in the Academy of Painting and Sculpture and I was registered in the Academy of Architecture. It was there that I first met Professor Henry Davidson. He was working toward his doctoral at the time. After we graduated, there weren't a lot of studios that would show sculpture carvings from a recent graduate, even one from a school as prominent as the École des Beaux-Arts. My father was very well-off and I had a sizeable inheritance, so I took some of it, and designed and opened a studio in Spain, *Mi Alma*. It specialized in three-dimensional art so Camilla would have a place to display and sell her work. She was particularly fond of sculpting gargoyles." He smiles at a memory, but it doesn't match the lost expression etched in every line of his perfect face.

"I think that has to be the most romantic thing I have ever heard," I say honestly.

He inhales harshly. "When my father noticed the money had been removed from my account, he investigated, learning that I had not only fallen in love but also secretly mated with Camilla, breaking my protector oath. The rest, as they say, is history." He swallows hard, fighting off the shadows.

"What does *Mi Alma* mean?" I ask with a gentle voice.

His eyes catch mine in a fleeting moment of sentiment. "My soul."

My heart breaks. "I'm so sorry, Gage."

"As I said before, love, don't be. She's dead," he bristles and puts his mask back on. "I was the one who actually designed and built Katana."

"Really?" I ask, surprised. "Asher never mentioned it."

The right side of his mouth tilts. "No. I imagine he didn't, love."

We're silent for a while. Lost in our own memories and emotional turmoil.

"I'm scared," I admit in a low whisper. "That Asher won't come back. And if he does, that what I feel isn't real. I'm even more terrified that he doesn't feel the same," I continue, barely audible.

"He loves you," Gage says with firmness.

I hold his eyes. "How can you be sure?"

"I know," he states, reaching out and wiping away a lone tear that has fallen on my cheek.

"Eve? Oh, sorry. I thought you were studying?" Abby floats into the room, making her way to stand in front of us, narrowing her eyes at Gage's hand on my cheek.

I plaster on a fake smile. "I was. What's up?"

"Callan and I were going to take you out for ice cream. You know, to cheer you up. I can come back, though . . . if it's not a good time," she shuffles awkwardly.

"I'd love some ice cream. I'll meet you guys outside in a minute." My pitch is high.

"Okay." She looks between Gage and me for a moment before slowly leaving.

Gage smirks sexily at me.

I huff. "They treat me like a child."

"I have an engagement this evening, so they offered to babysit you."

"I thought you didn't babysit?"

He shrugs. "If they're buying, I suggest rainbow sprinkles."

I nudge him with my shoulder. "Go . . . drop some panties. Break some hearts. Or whatever it is you're doing tonight," I say and he stands, heading to the doorway.

"Oh, and Gage?"

"Yeah, love?"

"Thanks for letting me in."

Gage nervously smiles and leaves.

෯෯

"I can't even believe that I am mated to you," Abby screeches. I cringe. An hour. This has been going on for an hour. *Please, God, make it stop.* I sigh and swallow another spoonful.

"Baby, don't be like that. You know it's totally true. Ben & Jerry's Hazed and Confused is honestly the best ice-cream flavor in the history of the world," Callan argues.

Abby's eyes are like saucers. Big, blue, angry saucers. "Callan Thomas St. Michael, I may have to break our bond. McConnell's Eureka Lemon and Marion Berries is by far the best flavor ever made. Right, Eve?" They both stare at me, waiting for me to pick a side. I groan.

"I'm partial to black raspberry," I offer quietly, not really wanting to be in the middle.

Callan's jaw drops and Abby beams before clearly declaring that she's won. *Good Lord.*

"That's closer to my flavor, and since they're both fruit flavors, I win," she declares.

"No way. Babe, her pick doesn't count. That flavor isn't even an ice cream. It's a sorbet or frozen yogurt, or something. I mean, who picks a fruit-flavored ice cream?" Callan disputes.

Abby's mouth drops. "I JUST DID!"

"Would you two please tone it down? Christ, it's like I'm out with my parents. People are staring and you're embarrassing me with your bickering."

God, they're like children.

They both look around with perplexed expressions.

"Cutie, there's like, no one here. How could we possibly be embarrassing you? Are you telling me the opinion of one scoop girl is going to keep you up all night?" He laughs lightly.

"You're so immature." I roll my eyes at his antics.

"All right, babe. Eves doesn't want our ice-cream war to humiliate her. Apparently, she's too cool for school. So what do you say, just admit I'm right and we'll call it a night," he suggests.

Just as Abby is about to make her case, again, the front window of the ice-cream shop shatters, sending shards of glass everywhere. The three of us hit the floor. On our hands and knees, both gargoyles move to protect me from whatever blew the window out. *Shit.*

Thoren emerges from the darkness with two large men, mirror images of one another, flanking him, one on each side. They lithely walk through the nonexistent window as glass crunches under the weight of their heavy black combat boots.

Uninterested in the scene in front of him, Thoren walks over to the whimpering girl behind the counter and runs his sword right through her throat, ending her life by decapitation. My stomach roils at the cruel display of evil as her head hits the ground.

"Oh. My. God," I gasp and bile rises into my throat.

He didn't even blink.

At the sound of my voice, Thoren swings his head in my direction. Callan and Abby both stand and move into a warrior stance. I follow suit behind them. The demon takes a step toward us, his samurai sword dripping with blood.

Crap. This isn't going to end well.

"What the fuck, dude?" Callan says to him from in front of me.

"Eve," Thoren addresses me, his voice deep and ominous.

"Friend of yours?" Callan questions.

Shit. I'd forgotten to tell the clan about him.

"Um . . . Thoren is a higher-level demon, and apparently a stalker," I answer, scared shitless.

"Higher-level demon?" Abby repeats to herself, somewhat perturbed.

"What can we do for you gentlemen this evening?" Callan asks in a friendly, relaxed tone.

Thoren just tilts his head in a threatening fashion. "I've come for the girl."

I peek around Callan to see the other two imposing soldiers. Twins. Neither has hair. Their heads are as bald as a baby's bottom. Both demons also have black eyes and pale skin, almost albino, which looks ghastly against their all-black army fatigues. I cringe.

Callan sighs dramatically. "Thoren, was it? Listen, dude, I'm not one of those guys who likes to disappoint others. I have this unhealthy need-to-be-liked complex. Right, babe?"

"It's true. He sulks for weeks if someone doesn't like him," Abby adds. *Oh my God, these two.*

"That said, we've become quite fond of and attached to Eve. Which means there is no way in hell we're handing her over to you. If you want her, you'll have to go through us. Sorry to disappoint you guys. I'd be happy to buy you a fruit-flavored ice cream to make up for it, though. Wait." Callan tsks. "You killed the scoop girl."

Holy shit. I'm so screwed.

Tiring of Callan's clowning around, Thoren stretches his head from side to side before taking a threatening step toward us. At the movement, both gargoyles protrude their raven wings, morphing into combat mode. Withdrawing their weapons, they're vigilantly ready to fight.

It's starting to rain, and the wind is whipping droplets of water into the deserted shop, causing puddles to form and mix with the young girl's blood. I'm trying to stay calm, but after watching Thoren kill that innocent girl, without thought or emotion, I'm becoming gut-wrenchingly terrified.

Callan and Abby aren't just protectors, they're my family. I love them and if anything were to happen to either of them, I wouldn't survive the loss. My heart is racing as I take in the scene in front of me.

"I do not play games, gargoyle," Thoren spits out spitefully at Callan.

"I guess you won't be invited to family game night, then," Abby murmurs.

Callan's focus flicks to Abby. "Good one, babe."

"Thanks." She blushes under his adoration.

"ENOUGH!" Thoren's explosive voice rocks the shop.

The remaining window glass falls from the frame and clanks on the tile. My stomach drops at the command and my hands automatically move to my daggers.

Callan's face contorts in rage before he snaps forward toward Thoren. "Agreed, demon."

Out of the blue, the twins morph into one body. I blink rapidly, trying to figure out if what I'm seeing is accurate. Unexpectedly, they teleport behind Abby and grab her around the throat. She's fast, though, bending at the waist and escaping their grasp.

I turn my focus onto Callan. He and Thoren are in a battle of mind control. Callan's face is marred by frustration. Thoren just looks pleased. The higher-level demon's eyes are no longer black, but a chilling red, while he chants in Latin.

The twin demon splits again and one of them shoots toward me at an inhuman speed. Abby manipulates the air around us, locking the first clone in an invisible hold. Without even realizing what I'm doing, I start focusing on the darkness, pulling Asher's gift to me, blanketing us all in black. The only light is the soft blue glow from Callan and Abby's eyes.

The momentary obscurity confuses the demons as the twins stare at me in disbelief. Abby takes advantage of the distraction and wields her sword into the trapped demon's heart. The wound causes him to vanish into blue flames. She turns angrily to the second demon, which is also just standing in awe, watching me. The angelic gargoyle plunges her knife into his back, through his heart, before he exits the shop in the same manner as his brother.

I smile at Abby as she winks at me. We turn to see Callan in the air, rotating to the right as Thoren's sword connects with his black wing, slicing into it painfully. He grunts in pain before landing on the black-and-white-tiled floor. Abby doesn't flinch, but the worry is evident by her slight intake of breath. Out of nowhere, a vicious circle of fire appears around the injured gargoyle, caging him in, no doubt produced by Thoren.

"Abby, focus your energies on Callan. I've got Thoren," I plead through the dark.

Her conflicted, glowing eyes transfer to me. "I-I can't do that, Eve. You're the charge."

"You have to. Please. I've got this." I point to Thoren. "Save Callan," I beg.

"Shit!" She pulls the rain, sourcing her powers to create a water tornado then moves it toward the flames in front of Callan to fight off the fire, which is growing wilder by the minute.

Thoren chooses that moment to teleport. None of us see it until it is too late. His hand whips out and snatches my throat, squeezing it tightly and lifting me off the ground.

The wind from the waterspout flies around the store, creating chaos with the shards of glass, but Abby has to keep it up to keep Callan safe.

I use every last bit of energy I have to raise my arms and bring my daggers downward. The sharp points slice into each of the demon's cheeks as thick, black tar oozes out.

Thoren doesn't even recoil. He just walks us backwards effortlessly through the chaos.

Cold, lifeless eyes bore into me with hatred. "You're mine now, daughter of Heaven."

"Actually, she's mine, asshole." At the sound of his deep voice, my heart rate slows.

The demon twists me so my back is pressed against his chest, never letting go of the tight chokehold. My eyes lift and connect with a pair of glowing indigo ones. I stop breathing, and not because Thoren is cutting off my circulation. Asher looks menacing and untamed, like at any moment, my beautiful dark prince would light the world on fire to get to me.

With the Angelic Sword in his hand, he rushes for Thoren. In one sharp movement, the arm that was squeezing my neck is removed from the demon's body. I drop to the ground, gasping for air. My gaze darts around, and I see the fire around Callan has disappeared. Then I'm being yanked back and wrapped in Abby's protection next to Callan.

Taking advantage of Thoren's pain, Asher lunges and spins again, making contact with and effortlessly removing the other arm from the demon. Thoren releases a painful howl before Asher's sword slices through the air and removes his legs. Black blood seeps and flows everywhere as my stomach roils again. Abby pulls me tighter into her embrace so I can't watch Asher torturing the demon.

Thoren growls. "Dark prince. You end me and you will seal your fate."

Worried, I look up to see that Asher isn't moving and his eyes are feral. "She is my fate." In an instant, he lunges forward and plunges the sword into the demon's heart. Seconds later, Thoren vanishes in blue flames and it's over.

Not even out of breath, Asher just stands there, like a dark avenging angel, his raven wings extended while the sword in his hand drips with the demon's remains. Soft, glowing eyes connect with mine. Behind him, the rain pours down outside and the wind whips through the storefront.

"Ash, so good to see you, bro," Callan says through the deep breaths he's taking.

"You too, man," Asher replies, never taking his eyes from me.

"Let me ask you something, would you order fruit-flavored ice cream?" Callan asks.

Asher gives me his sexy signature smirk. "Forbidden fruit is my favorite flavor."

My heart just stopped.

8 Broken

I let my eyes soak him in. They've been starved of his beauty for too long. The rain drips over Asher's face and his lips part. We stand there, unmoving, holding one another's gaze. While Abby tends to Callan's injuries, I fight every instinct I have telling me to run and jump into Asher's strong arms. *He's here. He's really here.*

Curbing the need to crawl inside his soul, I do the only thing I can in this moment. I walk right past him toward the opening of the broken window. With the wind and rain whipping at me, I twist slowly and hold his stare, then walk backwards into the rainfall. *God, I love him, and at the same time, I'm still so angry with him for lying to me. I'm a hot mess.*

As soon as the warm drops hit my face, I lift my daggers and throw the weapons at him, one on each side. I don't wait to see if they hit their mark, I simply turn and walk away.

"Is that any way to greet me, siren?" Asher's voice cuts through the downpour.

I keep my focus trained ahead of me as I continue to escape. Each step weighs me down. My chest begins to burn. *What the hell is he doing here?* Without warning, strong arms wrap around my waist, pulling me tight against a warm, muscular body. Asher's minty breath crosses my ear, and the butterflies in my stomach awaken from their long slumber. *Oh God.*

"If I wanted to play rough, I would take you to the chamber." I shudder in his arms.

Yanking out of his grip, I keep moving forward. I don't get far before his large hand grabs my upper arm. He spins me so we're face-to-face. He looks at me, memorizing every detail, devouring me with his eyes. With every caress, the months of absence from one another fade away, and we just absorb each other.

Damn, he's so beautiful. I scan the depths of his eyes as water drips from his long, sooty lashes and runs down his stubble-dusted cheeks, onto his perfectly kissable lips. My body hums with longing and energy. All my senses reawaken, igniting my skin. The darkness recedes, and in its place, light fills me, making me whole. I can finally breathe again.

No, Eve, focus. He hurt you.

Asher leans his forehead on mine while his hands bury themselves into my soaked hair. He tugs once, forcing my head up as his eyes dart to my lips. This feeling is addicting.

It's official. Asher is my drug. The way he's studying me is intense, empowering.

"I've fucking missed you, siren." His voice is raw with need. "Tell me you missed me."

I have. With everything that I am, I have.

"No," I murmur in a stubborn tone.

Asher takes my denial as a challenge. He raises his eyebrows and smirks at me. "Say it."

"Go to hell," I bite out, allowing his betrayals to fuel my anger and frustration.

"I've already been there, sweetheart," Asher taunts, using the nickname I hate.

My eyes turn to slits, pinning him. Rain continues to trickle down his body and his eyes darken with desire. He jerks my hair again, roughly. My chest begins to rise and fall rapidly at his proximity.

Damn traitorous body.

"Tell me, siren," he demands, becoming irritated. Good, he's getting mad. So am I.

"No!" I push at his chest and back away an inch, before his arm shoots out and grabs me again, yanking me to him. His wet body presses against me everywhere I need it to. I moan at the contact, unable to control it. I'm lost in the sensation of him near me after a long absence.

Our breathing is ragged, coming out in angry pants as we stare one another down. Asher's hands lock onto my waist, forcing me even tighter against him. Passionate dark eyes bore into me, weakening my resolve.

He lied to you and he left. Stay focused.

"Let me walk away." I whisper the plea.

"Never!" His face is furious and intense.

"I hate you," I speak softly.

"You love me," he counters.

Asher's gaze narrows before he leans in and lightly brushes his lips across mine. A soft whimper escapes me, parting my lips, granting him full access. Breathing him in.

He takes the invitation without thought. His lips press forcefully to mine, and his tongue invades me. This kiss isn't sweet or adoring. It's angry and raw, punishing. Each of us gives just as good as we're getting. It's maddening and intoxicating. He's all around me. His scent. His body. His touch. I'm drowning in all that is Asher St. Michael.

My fingers tangle into his damp hair and pull, hard. At the painful grip, he growls into my mouth. We match one another stroke for stroke, each swallowing the primal noises the other makes.

A clap of loud thunder booms in the distance. At the intrusion, I realize I can't breathe and have to pull away. The momentary oxygen reprieve brings me back to my senses. Tears of rage, and relief that he's here, begin to form, stinging my eyes.

"You're right, I do love you. It's why it shattered me when you left," I snap, and lift my eyes to meet his.

"I'm sorry, siren." Asher's face is pained as he releases the apology.

"That's not even the worst part. At least when you're shattered, you can eventually put the pieces back together and become whole again. But then, I discovered that you've been lying to me this entire time about my parents and the divination, breaking my faith in you. Putting an end to my allegiance to you. You've broken us, forever." My voice is resolute.

Asher stops breathing. "What?" he says, with fear lining his voice.

"I know everything. I know that Michael and Elizabeth are my biological parents. I know that your bloodline carries the mark of Lilith and Adam. I know that we were created to fall in love and fulfill the divination." My voice rises with each statement. "This entire time, you pretended to feel for me so we could fulfill a prophecy. Knowing how I craved normalcy and a sense of family, you kept me in the dark about my biological parents. All you've done is lie to me. You've broken my loyalty to you," I fume.

"I didn't lie to you, siren." He runs a frustrated hand through his damp hair and down the back of his neck. "Is that the shit Gage has been feeding you while I was away?"

I'm not sure why, but bringing Gage into this seems below the belt, which makes my blood boil. "YOU LEFT ME WITH HIM!" I shout and point at him.

Asher's face turns dangerous. "YES! I FUCKING DID!" he yells back. "And for the record," his voice cracks with anger, "I'd do it again."

"WHY?" My temper flares as I seethe at him.

"I HAD NO CHOICE," he screams. The veins in his neck bulge. "Christ, siren, the fucking council was down my back. I TOOK AN OATH!" Asher takes an angry step toward me, and I retreat. "By the grace, I'm the next in line to the royal throne. For shit's sake, I'm a member of the protector council. I was accused of breaking my oath to my people and family. That kind of accusation doesn't come with a slap on the goddamn wrist." His voice drops to a heated calm, vibrating straight through me.

I look away, not knowing how to respond to him. My tears are flowing freely now, mixing with the rain. Another clap of thunder sounds as Asher pulls in air, reining in his temper.

"I've never fucking lied to you, siren. Not about the divination or your biological parents. I had my suspicions about Michael and Elizabeth. Believe it or not, I'm not privy to all that is the Angelic Council. It was on the tip of my tongue to tell you on numerous occasions, but without any real proof, I didn't want to get your hopes up, only to crush them if it wasn't true. I'm not sure what Gage told you about the divination, but I haven't seen the scrolls for myself. So no, I don't fucking know what it prophesizes about you and me. As far as having Lilith's blood running through me . . . it's demon blood. That's not something to be shouting about from the rooftops. When I was stabbed by Dimia, Callan explained the demon blood to you, perhaps not in divination detail, but you knew."

"Omitting the facts to me is the same as lying," I counter, as my anger dissipates.

"In that moment, my brother didn't feel you were in the right emotional state to hear every minor detail of the bloodline. Looking back, I think you'd agree. I've never looked you in the eyes and lied to you. I swear to you, on my honor." I watch Asher's face. The hurt on it hits me in the gut, crushing my resolve.

No. Eve, you have to be strong.

"Asher, the divin—" Cold eyes meet mine, stopping the progression of my sentence.

"I told you early on not to look too deeply into who I am. That all you would find is darkness, siren. All I know about the divination is that the lineage grants me the gift to sense higher-level demons, like Thoren, and it protects me from turning into stone dust if stabbed. Beyond that, you've lost me. I have no knowledge of what else the scrolls state," he says, his voice returning to a more tolerable decibel.

I can't think straight. Between watching an innocent girl get beheaded tonight, fighting for my life, and now having Asher back, twisting the beliefs I've accepted, I'm exhausted. I have no fight left in me.

Sensing my surrender, Asher takes a step toward me again. "As far as Gage Gallagher goes, yeah, siren, I fucking left the one thing in the world that I care about under that piece of shit's protection. Do you want to know why?"

I shake my head slowly back and forth, because I can't handle any more. Asher frowns and remains silent for a moment. The only things between us are the sounds of the rain and our heavy breathing.

Asher closes his eyes and drops his head back. When they reopen, he's looking up at the inky sky. Slowly, his focus returns to face me. His gaze is glowing as he steps up to me, taking my face in his hands. The water pours off us now, since we're both completely drenched. I keep my arms in a tight grasp, hugging myself to prevent my hands from reaching out and touching him.

"Why?" I whisper.

"Because you're mine. Because I knew that Gage knew that I love you. Because, siren, hear me when I say this to you. I would give it all up. Break every fucking oath and loyalty I've taken to keep the one I made to you. Forever," he whispers firmly. "I love you."

I stop breathing. My eyes dart around, praying no one is around to hear him break his vow. Yet, at the same time, my heart and mind work overtime to grasp what he just said.

"That's just it, Asher. I'm not yours. I can never be," I remind him in a timid voice.

"You are mine, siren. I trusted Gage with your safety because I recognized that he is the only fucking person in this crazy-ass world that understands our situation. It was the same for him and Camilla," he confesses. "You're mine . . . and I'm yours, forever."

In the silence of the night, his words hang in the air. I sink to my knees, my body crumbling at his admission. Asher follows suit and kneels down in front of me.

"You shattered my trust and ended whatever amazing future we could have had." My voice is gentle and confused. "We're broken."

Asher lowers his head to my ear. "We're not broken. I love you."

My world tilts again. I have to close my eyes and focus on breathing before I completely pass out. The tears start coming again as Asher pulls me into an embrace. I clutch at him, needing to be close. He strokes my back gently while I sob into his shoulder.

"I'm sorry. I swear to fucking God, I'm sorry," he mumbles into my wet hair.

My resolve finally breaks, and I say the only thing I can. "I missed you so much."

As soon as the words are released from my mouth, Asher's entire body relaxes as he pulls back to look at me. Within the blue layers, I can see the underlying desire, but now, there's something else, something deeper, more permanent.

Its presence causes me to tremble.

"Cold?" Asher gives me his signature sexy smile.

"In love," I whisper.

Asher arches a brow. "Who is this asshole? Give me a name. I'll end his existence."

My mouth tilts into a smile. "No. I'll protect him, always."

❧

The steam from the shower billows out of the glass enclosure into the room. I allow the hot water to run over me, helping me wash away the insanity of the evening. Now that the adrenaline is wearing off, the reminder of that poor girl's death looms over me.

Abby and Callan were assigned to protect me. I was their charge tonight. Not her. That knowledge sickens me.

"Oh God," I speak softly into the warm mist. The realization hits me hard that Gage is right. These aren't cartoon characters I'm dealing with. They're killers with no regard for life.

I close my eyes and send a little plea that her spirit is at peace. I can't help but feel, once again, that I'm responsible for another innocent life having been ended before its time.

I study the shampoo and dirty rainwater as it twirls around the drain before sinking into it. Part of me wishes I could disappear too. Dragging myself out of the warmth, I throw on flannel pajama bottoms and a tank top. I dry my hair and head downstairs to find everyone.

The manor is silent. Oddly quiet. I move around in the stillness until I come into the Tension Room and see five beautiful gargoyles speaking in hushed tones. As soon as Abby sees me, she smiles brightly and waves me in.

I enter as Asher turns his attention to me, taking my breath away. He's showered and in black pajama bottoms and his gray *Property of London* shirt. It's all I can do not to run over and curl up on his lap like a kitten.

He's here. It wasn't a dream.

"Come here." Asher holds his hand out, and with tunnel vision, I walk over, allowing him to capture mine in his, pulling me into his side on the sectional. Not caring that everyone is watching us, he places the lightest kiss on my lips, causing me to blush.

Asher smirks. The hand not holding mine lifts, his thumb brushing over the pink hue on my cheeks, trying to wipe it away. I sigh as he pulls me closer, planting another kiss on my forehead.

"What precautions have been taken at the scene to avoid attention?" Keegan's voice slithers its way through my Asher focus, shoving me back into reality.

"We staged a large tree branch to appear as if the wind had broken it off, pushing it through the window, beheading and killing the girl. There were no other witnesses," Abby answers. Her worried gaze slides to Callan, who is lying on the couch, wings out, healing.

His injured wing is still covered in a blood-soaked bandage. Even though Callan's eyes are shut, I can tell he's already restoring his vigor. The color is slowly returning to his relaxed face. Guilt crawls up my throat. He's hurt because of me.

"I'm sorry," I blurt out. "I should have told you earlier about Thoren. With everything else going on, it . . . it just slipped my mind." I rub my forehead. *I'm so tired.*

McKenna scoffs. "It's about time you take responsibility, blood of Eden," she barks from across the room. "You're a serious fucking nightmare. You need to smarten the fuck up. This is not a game. It's our world. Your lack of respect for it is affecting my family."

"McKenna! That's enough." Asher throws out the warning in a growl.

"She's right. I know it's my fault. I take full responsibility for what happened this evening. I was preoccupied and I failed to mention Thoren earlier to the clan. I get it."

"Didn't I warn you, in England, about being unfocused?" McKenna bites out coolly.

"It's not entirely Eve's fault." Callan sighs from the couch. "Yes, she should have told us, but none of us sensed him. The fact that he was a higher-level demon means he got by us. All of us." The last part of his statement was pointed at McKenna. "So lay off a bit, Kenna."

"How did you know we needed help?" Abby asks Asher.

"I felt Eve pull my dark energy. I figured that she was in some sort of danger if she managed to successfully steal my gifts. Again," he replies cockily.

"Borrowed. I borrowed them. Not stole," I remind him, attempting not to roll my eyes.

"And the council?" Keegan asks, his voice stern.

"They've pardoned me due to lack of physical evidence. They did an extensive investigation and came up empty-handed," Asher explains with a sly smirk. "I was actually planning to call you this evening to let you know I was coming back tomorrow, before all hell literally broke loose."

"Do we really think they're going to let this go? Allow you to return to protecting Eve as if nothing happened?" Keegan asks.

Asher blows out a breath and his eyes find mine. "No more secrets, yeah?"

"Yeah." I squeeze his hand, relieved but also waiting for the other shoe to drop.

"They're consenting to my protection return on a probation period. Gage will still have to remain on for a bit while they continue to clear me." He watches me closely, probably expecting me to blow up that Gage will still be around. I won't. He's grown on me.

"Fabulous, we're stuck with the traitor even longer." McKenna sulks, sinking into a chair.

"Speaking of the devil," Keegan states, as Gage swaggers into the room.

"Well. Well. Well. Look who's back. Nice to see you, old friend," Gage taunts Asher.

With lightning speed, Asher is off the couch. His fist connects with Gage's jaw with a loud pop. *Lovely.*

"WHERE THE FUCK WERE YOU TONIGHT?" Asher shouts.

Gage just rubs his hand over his jawline, soothing the spot where Asher punched him. "Out."

At the reply, I close my eyes because Asher's entire body has gone rigid. "OUT? Eve was attacked tonight. By. A. Higher-Level. Demon. You're supposed to be fucking protecting her, asshole. Not getting laid!" Asher roars through a tight jaw.

"HEY!" Keegan barks. "Enough! Back off, Asher. Even if he were there, Gage wouldn't have sensed Thoren any more than the rest of us."

Gage's eyes flick to mine. "You okay, love?"

Asher steps in front of me, blocking me from Gage.

"Don't. Fucking. Speak to her."

"Asher," I warn.

"Eve and I have an understanding of how our protector relationship works. I left her under the safeguard of Callan and Abby this evening. I assumed that you would have been okay with that. Unless, of course, you're saying you don't trust your family with her safety?" Gage cocks an eyebrow up in challenge.

Holy fuck, this isn't good.

Asher lunges for him. Before he can wrap his hands around Gage's throat, Callan is holding back Gage and Keegan managed to grab Asher. They're in a stare-down.

"Enough," I say in a low voice, moving in between the two. "You two better learn how to get along if you're both going to be protecting me. I won't tolerate daily fights," I inform.

"What are you talking about, love?" Gage questions.

"Stop fucking using that term of endearment when addressing her," Asher warns.

I turn to Gage, ignoring Asher's tantrum. "It turns out Asher is back but on probation. The council has granted me both of your protection for the time being."

"Is that okay with you? His return and protection?" Gage asks.

"There's no reason to ask her if she wants my protection," Asher bites out tersely.

"I'm her new protector. It's my job to make sure she feels safe," Gage baits.

"Temporary. *I* am her protector," Asher counters.

Gage shrugs. "Or you're the old and I'm the new."

"Stop!" I plead with Gage. "I won't permit you to provoke him." I turn to Asher. "And I won't allow you to hit him every chance you get. Figure out how to work together or I'll request Marcus from the Manhattan clan as my new protector."

There's silence for a few moments before Keegan and Callan decide that both gargoyles are calm enough to be released from their holds.

"You do realize what this means?" Callan asks, amusement clear on his face. "I'm going to have to call you Gasher from now on." He smirks. "Get it? It's like Brangelina. Asher and Gage. Gasher. A forbidden bromance," he chuckles.

I roll my eyes. "I'm going to bed. Try not to murder one another before sunrise."

"I'll walk you up." Asher doesn't ask and I don't argue. I'm too tired. He snatches my hand and in a mature moment, bumps Gage with his shoulder as we walk by.

I sigh. The sound echoes in the hallway.

"Was that really necessary?"

Asher pushes me against the wall, caging me in. His stunning face is intense. Those damn beautiful eyes of his are unforgiving as they peruse down my body.

"When it comes to you, siren, everything I do is necessary."

"You lie to me."

"For your protection."

Redemption

"You left."
"For your protection."
"You broke your oath."
"Never. To. You."

Randi Cooley Wilson

9 Forgiveness

I finish my nighttime routine and walk out to witness Asher sliding into my bed, getting all cozy on my side no less. Once he notices me, he takes me in and bestows his sexy smirk, followed by a come-hither look that makes my insides go all girlie and gooey.

I seriously need to get control of that.

"What do you think you're doing, gargoyle?" I ask with my eyebrow arched.

"Get your beautiful ass over here and snuggle me," he orders playfully.

I release a quiet laugh. "Are you saying the big, bad protector needs to be cuddled?"

Asher shrugs. "I'm feeling emotional," he throws out.

My lips tilt at his dramatic knack. Uncrossing my arms, I move toward the bed. Without warning, Asher grabs me and pulls me down. I squeal in laughter. He tugs me close and kisses me lightly on the forehead before wrapping me in his arms. I can't help but release a sigh of contentment. *I must have lost brain cells, because after everything, I still want only him.*

"Now that I have you where I want you, siren, say it so I can go to sleep." He snuggles in.

My lips form a slight smirk, knowing what he's asking.

"Just because you're the prince of the gargoyle race, does not mean you can demand things of me, Your Highness. I'm human."

"I've been dying to hear it fall from your pretty, pouty lips for way too long. Oh, and when you say it, be sure to put some feeling behind it. Don't just half-ass it, siren. I want to feel as if you mean it." *What the hell?*

"You can't force me," I retort with wide eyes.

"Want to bet?" His tone is suggestive.

"Um, no. That's a bet I'll definitely lose."

"Just say it. The faster you do, the sooner I can feel you up." He bites his lip.

"What?" I laugh, causing a stern look from my protector. "Fine," I exhale.

"Wait," he commands, settling back in. "Okay, ready. You may sweet-talk me."

"Now, I really don't want to," I huff.

"Siren." It's a warning for compliance.

"Asher St. Michael, you're full of gargoyle awesomeness," I murmur begrudgingly.

His lips tilt into a wicked smirk. "I'll never get tired of hearing you say that."

"What if I get tired of saying it?" I tease, and try to escape his clutches.

Suddenly, I'm on my back. Asher is above me, staring at me with a fierce concentration.

"You won't. Not ever, because you're mine." His tone leaves no room for argument.

"That's not barbaric or anything." I push at his shoulder.

"I'm a gargoyle. We're intense and hot-blooded when it comes to our mates." Asher's face is unyielding.

After holding his stare for a bit, I choke out, "Mate?"

His eyes darken with resolve. "Mate," he confirms with authority.

This is too much, too soon. I'm still working on forgiving him. He can't just come back and claim me.

Oh shit, I can't breathe.

"Ash." I try to move out from beneath him.

My motion causes his body to press me firmly into the bed. "Listen to me, siren."

At his pointed tone, I stop fidgeting and nod that I'm paying attention.

"I know I fucked up by leaving. I'm sorry. If there had been another way, I would have done it. I swear to you. I'm still the next in line to the throne and there are rules I must follow. There's also the tiny issue of your ascension, and the demonic legion hunting you. We have some heavy burdens, yeah? But when this is all over, when all the battles have been fought and won, it's you and me. I promise. I'll fight for us. I'll light the world on fire if I have to. If it takes my last damn breath, I will lay my sword at your feet in front of every realm and being in existence. Claiming you as mine, forever."

My heart soars at his words, then falls at the reality. "It's not that simple, Ash."

"It *IS* that simple, siren." His tone is firm.

"Professor Davidson told me the divination of redemption prophesizes this, us. I don't want what we have to be based off a plan that was predestined. I want us to be real."

Asher goes quiet for a moment, in deep thought, before his eyes search mine.

"Hear me when I say this to you, yeah? I don't give a fuck what the scrolls say. If our souls are fated for one another, then fucking perfect. That just proves that you're meant to be mine," he determines.

"If the divination is true, how do I know what we feel is genuine?" I ask worriedly.

Piercing my eyes with his, Asher interlaces one of each of our hands. He pulls them toward his mouth before taking mine and flipping it over in his. Slowly, he lifts my palm to his lips, dropping the barest of kisses into the middle, searing my soul.

"It's real, because I say it's real," he says, ending the discussion.

Damn. Who could really argue with that? Especially when Asher's entire body is pressing against me. *Oh. My. God.* After the longest few seconds of my life, Asher shifts so he's leaning on his elbows. His hands come up and cradle my head, preventing me from moving.

"Siren."

My eyes flick to his mouth before locking with his. I swallow hard because my throat is dry from the hungry way he's looking at me. Asher looks like a predator ready to pounce on its prey. My body hums with energy and anticipation as he slowly lowers his mouth to mine.

"I've fucking missed touching you," he growls against my lips, before teasing my mouth by brushing his lips back and forth over them. The light contact sends shivers down my spine, leaving my body wanting more.

My hips lift, trying to bring his aroused body closer as he consumes me. He pulls his mouth back so there's only a sliver of air between us. His gaze penetrates each of my layers until finally it hits its mark. I know the exact moment it happens, because I can literally feel my soul shudder inside my body, clawing to get out and attach to his.

Asher moves his hips the slightest bit, and the friction causes me to release a soft mewl. At the sound, desire falls across his expression. I lift my lips to his, aching for contact so I can have the relief I'm so desperately craving. Yet, he pulls away, denying me.

"Asher." His name comes out a breathy plea.

He licks his lips. "Say it," he demands.

My brows pull together, not understanding.

"Say what?" I pant out.

Asher rocks his lower body into mine again and my entire body arches into his. I let out a sharp breath at the roughness of my breasts touching his chest. He pulls his lower lip into his mouth as his top teeth rake across the spot I want my lips sucking on.

"Tell me you believe this is real." He waits.

I whimper, because my body is hungering for more. Each of my hands moves up, wrapping themselves around his wrists. The feel of his leather bands increase my already sensitive response to him.

He's still holding my body hostage with his, my head firmly trapped between his hands. If I wasn't in such a lust-filled daze, I might be embarrassed by how I'm literally breathless for his touch. *This has to be real, right?* My feelings for him can't just be about the bond or divination.

Asher's tongue darts out, running along my bottom lip, wetting it with promises of release and bliss. He hasn't even blinked. His intense stare bores into me, stirring the want.

"Siren?" He pulls back again, watching me, waiting for me to answer.

I close my eyes and tighten my grip on his leather bands, as my brain plays back all the moments we've shared together and apart. I recall every emotion and feeling he's awakened in me. I try to imagine my future with him, and then without him. I can't. If he's not in it, there is only darkness. He. Is. It. Asher is my sole purpose for being.

I begin and end with him.

Slowly my eyes flutter open. I take in his face, marred with an anxious expression.

"It's real."

Without hesitation, Asher's mouth fuses to mine, inhaling my words.

The inviting scents of honeysuckle and lavender trickle into my nose as I glide quietly through the lush, green forest. I admire the sunlight bouncing off the tiny flecks of glitter in the cobblestone pathway leading to the Emerald Castle. A light, warm breeze washes over me, while tiny giggles tag along, following my journey toward the castle.

Some of the twinkling fairies place flowers in my hair as we walk. Others just express amusement at my presence in the Kingdom of the Fae as they guide my expedition through their land.

I make my way to the large glass doors that protect the castle's opening. The fairies release the double gateway, allowing me entrance into the grand foyer gardens. The sun beams through the translucent walls, draping everything in a calming green hue. My presence wakes the vegetation.

The flowers stretch and bow, greeting me during my walk down the elegant entrance hall. It's lined on each side by crystal-blue streams of water.

Miniature waterfalls cascade down the glass walls as the sound of the collecting water bounces off the high glass ceilings. Pink and white water lilies float dramatically through a web of green lily pads in the collecting pools.

All around me, nature is alive. The flora is so bright and lush. It's easier to breathe and feel the tranquility of life here. Following the labyrinth of glass corridors, I finally come to the arched doorway I'm in search of. I knock once, then enter the exquisite domed study.

I discover Lady Finella on her outdoor veranda, overlooking her kingdom. A warm, flower-scented breeze trickles through the arched aperture and washes over me.

The queen of the fae is always so regal, yet seeing her pose on the terrace strikes a chord, a reminder that she is truly a supernatural ruler of this magical dominion.

I fidget for a moment. Even though I've visited this place so many times the guards no longer escort me or announce when I arrive, I'm still unsure how to address her. She's in deep in thought and I don't want to startle her, so as gracefully as I can, I clear my throat to announce my presence.

When she turns, her long, red ringlets drape elegantly over her slender shoulders. The color offsets the emerald green of her dress and eyes. Her peach lips pull into a warm smile as the golden runes on her arms begin to move. She bows her head ever so slightly.

"Eve, as always, it is a pleasure to have you visit our realm," the queen offers.

I bow my head in respect. "Your Grace, I'm sorry if I'm late for our tea. I had an urgent matter that had to be dealt with prior to my realm jumping."

The stunning fairy flitters her translucent wings in delight before smirking at me. She ambles toward me, drawing me into a warmhearted embrace. When she pulls back, she takes my hands in hers and looks me directly in the eyes.

"This pressing issue, did it perhaps have something to do with the return of a certain gargoyle protector?" she muses.

Damn fairy insight. "Maybe," I allude mysteriously.

Lady Finella laughs softly at my antics. "Well then, daughter of Heaven, now that you have made the journey, shall we converse about the occurrences in your realm since we last saw one another?" The queen motions to the sitting area in the large room.

I sit while she pours tea. My eyes scan the lovely chamber, taking in the white flowers climbing the walls.

They almost give the impression of wallpaper, though I know they're real by the perfume they're giving off.

"I love being here," I blurt out without thought. "It always feels like home when I'm here, and no matter how busy you are, you always find time to see me," I offer appreciatively.

The regal fairy sits back in her chair and smiles at me. "I adore having you, Eve. I could not be more pleased that you feel welcome in our realm. Now, daughter of Heaven, please be kind enough to discontinue distracting me with flattery. In its place, enlighten me to your happenings."

I'm not sure how long I've been in the queen's sitting room, rambling. I explain in great detail about my aunt and Michael, as well as Asher's return, and my visit with Gage to the Land of the Leprechauns. I end with the scrolls, and lay out my fears about my feelings for Asher and my concerns with being manipulated by the divine path.

Since Aria's death, Lady Finella seems to be the only being I can confide in. When I finally finish, she's watching me with deep intrigue before placing her teacup and saucer on a tree stump, her version of a coffee table.

"Heavens, you have certainly been through a great deal since our last appointment."

I chew on the inside of my cheek nervously. "I know."

"I must admit that my fondness for those pesky leprechauns is nonexistent. They have become quite a poor representation of the magical realms. Though I do hope that Mr. Gallagher explained that their land is overseen by the darkness," she ends solemnly.

"He did. I was surprised to hear that each dominion has light and dark in it. I haven't seen any dark in this realm. Is there?" I ask, and take a sip of rose-infused tea.

I'm met with silence, as Lady Finella becomes less regal and more rigid at the question.

"Where there is light, Eve, there is also dark. It is the law of balance. Each of the realms must maintain that equilibrium in order to exist. So yes, in this kingdom, as in all others, sadly there is darkness. Its presence is perhaps not as visible as in other worlds."

I'm not sure why, but I find her response unsettling. I awkwardly smile at her answer. As if shaking something off, her posture becomes more relaxed, and I see her warmness return.

"As for Mr. St. Michael and the scrolls, an appointment with Sorceress Lunette is in order. The magic dimension is home to the sorceresses of the Black Circle. Lunette is very wise and powerful. If she is guarding the scrolls, as you say, then be assured they are in good hands. I must forewarn you, however, that you ought to enter the dimension with your protector. There is treacherous and dark magic lurking within the enchanted forest," she offers the caveat without a smile.

I swallow. "I'll talk to Asher and Gage when I get back to confirm the visit."

The fairy's face takes on a maternal expression. I brace myself for the lecture. Crap.

"Eve, forgive me for speaking out of turn, however, such a journey will require the warrior of Heaven to be in agreement as well."

I roll my eyes and sit back on the couch. "We aren't on speaking terms, Your Grace."

Her mouth tilts slightly. "I appreciate that you are suffering from the angel's untruths. It is amenable that you embrace those feelings. Conversely, it is my wish that you also grant acceptance of your lineage. Elizabeth and Michael meant well. They love you deeply, Eve. I trust when your antagonism dissipates, your love will resurface," she says gently.

I sigh and remain silent.

"Patience and acceptance are commendable divine gifts. Nonetheless, amongst all the human attributes, forgiveness is by far the most revered by supernatural beings."

My eyes meet hers. "Forgiveness is not something that is easy to do when those who are supposed to love you lie to you," I throw back.

"In spite of that, forgiveness has come effortlessly for you as it relates to your protector, and for him to you. Deceit is a mirage. Love is an oasis. I do not presume to be familiar with your emotions when it comes to Michael and Elizabeth. Though, if you were my daughter, I hope that your heart would be open and forgiving to whatever treachery was committed in the name of love, sacrifice and protection," she offers in a chiding tone.

We sit in comfortable silence for a moment before Ainsley, the duchess of sprites, enters the study. She seems jittery and unfocused. "Forgive the intrusion, Your Grace. I'm afraid Lucian awaits you in the rose garden."

I smile at Ainsley and she responds with a curt nod back. Odd.

"Thank you, Duchess. Eve, sorrowfully, I am obliged to take my leave and convene with the werewolf. I do hope you understand."

"Of course, Your Grace. Thank you again for having me today." I stand and hug her.

"Until we meet again," she promises, before blowing her golden fairy dust at me, returning me to the earth realm and Asher's arms.

My eyes flick open before I blink a few times, adjusting to the bright sunlight filtering into my room. For a moment, I stretch and bask in its warmth before turning to my side to greet Asher. My heart sinks when I see the bed is empty beside me. Downhearted, I rub my palm over the warm spot he was in last night.

A small smile crosses my lips at knowing that Asher is back, followed by a ball of worry knotting in my chest about the council. They may not have found evidence, but his newfound stance on us isn't going to help keep him safe either. *Damn stubborn gargoyle.*

I shift my focus to the pillow and see a note with two words that make me groan in annoyance at him.

Training Room.

10 Breathing You In

"Do you forgive me now?" I plead with Callan, while standing across from him on the mat. We're both out of breath, having just finished a round of hand-to-hand combat training. He's watching me, trying not to break out into hysterical laughter. *Asshat.*

"I'm not sure, cutie. My wing is still slightly bruised. It hurts every time I twitch it. Why don't you do it again and then we'll see," he bellyaches.

"What? You said I only had to do it once. This is ridiculous."

He rubs his hand over his extracted raven wing, now healed. However, Callan being Callan, he continues to hold it over my head while giving me puppy dog eyes. *Crap.*

The sad part is it's totally working.

"Does that face work with Abby?" I squint my eyes in disbelief.

The adorable gargoyle wiggles his eyebrows at me.

"Did last night."

I scrunch may face. "Ew. Way too much information, Callan."

"I'm in pain, cutie," he argues.

"No, you ARE the pain," I retort.

He shrugs and chuckles. "One more time and then I promise to stop."

I sigh, facing him. "Fine," I reply through my tight jaw.

Callan jumps up and down, clapping like a fangirl.

Good Lord.

"I, Eve Marie Collins, agree that Callan Thomas St. Michael is absolutely correct. Fruit-flavored ice cream is not, in fact, an appropriate ice-cream flavor. Furthermore, I hereby solemnly swear to never order black raspberry ice cream again in the presence of the greatest gargoyle to ever live, Callan St. Michael." *Christ, this clan is nuts.*

Callan is tearing up, he's laughing so hard.

"Torturing you is so much fun."

I narrow my eyes at him. "You suck, gargoyle."

That earns me a headlock. "If you fight, it will only make it worse for you," he laughs.

Suddenly, the air shifts in the room. Callan lets go of my neck and I straighten myself out.

"I see now that Asher is back, you're no longer allowed to run free, love," Gage muses.

"It's easier to get Eve trained in a controlled environment, Gage. If you have an issue with it, take it up with Asher or the council," Callan warns.

Gage smirks. "Running on a piece of machinery and hand-to-hand combat training won't help her. Demons will still outrun her. You are providing her with a false sense of security."

Callan's face goes red as he steps up to Gage, chest to chest. "What the fuck is your problem, man?"

Gage doesn't back down. "My problem, as you so eloquently put it, is that she is not adequately experienced to fight in a war between Heaven and Hell."

Callan tips his chin up. "She's human, asshole. Of course she's not capable enough to fight. We're simply trying to show her how to keep herself alive, if the need should arise."

Gage laughs. "Good luck with that."

"HEY!" I shout before stepping in between the two heated gargoyles. "I'm standing right here. If you want to talk about me, include me. Otherwise, stop it. Both of you." I turn to Gage. "It would be impossible for me to fight off every demon that attacks me. The St. Michaels are training me to self-defend."

Gage's face goes soft. "That isn't possible, love, even with your extra gifts."

I swallow hard, knowing he's right. "Well, I have to try."

"Try in the name of the ascension, or love?" Gage asks with a questioning stare.

I force my shoulders back. "Both," I respond firmly, and leave the training room.

I'm in my head, talking to myself again. I keep going over all the ways my life sucks as I make my way back to my room. I need to shower and get ready for class because I'm running late. I rush by the Tension Room when I hear Keegan and Asher's voices.

"What are you asking of me, Asher?" Keegan sighs, sounding tired and defeated. It's very unlike his usual calm and cool tone. The change stops me in my tracks to eavesdrop.

"I need to hear from you that if something were to happen to me, you would step up and claim the throne," Asher states calmly.

My heart drops. *What is he talking about?*

"Define something happening to you," Keegan asks, with caution lining the question.

"I love her," Asher exhales. "The oath is broken."

Silence.

I pinch my eyes shut and squeeze. *Shit.*

"It's not the bond or the divination. It's her. I want her. Forever," Asher continues.

More silence.

"Say something, Keegan," Asher demands of his brother.

"It's not allowed, Asher. There are rules," Keegan reminds him in a cold tone.

Asher exhales roughly and sits back on the couch. His eyes focus on his older brother.

"I'm the next in line. I could petition the council and change the oaths," Asher argues.

Keegan rubs his hands over his face, obviously exhausted with Asher's thought process. He studies my protector for what feels like an eternity before his expression finally softens.

"When we were kids, there was this tree at the Wiltshire manor, in the gardens. Do you recall it?" Keegan waits as Asher shakes his head. "It was tall, lush, and beautiful. It had these light pink flowers that would fall all around it. Anyway, Mom would sit under it for hours while reading."

Asher smiles briefly before it drops. "I don't remember. What does this have to do with what I'm asking, Keegan?"

"When I used to walk back from my training sessions, I would pass Dad's office and glance in. He would always be standing in the same place, at the same time every day, looking out the window. I never knew what he was so infatuated with, until one day, I walked by as he was called into a meeting. Begrudgingly, he tore himself away from the view and left. I marched over to the spot and saw Mom sitting with her dress floating in the light summer breeze, reading. She looked so peaceful under the tree, surrounded by sunshine and pink petals. Like an angel bathed in light."

"Sounds like a nice memory to have," Asher replies, his voice quiet, wishful.

"It took me years to figure out why, for those thirty minutes each day, the king of the gargoyle race would just stand there, watching his mate. In our position, the darkness is overwhelming. She was his light. His refuge. His place of peace in the shitstorm that is a protector's life." Keegan stands and moves toward the fireplace, his back now to Asher. "If you think I am unsympathetic to your feelings for Eve, you are wrong, brother. I'm mated. I grew up with the same parents you did. I watched them dote on one another, as did you. I understand love, Asher. I identify with the need for light in a world of darkness."

"Then you grasp what I am asking?" Asher confirms.

"Yes." Keegan exhales roughly. "However, my answer is no."

Asher is quiet. I fidget, realizing I'm probably going to miss class today. My heart hurts for Asher. It's all I can do not to go into the room and punch Keegan in the face.

Keegan turns slowly and moves toward the coffee table, sitting so they are eye to eye.

"There are rules in place for reasons, Asher. A protector is forbidden to love his charge because it clouds his judgment and ability to protect her. Even now, you come to me, asking this of me, knowing that there is a war on the horizon. A war in which Eve will die if you don't protect her. If you love her the way you claim to, the way each member of this clan feels you do, then you must stop allowing that love to cloud your protector judgment." Keegan's voice is softer now.

"My love for her enhances my protector instincts," Asher argues.

"Asher, you were just removed as her guardian for this very accusation. Stone petrifaction is the punishment for breaking your oath. Yet here you are, declaring your undying love for her. Placing yourself and this clan in the line of fire. Once again," Keegan whisper-shouts.

"I know. I don't need a lecture or reminder," Asher grits out of a tight jaw.

"On the contrary, brother. You do. You are not only a protector but next in line to rule our people. That is a great responsibility. Something that you've never taken lightly, until her." Keegan positions his elbows on his knees, reining in his temper. "I can't do it again, Ash. When Mom and Dad went missing, I was too young to step into the role of clan leader. I did. Out of love for this family. Out of sacrifice. Someone needed to be there to pick up the pieces and move us forward. I will not fail you. You will be the next king. There is no question."

"You are failing me by denying me happiness," Asher spits out.

"By the grace, grow up. You are not a child. You are the next king. Start acting like it," Keegan scolds.

"If it was Kenna, would you feel this way?" Asher asks.

"What?"

"If you were next in line and McKenna was your charge, would you deny yourself?"

"I am a gargoyle. I am bound to my oaths, my race, and my kin, above all else."

"If I choose her, what will you do?" Asher questions.

"Asher."

"Tell me, brother. If I choose her over everything else, will you step up?"

"It's my role within this clan to step up, Your Highness," Keegan seethes.

"Have you always been this fucking nosey, or is eavesdropping a new thing with you?" Kenna barks from behind me. *Crap.* I didn't even hear her approach.

I whip around. "It's nice to see you too, McKenna."

"Fuck off, blood of Eden," she spits.

I cross my arms. "Why do you despise me so much? What have I ever done to you?"

Her sapphire eyes glare at me. "You exist. It's that simple."

"Want to know my theory?" I ask, knowing she doesn't.

"No," she barks, and walks past me, down the hallway.

"I think you're afraid to like me," I yell to her back, while following.

She releases a light laugh. "Oh, and why would that be?"

I pause for a moment. "If you're partial to me, then you can't protect Keegan."

McKenna turns and narrows her eyes at me. "Enlighten me." *Fuck, she's intimidating.*

I stand taller. "If you embrace me into the clan and allow Asher to love me, you think he will be taken from you. Leaving Keegan to step into his role, like before, when he was forced to lead this clan when Garrick left, and that terrifies you."

The warrior just stands there, glaring at me, unmoving. I notice the slight tic by her right eye, and that confirms all I need to know. I'm right. It's about Keegan, not me.

I drop my voice in comprehension. "It scares the shit out of you because you love him. Not like the love that most people share, though. It's the earth-shattering, can't-breathe-without-him kind of love. The kind where you would lay down your life for him. Right?"

"My love for Keegan is not insight, blood of Eden," she states coolly.

"No, it's not. What is, though, is that beneath the thick skin you hide behind is a scared woman who is afraid that the man she loves will suffer at the hands of his brother and the woman he loves. The fear is there because you witnessed Keegan picking up the pieces before, when Garrick and Vivian disappeared. I think that terrifies you, Kenna, because you don't want to see him suffer again. Your heart wouldn't survive having to hold him while he cries behind closed doors. In front of the clan, he's the strong one. The true leader of this family is Keegan. He is the one who steps in and keeps everyone together and on track. In that role, there is no room for grieving or fear. So as his mate, you take it on, because for every tear that he silently let slide, I know that you held him, wiping them away while a piece of you died. That—that piece of insight is why you can't bear taking on his pain and suffering again."

McKenna gets in my face so fast that I'm fearful for a moment. "Don't presume to know anything about me or my mate. You have no right to psychoanalyze anything I do. You. Know. Nothing."

"Maybe not. I do know this: breathing him in is what keeps you alive and whole. It's why you fight so hard and are completely guarded. You're protecting him. We're on the same team, Kenna. I feel that for Asher. I'm not a threat. I'm not the enemy. I'm not going to stop loving and protecting him," I vow.

I walk around her and up the stairs.

She lets me.

❧

After realizing I'm not going to class, I shower to try to calm myself. Keegan's and McKenna's words keep swirling in my mind. Every emotion from the last few months begins to climb into my throat as I blow-dry my hair. I can feel my resolve slip away.

Throwing down my brush and the dryer on the counter, I close my eyes, giving myself a moment to absorb everything. I'm so tired. Weary from everyone telling me what to do all the time and making decisions for me, instead of with me, under the guise of protection. It's too hard. I don't want to fight what Asher and I have, or don't have. I don't even know anymore. There are so many other things I'm fighting.

I take one last look at myself in the mirror, pushing my shoulders back in defiance, before I storm downstairs and head into the library. Asher is sitting in a large leather chair with a book in hand, looking delicious and relaxed. As if the conversation with Keegan never happened.

Standing in the doorway, I'm completely still. Asher cocks his head to the side and smiles at me. My eyes roam the empty room before landing on his face. I hold his questioning gaze for a moment before I start toward him, playing with the bottom of his shirt that I'm wearing.

"I can't do this anymore," I whisper.

Asher closes the book and places it on the table next to him. His eyes never leave mine.

"Can't do what, siren?" His voice is laced with a seriousness that unnerves me.

"Any of it. All of it. It's too hard." My voice trails off.

Asher doesn't say anything. His eyes travel over me intimately. That's when I realize that I forgot to throw pants on. *Wonderful.* He stands and purposely walks over to the library doors, pulling them shut and locking them before turning back to face me.

He leans back against them, arms folded. Both of our breathing has picked up. The heat from his look radiates onto me, igniting me as desire spreads throughout my veins.

Pushing off from the door, he stalks toward me while lifting his hand behind his neck and removing his T-shirt. My thoughts disappear. I'm frozen in place at the raw emotion and passion in his eyes. All I can do is stare into them, unmoving.

Once Asher is in front of me, he takes both of his hands and cups my cheeks. I close my eyes and lean into his touch. After a moment, his hands slide through my hair, pushing it off my shoulders on both sides before he brings them down my back. As soon as they reach the back of my upper thighs, he grips each one.

With ease, he lifts me, forcing my legs to wrap around his waist as he walks us backwards. In seconds, he's got me pressed against the wall. The feeling of my body pushed against his, and the intensity of our breathing, snaps me out of my previous thought process.

Slowly, he thrusts farther into me. Pinning my body tighter with his hips. I have no choice but to clutch on to his naked shoulders. After releasing a deep, raw rumble from his chest, Asher sucks in a breath as my hands wander over him, tracing every line and crease with an unhealthy fixation.

My body responds by pushing closer to his. Asher's left hand finds its way under my shirt, setting off longing sensations. Impatiently, I take my hands away from him and yank my shirt off, throwing it on the floor. He releases an appreciative noise when he realizes I'm not wearing a bra, only my cotton panties now.

"You're trying to kill me," he releases in a ragged pant.

"Take your wings out," I demand in a soft tone.

"What?" He pulls his face back, and uncertainty crosses his expression.

"I want to feel all of you," I explain, while leaving kisses along his jawline.

Asher stops breathing. I gather my courage and lift my eyes to his. He's pulled his brows together in hesitation. I take his cheeks in my palms, pulling him closer.

"I want all of you, gargoyle," I repeat across his soft lips.

He exhales roughly and discharges his midnight-black wings. The sight causes me to shudder. I swallow and allow one of my hands to run along the feathers. A deep noise releases from his throat, and his entire body trembles.

"You're so striking," I murmur, as he swallows.

Asher responds by running his warm palm down my neck, over my chest, stopping over one of my breasts to tease me. My breath comes out in short pants at the circular motion of his thumb over the sensitive area. I grip tighter onto his shoulders.

Each of his touches forces me to arch deeper into him. I release a primal cry when his lips and tongue pay meticulous attention to the other breast.

"Holy shit," I exhale.

Asher's lips pull into a smile before his mouth and tongue continue their assault. Fingertips push into my skin as he drags his other hand slowly over my chest and stomach before landing inside my panties.

Long, skillful fingers make their way inside me, and I have to lightly bite Asher's shoulder to keep from screaming out in ecstasy as he pleasures me without mercy.

All of the sensations at once become too overwhelming, and just as quickly as it all started, I fall, giving in to the need for release. When the last shudder of my orgasm passes through me, I eagerly push Asher's hips away from me, forcing him to place me on my feet.

I coerce him to turn, then shove his chest so he's pressed against the wall. Asher groans with need as I hold his gaze and slowly descend to my knees, taking his pants with me.

Stopping for a moment, I take him in. A thrill of power runs through me as I become conscious that I have him trapped against the wall—wings out, exposed to me, only for me. The knowledge heightens the need I have to own Asher, to make him mine, completely.

Watching him through my eyelashes, I run my fingers down his length with the lightest of touches. Asher's head falls back against the wall in bliss.

"Fuck, siren."

Smiling, I run the top of my tongue in circles over the tip of his arousal. He entangles his hands in my hair, holding my head still. His roughness only fuels my desire to do it again, to make him fall to his knees for me. So I do, and he grunts.

Asher pushes his hips toward my mouth. I jerk back in a tease, causing him to growl like an animal. I lick my lips and let my tongue travel down the length of him. I do this a few times, while he releases short breaths. He tightens his hold on my hair.

Unhurriedly, I play with the apadravya piercing, letting the cool balls caress my tongue until I hear Asher whimper. At the sound, I moan on him and take him fully into my mouth.

"Fuck," he draws out.

My gaze lifts and locks onto his. His mouth falls open, and a crease forms between his eyebrows from deep concentration as he watches me pleasure him.

His indigo gaze follows every move I make. His violent hold on my hair keeps me still as he plunges deeper and deeper with gentle, yet forceful, movements. I eagerly meet him thrust for thrust. Taking him all in, my only want is to please him and satisfy the ache building in him.

I'm not sure how long this goes on. It doesn't matter. I don't want it to stop. I continue my assault until I think he can't hold on any longer. When that time comes, I run my hands gently over the bottom portion of his wings, caressing them.

"Holy shit, siren. Take your mouth off me," Asher grounds out, trying to move me.

I know why he demands this, but I'm in control tonight. So I don't. Instead, I challenge him with my eyes to stop me and continue sucking so he can find his release.

With a deep, raw grunt, he does, and I swallow every ounce of him without thought. When he's finished, he pulls me up by my hair, then twists and shoves me against the wall before dropping his nose to my neck.

"What are you doing," I whimper at the intensity of it all.

"Breathing you in," he whispers, inhaling.

11 Sorceress Lunette

Blackness. It's all I see and feel. My fight-or-flight instinct kicks in, as the vast darkness has set in motion an overwhelming panic in me. It begins to inch up my throat, and my heart slams against my rib cage in a violent beat.

My eyes can't adjust. It's as if someone has turned off the lights and I've been thrust into pitch-blackness. I blink several times, trying to adapt. A deep heaviness settles into my skin. The unnatural feeling of barrenness and frigid air soaks into my bones.

I startle when a balmy, bulky hand enfolds mine into it, gripping it tightly as warmth pushes into me, penetrating the layers of my body.

Randi Cooley Wilson

My focus moves to the right, where the physical connection is, and I'm bathed in a soft blue glow coming from Asher's eyes. Behind him, the radiant eyes of both Keegan and McKenna and, to my left, the light-green smolder from Gage's, pull me out of the dimness.

I'm unsuccessful at getting my rapid breathing under control, though. I squeeze my eyes shut so I don't pass out or have a panic attack.

"You're safe." Asher's voice vibrates through my fear.

"Where are we?" My voice is shaky as I cling to Asher.

"The magic dimension," Keegan answers pointedly.

"Why is it completely black? Where is the actual land?" I ask, dumbfounded.

"The dimension's entrance is a void. A black hole, if you will. Unless the sorceresses of the Black Circle embrace your presence, it will stay pitch-black, love," Gage responds.

"How do we know when they accept our being here?" I inquire with a shiver.

At the release of my question, a large ring of violet fire appears. The blaze roars to life in the middle of the nothingness. The flames are short, maybe three feet in height, and sway in a perfectly round formation. I swallow, waiting. Unsure of what I should do.

The five of us stand motionless, entranced while the flames move in a choreographed dance. I've never seen fire so controlled or such an odd color. I blink rapidly for a moment, thinking I'm hallucinating as a black spotted jaguar suddenly appears in the center of the ring. Its amber eyes are fierce as it watches us, pacing back and forth like a calm, caged animal amongst the flames.

"Everyone else sees the large wild cat, right?" I whisper.

144

"Yes, blood of Eden," McKenna sighs in aggravation.

"Just confirming that I haven't lost my mind," I answer.

My voice causes the jaguar to stop and face me. Oddly, it lifts its head to me, stretching its neck in an elegant motion. With grace, the animal drops its head and lowers the front half of its body onto the ground in a submissive stance, almost like it's bowing to me.

Crap. Maybe I have lost my mind.

At the feline's shift, the flames grow taller before a loud gush of wind occurs. I watch in fascination as the blaze morphs into thousands of lavender monarch butterflies and the blackness peels away, revealing an enchanted cottage, surrounded by fields of lilacs and wildflowers. The dimension warms with the presence of the sun, sky, and land.

"I guess we've been accepted, love." Gage moves toward the stationary cat.

At his progression, the jaguar roars, baring its teeth at him, and forcing Gage's retreat.

"Eve, since the animal has chosen to submit to you, perhaps you should be the one to lead," Keegan suggests in an even, quiet tone.

"The fuck she will," Asher snips, and tightens his grip on my hand, stepping in front of me before turning his focus to Gage. "Stop calling her 'love.'"

Once again, the jaguar growls at his movement. *Good Lord.* I yank Asher back by his hand and cut him a side-glance.

"Settle down, protector. I don't think it's going to hurt me and leave Gage alone," I warn.

"Eve," Asher bites out, as I pry free of his hold after several attempts.

"I've got this. Keegan might be right." I slowly approach the animal.

The feline doesn't move or make a sound. It just sits patiently until I get close enough to know Asher is having a mild heart attack behind me. Once I'm directly in front of the massive cat, it purrs. Honest to God. The freaking thing purrs like a damn house cat and rolls onto its back, showing me its black-and-brown-spotted stomach.

I look back at the stunned and speechless gargoyles. *Crap.* My eyes scan the beautiful meadow of wildflowers, then return to the purring feline. It's not going anywhere, so I bend down and begrudgingly rub its belly. Apparently happy at my show of affection, the jaguar licks me. *Gross. Good God.*

Once it's had enough, it smoothly stands and turns toward the cottage, waiting for us to follow. Swinging its tail, the beautiful creature takes the lead and escorts us through the field.

"Guess this one isn't a relative of Fiona," Asher smirks. "The woman would kill us on the spot if we tried massaging her tummy."

Keegan and he break out into a laughing fit. McKenna rolls her eyes, walking past them, irritated at their child-like antics.

"We're following it, then?" I ask.

"I believe so, love," Gage answers, fidgeting with an unlit cigarette and shooting a *fuck off* look toward Asher after my nickname as we begin our journey, following the cat down a cobblestone pathway through the flowers.

Aside from the completely weird entry, this dimension is visually stunning. My eyes take in the sight of thousands upon thousands of monarch butterflies. They encircle us, and land among the fields of lavender that run as far as the eye can see. The smell is intoxicating.

The soaring jewels of nature are in constant motion, emanating the sound of millions of flapping wings in steady movement. The hum of their continuous flight echoes like a breeze, but there is no air moving. It's magical.

As they flutter, the sun strikes each monarch, causing them to glow. The effect is a warm amethyst radiance that enfolds us. It's indescribable.

Asher comes up behind me, wrapping his arms around my waist. He lifts one of my hands in his and leans in, speaking very softly. "If you put your hand out and stand very still, they'll come to you."

I hold my breath and become motionless as the beautiful creatures land effortlessly on my arm and hand. Their small bodies tickle my skin as their wings flap with a slow ease.

"Oh. My. God. Asher," I say in subdued excitement, so as not to scare the monarchs.

He moans. "Fuck, siren, you can't say that here if you don't want me to throw you down and have my way with you," Asher scolds, nuzzling my neck.

I ignore him. "It's like a *National Geographic* picture," I breathe out in appreciation.

"The warm climate is why the monarchs thrive here. It's similar to Mexico when they migrate," Keegan offers next to us, stopping my body from sinking into Asher's touch.

"I thought monarch butterflies were orange?" I question.

"On earth. Here in the magic dimension, love, they're purple. For the sorceresses, violet signifies spiritual awakening, protection and power," Gage answers flatly.

"It's amazing," I reply, lowering my arm as the butterflies retreat.

Asher lifts his mouth to my ear. "You're amazing."

"Christ. I hate these damn insects," Gage spits out around his nicotine stick, watching us.

I spin and narrow my eyes at him. "You're not going to light up, are you?" I challenge, stepping away from Asher and planting my hands on my hips.

The jaguar comes up beside me, studying Gage with disdain. Gage just holds my gaze for a moment before angrily stomping off, mumbling something under his breath about me being a pain in the ass.

"I agree with the traitor." McKenna offers a pointed glance at me. *Have I mentioned how awesome it is to have her on this journey today? So. Much. Fun.*

My eyes drop to the cat's amber ones before we both turn and continue toward the dark gray stone cottage.

The chalet gives new meaning to the word *enchanted*. It's nestled among oak trees, and has smoke coming out of the chimney, signaling that whoever is there has a fire going. The entrance door is located in a turret that juts out from the front of the home. It's very quaint.

"Are you nervous?" I ask Asher, as we make our way through the meadow.

"About our engagement with Sorceress Lunette? No," he answers.

"I was referring to the scrolls and what they'll say." I slide my eyes to him.

Asher kicks a rock on the ground and shrugs casually. "It doesn't mean anything, siren. Either they say we were created to fulfill the divination, proving we're meant to be, or they don't. Whichever, I'll still feel the way I do about you. It won't change."

I inhale and chance a nervous look behind us at Keegan, McKenna, and Gage before returning my eyes forward to the cat leading us.

"What about the council? You can't just break your oath, Ash," I speak softly.

He stops and faces me. The rest of the clan moves around us and keeps on walking.

"Trust me to handle the council, yeah?"

There's that damn word again. Trust.

I drop my voice. "I won't survive if you end up a stone statue for eternity. The time I was without you . . . it will kill me if you actually become a gargoyle sculpture."

Giving me a boyish grin, he brushes the hair off my shoulder. "I won't. I'll figure it out."

"You mean *we'll* figure it out?" I correct.

He exhales, his expression morphing into a heated look. "Yeah, siren. *We'll* figure it out."

A high-pitched woman's voice cuts through my Asher stare. "Here kitty, kitty, kitty."

My eyes go wide as I watch the jaguar run up to a petite lady. Her hair is so blonde it's almost white. With joy, she bends down and pets the cat, cooing in its ear.

"There you are, Malefica. What a good familiar you are, baby girl. Did you find her, sweetheart? Did you?" She talks to and plays with the animal like a baby.

As we approach, the older woman's steel-gray eyes lift and meet mine in welcome. Her lips draw into a smile. The slight wrinkles around her eyes pull, then disappear as her face softens. She straightens her slender body to greet us, while wiping her hands absently on her bluish-purple medieval dress.

The old-world material is adorned with bell sleeves and a lovely metal belt, decorated with crescent-shaped charms, hanging off her skinny hips. As she moves forward to us, the long braid she has in her hair falls over her right shoulder, showing off the lilacs she's weaved throughout the design. Her flat, open sandals are barely noticeable under the length of her outfit.

"Welcome. You must be Eve. It's lovely to finally meet you, dear." She holds out her frail hand and extends her fingers covered in gemstone rings, one adorning each finger.

I step up to greet her, offering mine as well. "I am."

We hold this pose for a few awkward moments of silence. Unsure of what to do, I begin to pull my hand away.

"Oh my," she blows out dramatically, and facepalms herself. "I can be so scattered sometimes. Perhaps I should familiarize myself to you as well. Yes, that would be proper."

I wait for her to introduce herself, but she's just looking at me and smiling, as if she's waiting for me to say something. This goes on for several seconds before my eyes shift to Gage. He looks just as perplexed as I feel. He simply shrugs his bewilderment.

"OH, RIGHT. Me again." She laughs boisterously. "Oh dear. I am Sorceress Lunette."

THIS is Sorceress Lunette? I was expecting someone a little more majestic and well . . . put together, and less . . . um, outlandish.

"It's nice to meet you," I say, and go to introduce the gargoyles before she waves me off.

"No need, dear. When it comes to handsome men, I prefer to reacquaint or introduce myself," she answers, and stalks to the boys like a cougar.

McKenna's eyes catch mine as I just watch the batshit crazy sorceress.

"Sorry," Lunette says, fanning herself. "Good-looking supernatural beings make me nervous," she giggles, sidling up to Gage. "How do you do, sir? I am Lunette." The sorceress gives him her hand to kiss, along with bedroom eyes.

Playing along, Gage releases his panty-dropping smile while taking her hand and kissing it gallantly. "Sorceress Lunette, it's a pleasure. Gage Gallagher, Eve's protector." *Poor woman didn't have a chance.*

"Backup protector," Asher snaps out.

It takes Lunette a few minutes of batting her lashes before she moves on to Keegan.

"I've always had a thing for tall, dark, and silently strong," she coos, and moves closer to him, running a dark purple fingernail down his chest.

Keegan squirms.

McKenna sees red.

"Nice to meet you," Keegan replies uncomfortably while Kenna moves in front of him.

"Remove your hand from my mate, witch," she seethes at the fanatical being.

The sorceress places her hand over her heart in mock shock at McKenna's clipped tone.

"You must be McKenna. Apologies dear. I didn't realize he was spoken for." Her tone is anything but apologetic as she winks at Keegan before making her way to Asher, who I have to admit, looks terrified.

"Prince Asher," Lunette purrs, and curtsies.

My eyebrows rise in curiosity.

"Lunette," he replies guardedly.

"How's the piercing?" she asks in a seductive voice.

Asher blushes. Actually fucking blushes.

He clears his throat in an uneasy manner. "It's fine. Thank you."

"I knew it would be." The sorceress's eyes sparkle as she turns to me.

"Oh my God," I whisper under my breath.

"It's a thing of beauty, isn't it, dear?" Lunette asks me, licking her lips.

The blush stains my neck and cheeks at her boldness. How the hell does she know about the piercing and is she really discussing this in front of everyone?

"I'm guessing by your reaction, it's made you writhe more times than you care to share," she says in a conspiratorial tone. *Yep, she's really asking.*

Asher grabs Lunette by the arm. "Shall we visit?" he asks with a cracked voice.

The eccentric woman clasps her hands together in delight, and motions to the cottage.

"Yes. Yes. Of course, I've been waiting for you. I'm so glad that Malefica found you and guided you to me safely for our appointment." She beams, petting the cat. "Such a good familiar."

"Familiar?" I question with a small voice, trying to forget the last ten minutes.

"Sorceresses have familiars, dear. They're like magical helpers. Malefica was given to me by an incubus I once bedded," she answers, and wiggles her eyebrows.

McKenna groans. "By the grace."

Lunette dismisses her with a wave of her hand. "Apparently, I was the best he'd ever had. As a gesture of appreciation for my . . . talents, shall we say, he gave me Malefica."

"I need to smoke," Gage mumbles and escapes the discussion.

Lunette hums and smiles before shooing us into the house. I brush off her rant and enter the cottage. It looks like a page right out of a storybook fairy tale.

The sitting room is cluttered with spell books, candles, gemstones, and vases of lavender. I feel like it should be disorderly, yet somehow it's cozy and warmly inviting.

That is, until I notice all the *Kama Sutra* sculptures of couples in various sexual positions. It's then that I see that, mixed in with her spell library, Lunette has various books of a tantric sexual nature that match the themed artwork on the walls. *Holy hell.*

"A hobby of mine." She winks.

I smile awkwardly and continue to study her home. A painting on the wall catches my eye, when Lunette's voice makes an appearance behind me.

"Interesting that you are drawn to that piece of artwork, dear," she states.

"Why is that?" I question, fixated on the picture.

"It's from the collection of the Mauritshuis. It's Rubens & Brueghel's *Adam and Eve in Paradise*. Rubens painted the figures and Brueghel the landscape, as well as the native and exotic animals surrounding the soul mates. Such a masterpiece, wouldn't you agree, daughter of Heaven?" Lunette asks peculiarly.

"It's lovely," I answer, even though I get the feeling her question was rhetorical.

Lunette runs her hand over Adam's naked body, and for some absurd reason, it bothers me.

"Forbidden desire is a yummy thing, isn't it? The tempting act of pleasure is one of the finest and most powerful gifts we've been granted," the sorceress seduces.

I just politely nod because really, what the hell else am I going to say to the odd woman?

"Please make yourself at home while I fetch some brew." She shifts her focus.

"I think she's had enough brew," McKenna mutters under her breath.

Gage joins us just in time to see Lunette handing out goblets filled with some sort of red liquid that I'd rather not touch my lips to. Instead, I sit back on the antique sofa.

There's an odd silence. It goes on far too long before Asher finally breaks the quiet.

"Lunette, our appointment with you is so we can see the scrolls," he says point-blank.

The sorceress smiles brightly and folds her legs under her body on the wingback chair she's perched in. "Of course. Anything for an old friend," she agrees, while taking a sip of the infusion and holding Asher's eye contact in a seductive manner.

I clear my throat.

He fidgets under her gaze. "If you don't mind, we are pressed for time."

She smiles brightly and shifts her focus to me. "What has the keeper of the scrolls told you about what is written in them, dear?" Lunette asks.

My eyes roam from Gage's to Asher's. Both protectors nonverbally agree for me to answer Lunette's question.

"Professor Davidson explained that Asher's and my bloodlines have been created to fulfill the divination of redemption," I answer, while McKenna rolls her eyes.

Lunette throws her head back in laughter. "I suppose Henry never was one for flowery words. Although in bed, his bowtie is deceiving." She winks.

What the hell does that even mean?

Asher rubs his face in frustration. "Lunette, the scrolls, please."

"Yes. Right, of course, Your Highness. As the guardian of the scrolls, it's my job to safeguard them; therefore I'll only allow Asher and Eve to join me for a viewing. The rest of you may wait here at the cottage for us to arrive back," the sorceress states, oddly focused.

"Where are we going?" Asher questions.

"You don't think I would keep something as important as ancient documents in my cottage, prince. I might be flighty, but I am certainly not stupid." She gives him a look.

"I need to be present as well," Gage states.

"No," Lunette responds in a firm tone.

"No?" Gage repeats. "I'm Eve's protector. There's no way she goes without me."

Lunette shrugs, unaffected, while sipping her beverage. "Then we don't go."

"Look, witch, we don't have all day to play your fucking games," McKenna spits out.

"Kenna," Keegan warns.

"Lunette." Asher says her name gently. "Eve and I will go with you. Gage is fine to stay here with Keegan and McKenna." Asher gives Gage his *don't argue* face.

"Wonderful, then it's settled. The rest of you may make yourselves comfortable while Eve and Asher join me in the spell room," Lunette announces, standing.

"The spell room?" I question Asher quietly.

Lunette smiles brightly. "Yes, it's a room in my home where I do spells."

McKenna rolls her eyes. "Original."

Asher stands and laces our fingers together.

"We'll be back shortly."

Keegan leans in, whispering something to Asher that I can't make out. He nods and pulls me toward Lunette. We follow her tiny body into the small kitchen. She opens a door and nods her head down the set of stairs.

"Your spell room is in your basement?" I inquire.

"Where else?" Lunette cackles, and motions for us proceed.

Malefica follows behind as we descend into the darkness.

12 The Scrolls

If it weren't for the fact that Asher's hand is clutching mine in a death grip, I might run away. The basement of the cottage smells like incense, and the stairs creak as we make our way into the blackness. Within seconds, Lunette has a lit candle sitting in an old-fashioned holder. The sorceress uses the small light to guide us.

"I apologize, dears, for the dark dramatics. I use candle magic when I perform spells, therefore I don't have electricity down here," she explains in a light, airy tone.

I swallow. My life gets weirder and weirder. Shouldn't I be picking a major at this point? Instead I'm following sorceresses down to dark basements. I exhale loudly.

Asher tightens his hold on my hand, like he's in my head and knows at any minute, I plan to throw my hands in the air and say this is fucking ridiculous, which for the record, I'm seriously thinking about doing.

Lunette turns to face us. The single flame illuminates her face. "Please, have a seat." She motions to the floor. I stand, unsure before Asher tugs me down, still grasping my hand.

Lunette busies herself with lighting several candles haphazardly placed around an altar. *Fabulous. All she needs is a sacrificial virgin.* Malefica lies in front of me, snoring away as if this is an everyday occurrence.

"It's vervain," Lunette blurts out, breaking through my crazy internal rant.

My eyes shift to Asher in question, because I'm pretty sure neither of us said anything.

"I'm sorry?" I ask.

"The incense I use is vervain. It helps give my spells a little umph. That way, we don't get lost somewhere, or stuck with the vampires. Then again . . . nothing is ever set in stone," she says quietly, then begins to hoot. "Oh my dear, so sorry, Asher. I meant no disrespect." *Wow, maybe she's been sniffing the incense a bit too long.*

"None taken," Asher replies, but his tone is anything but forgiving and his body is rigid.

"Eve, dear, I use the incense because it symbolizes air. As the smoke rises, it takes our thoughts with it, protecting us from darkness. Vervain is also a weakness amongst vampires." Lunette smiles at me. "Sorceresses are targets for the bloodsuckers because our blood powers them. On occasion, while we spell, they like to snack."

Of course they do.

My wide eyes flick to Asher. He shrugs and inhales.

"Feel free to relax while I perform the cleansing and blessing," Lunette encourages.

I'll get right on that.

The candlelight has brightened the room now, allowing me to take in our surroundings. There's a large table pressed against the far wall with various candles in different sizes, shapes, and colors, as well as candelabras. Along with more gemstones and a few vintage books, a large circular throw rug covers the floor, while gigantic pillows adorn it.

Ironically, there's a brick fireplace that's unlit with a black cauldron on top of it, causing me to release a soft chuckle.

Lunette's eyes meet mine in whimsy. "That's just for show, dear." She nods to the cauldron. "Other supernatural beings tend to stereotype. Especially when they are in need of magic."

"I see."

Once Lunette is done with her cleansing, she takes two candles, one white and one black, and two lighters, and sits on the floor across from Asher and me, placing both candles in front of us.

"I make them myself." She motions to the wax lights. "They're made from beeswax, which makes them more powerful, because they come from nature."

I just smile.

"Asher, dear, please put out your hands for the oils," she asks and he does. Carefully, Lunette watches as three drops of oil drip onto Asher's hands. Then she proceeds to do the same with me. "I need you both to dress the candles."

"How do we do that?" Asher asks.

Lunette moves the white candle to him. "Take the lotus oil and run it on the candle in a downward motion. The direction is important. To bring something to you, like the scrolls, you must start at the top and move downward to the middle. Then from the bottom to the middle," she instructs and Asher complies.

Moving the black candle to me, the sorceress instructs me in the same manner. Once both candles have been dressed, Lunette dabs a portion of the lotus oil onto her third eye and breastbone. Asher and I copy the motions with what's remaining of the liquid on our hands.

"Repeat after me, please," she asks. "I cleanse and consecrate these candles in the name of the Sorceresses of the Black Circle. May they burn with strength in the service of the light. Sorceresses of the Black Circle, we ask you to guide the daughter of Heaven, the prince of the gargoyles, and the guardian of the scrolls to the Black Circle unharmed, then return us, when ready, with ease and safe passage to the magic dimension."

Lunette pulls a black-handled dagger from her metal belt. "It's an athame, dear," she answers my questioning expression. "I must inscribe each candle with a travel symbol so that when I do the spell, it will take us directly to the intended destination."

On each candle, she draws symbols I don't recognize in the same pattern we used to dress them. Top to middle, and then, bottom to middle. Once satisfied, she places the candles in front of us and hands Asher and I each a lighter.

"Eve, dear, please light the white candle in front of Asher. Then Asher will light the black candle in front of you."

Once we do, Lunette takes our unlaced hands in hers, forming a circle around the two lit candles. She closes her eyes and begins to chant quietly in Latin.

Everything goes black and quiet. I'm no longer able to feel Lunette's or Asher's hands.

"Asher?" I call into the darkness.

"Lunette?"

Silence.

The only sound is my breathing, which is coming out in short, frightened gasps. I start moving around, placing my hands out in front of me since I can't see anything, and that's when I trip.

"Shit," I curse as my hands and knees hit the hard ground.

I feel around the floor to see what I tripped over, and that's when I feel the wax. *Crap. Lunette and Asher must have traveled and left me in the basement.* Keeping one hand on the candle, I feel around in the dark for the lighter, figuring I dropped it when the room was engulfed in black. After several attempts, my hand lands on it.

I flick the top open so the flame appears, then light the candle. The small flame does nothing to illuminate the room.

I move the candle around, but I see nothing that resembles the spell room we were just in. *Awesome. The crazy witch sent me somewhere else.* This is just one big dungeon of dark.

"Asher?" I call out louder into the darkness.

This time, I hear a light pounding, like banging on plexiglass. I move the candle around to see where the sound is coming from, but see nothing. Sighing, I lower the candle back to the ground to sit, only to see another flame swaying in front of me at eye level. I crawl toward the second flame, but smash into something hard before I reach it.

My eyes water as my nose begins to sting.

"Ouch. Fuck. Shit!" I scream out, grabbing my now-bleeding appendage.

"Siren?" Asher's muffled voice barely makes it through the wall.

"Asher?" I call out with no answer, so I try again more forcefully.

"Siren! For fuck's sake . . . are you with Lunette?" I think that's what he said. It's hard to hear.

"No. Aren't you?" I scream at the top of my lungs.

"No. Why are you shouting?" he questions.

I exhale and drop my forehead to the wall while continuing to wipe away the blood trickling out of my bruised nose. "I can barely hear you. Where are you?"

He's quiet for a moment. "I'm not sure. I'm in an all-white room. The light in here is so fucking bright that I have to keep my eyes shut."

"Why do you have the candle lit?" I ask, closing my eyes, trying to push the pain away.

"It's always been lit. Where the fuck are you?" I hear him begin to bang on wall panels.

"I don't know. I'm in a dark room. There's no light. I had to crawl around to find the candle and lighter. More importantly, where the hell is Lunette?" I sniff in the blood.

"Are you crying? Don't panic. I'm going to get you out of there," he assures.

"I'm not crying. I bumped into the wall and I think I broke my nose," I yell.

There's silence before I hear a muffled version of Asher's laugh. *What the fuck?*

"You smacked into the wall?" he muses.

"It's pitch-black in here! You know what, you suck, gargoyle," I retort.

"All right, let me think," he says through the barrier.

I turn and push my back to the wall, because my face hurts and I know we'll be in here for a bit. After a long stretch of silence, and tons of overthinking, I need a diversion.

"Can I ask you something?"

"Yeah," he answers, distracted.

"How does Lunette know about your piercing?"

Silence.

"Asher?"

"She was the one who pierced me," he answers dryly.

"What?"

"I lost a bet with Callan. If I lost, I was to get the piercing. Lunette is into *Kama Sutra* and she is the one I trusted to do it." His tone is lined with aggravation.

"Well, that's . . . just . . . odd." I sigh and let my head fall back onto the wall.

"Is there anything else in your room, siren?"

"Ash, it's pitch-black. I can't even see my hand."

It goes quiet again, although I can hear Asher moving around in the connected space.

"What was the bet?" I ask.

"Huh?"

"The bet?" I raise my voice louder.

"Is that something you really want to know?"

"I asked, didn't I?"

It sounds like he released a heavy moan but it's hard to tell. "A few years ago, I was seeing a celestial nymph named Hesperia." *Oh God, do I really want to know?* "Anyway, being a human, you're probably not familiar with nymphs but they tend to be quite . . . beautiful, free, and sexually precocious."

"I see." I groan inside.

"They're also a bit selfish. You know, the attention-seeker type," he adds.

"Sounds like *your* type," I mutter quietly, thinking about Morgana, the beautiful dark-haired gargoyle from the Manhattan clan that threw herself at Asher in an attempt to rekindle his affections.

"Hesperia was free-spirited. She usually walked around naked and danced in the middle of forests and stuff. I liked that she was . . . animated." His voice is wistful.

"I'm sure you did." I roll my eyes.

He chuckles. "Nymphs are not known to exhibit a lot of self-control. They have a strong desire to engage in sexual behavior. Callan was tired of Hesperia walking around naked all the time whenever she'd visit with me."

"I'm sure he was," I mumble.

"Anyway, he bet me that I couldn't go a month without jumping her. Since I'm not one to back down from a challenge, I agreed. I bet Callan that if I could, he wasn't allowed to bake another cookie, ever again. If I lost, he wanted me to study *Kama Sutra* with Lunette to learn how to, um . . . control myself."

"I don't get it. How did the piercing come into play?"

"As we made the bet, Hesperia walked by us. Naked. At the sight, Callan upped the ante. If I were to lose the bet within an hour of making it, I had to get the apadravya piercing."

I scrunched my face in disgust. "Why that piercing?"

"In the history of *Kama Sutra*, it's the most painful piercing someone can get. That said, it's also the most pleasurable for women. So even though I lost, siren, I still won." His voice is cocky and smooth.

"That's the dumbest story I have ever heard," I reply while blushing. "Wait, you have the piercing. Are you saying you couldn't even go an HOUR?" I exclaim in disbelief.

"Siren, she was a naked nymph," he says slowly, as if I should understand.

"Oh my God, you're so gross," I huff.

"Say whatever you want, siren, but I know you like the silver balls," he mocks.

Still blushing, I stand. "You know what, I'm sorry I asked. Let's just get out of here, find Lunette, and maybe kill her."

"Deal."

My eyes scan the blackness before landing on a small shadow that my body is casting from the lit candle. "Ash, I have an idea. Maybe I can pull the dark energy and teleport into the room you're in."

"Are there shadows in the room?" he asks with caution.

"I can make some," I offer. "With the flame from the candle."

"I'll manipulate the dark energy. There are no shadows in this room for you to move into because it's too bright," he orders.

"Okay." I place the candle on the ground and stand in front of it, creating an outline of my silhouette on the wall. I close my eyes, hoping this works.

After a few moments, I feel warm palms on my cheeks and Asher's thumb moving over my bottom lip.

"Open your eyes, siren," he demands, his minty breath crossing my lips.

"It worked." I meet his gaze.

"It worked. Very clever." He smiles proudly at me.

The black room begins to fall away, and we're standing in a woodland scene, shrouded by evening. The moon is bright and unusually full. It looks larger than life. A cool night breeze floats over us, bringing with it the smell of spruce.

"You're not going to ask me to get naked and dance, are you?" I ask, with an arched brow.

Asher laughs. "You, dancing naked in the forest, bathed in moonlight? I'd pay to see that, siren." He wiggles his eyebrows and wraps his large arms around my waist, pulling me closer.

We both startle when a ring of violet fire appears out of nowhere, with eight women surrounding the flames. Each is covered in various colored silk robes.

Asher grabs my hand tightly, pulling me behind him in a protective stance.

Lunette approaches us with a smile. "Well done, dears. You have proven to the sorceresses of the Black Circle that you are, in fact, the divination bloodlines."

My gaze meets Asher's.

"Those rooms were a test?" he accuses.

Lunette's focus shifts to me. "The souls of the daughter of light and the prince of dark shall join together. United as one, the two souls will conquer the end of days and bring redemption to the universe and its people."

I turn toward Asher. His jaw is ticking and working hard. I exhale roughly.

"It's why I had Eve light the white candle, representing the light, and you, Asher, the black candle, representing darkness. You both have the bloodlines, the daughter of light and the prince of darkness. The prophecy has been fulfilled." She beams as if this is the greatest concept ever.

"Lunette, you'll forgive our wish to read the scrolls for ourselves," he demands, paling.

"Of course. First, dear, the sorceresses desire an introduction," she instructs.

"Wait—" I'm cut off by Lunette's whispers.

"Each sorceress is named after an equinox in our Wiccan lunar calendar," she explains, and hands me a small cloth, motioning to my nose. *Awesome.*

I wipe away the dried blood, hoping I got it all, even though I've already begun to heal.

"Sisters, it is with great honor that I present the daughter of Heaven and the prince of darkness," Lunette booms to the circle of ladies.

In unison, they all bow their heads and chant, "Blessed be."

Asher and I just tilt our heads politely in response. I'm not sure what I expected from a circle of sorceresses but these ladies are a wonderful collection of women of different nationalities, shapes, sizes and ages.

"We'll begin with Yule." Lunette motions to the mature, beautiful woman on her right. "Sorceress of the Northern Light."

"Blessed be," Yule offers to Asher and me.

We nod our head in respect.

"Imbolic, Sorceress of Fire." Lunette gestures to a younger woman with fire-red hair.

"Blessed be," Imbolic says.

"This is Ostara, Sorceress of Fertility," she continues to the stunning woman.

"Blessed be," Ostara returns.

"Beltane, Sorceress of Blessings," the sorceress introduces the older woman.

"Blessed be," Beltane states in a quiet voice.

"Litha, Sorceress of the Summer Solstice." Lunette squeezes the whimsical woman's hand with affection.

"Blessed be," Litha offers with a warm smile.

"Llughnassad, Sorceress of Prosperity."

"Blessed be," the youngest of the sorceresses rasps, and bows her head.

"Mabon. The White Sorceress," Lunette introduces.

"Blessed be," the woman with snow-white hair responds.

"And finally, the circle's elder, Samhain. Sorceress of Souls." Lunette bows to her.

"Blessed be, daughter of Eve and son of Adam."

Asher bristles next to me. "I do believe you are mistaken. I am Asher St. Michael, son to the late king, Garrick St. Michael, and next in line to the gargoyle throne."

Samhain nods her understanding. "Your bloodline and soul say differently, young prince."

Asher goes rigid. "You're incorrect, witch. I'm a gargoyle. We do not have souls."

Samhain's eyes meet Lunette's. "He has not been enlightened."

"No," Lunette answers in a quiet voice.

"I see," Samhain offers solemnly.

"As the guardian of the scrolls, I wish to petition the circle to allow the daughter of Heaven and the prince of darkness to view the divination for themselves," Lunette requests.

Samhain turns back to the seven other sorceresses surrounding the fire. In unison, they all bow their head in approval. "Granted. Blessed be you, Sorceress of the Moon," the elder offers, and returns to her spot in the circle.

"Come, dears. It's time to see the scrolls." Lunette motions us toward a mausoleum.

We walk into the cryptic burial chamber, which is covered in webs and dirt, and blanketed in darkness. *Wonderful.* Lunette lights a candle as we make our way through the cold tomb.

"Not creepy at all," I joke quietly.

Asher squeezes my hand in reassurance. Lunette pushes on a stone, and a hidden door opens as she motions for us to continue walking through the catacomb.

"I'll lead." Asher's voice is deep and authoritative.

"You'll get no argument from me on that," I reply.

He scoffs. "That's a first."

I roll my eyes and follow him as we come to a dead end. I turn back to Lunette, and she smiles knowingly before closing her eyes and speaking in Latin.

"Aperi, ex imperio auguratricis Lunette," the sorceress chants.

At the release of her words, the wall shifts and opens into a grotto. In the middle is an old crate, which Lunette approaches. "Ego praecipio tibi, ut liberare custodia clausum invernerunt," she continues.

The chest opens to reveal an aged tube. Carefully, she passes Asher the candle and pulls the cylinder out of the case. Turning, she hands it to me with an encouraging smile.

"I present the divination of redemption, daughter of Heaven," she says, and curtsies.

My eyes shift to Asher, and then back to Lunette, who nods her head in support. I pull the old parchment out of the case and lay it carefully on top of the crate, only to find there are no words written on it.

It's blank.

"It doesn't say anything," I say, sliding my glance to Lunette.

She faceplants again in her palm. "My bad. One second, dear."

Asher groans, rubbing his hands over his face and through his hair in aggravation.

I smile politely.

"Venit hora, et filius hominis, ut ostendat divination Evae filia redemptionis," she chants, and words suddenly appear.

"Thanks," I manage to squeak out, and return my gaze to the scrolls. "I'm sorry, I don't read Latin."

Asher steps forward. "Let me, siren."

I watch his lips move while he reads the document. For a moment, I actually have to close my eyes and try to focus on why we're here and not how good those lips feel against my own. *God, Eve, focus.*

Asher turns his ashen face to me.

"So?" I question. The anticipation is driving me insane.

"It's true," is all he says.

"Which part?"

"All of it. The bloodlines. The prophecy. Our connection. It's all predestined." He swallows roughly.

I inhale through my nose. "Oh shit."

"Everley, the cherub angel of ancestry, was ordered by Archangel Michael to touch our bloodlines at the time of conception. Yours was touched by Eve, a light of Heaven, and mine was touched by Lilith, a demon of darkness, and both were intertwined by Adam. Our souls have been predesigned to unite. Together, we're supposed to conquer the end of days and bring redemption to those in need," he summarizes in a quiet tone, assessing me.

"Souls?" I question, pulling my brows together.

"Souls," he confirms with a slow nod.

After a bit, it sinks in. "Asher, does this mean you have a soul?" I ask in disbelief.

"It's impossible. A gargoyle does not have a soul." He looks to Lunette for clarification.

Lunette's face is bright. She's excited and animated. "Yes, Asher dear, you have a soul. It only shines when it is connected to Eve's. You see, you need light to infuse the darkness and allow it to breathe and live. Without her, your soul cannot exist," she offers.

"Are you saying the only way for Asher to have a soul, and redemption, is if he loves me?" I ask Lunette, trying to follow.

"The divination has been predesigned so that your souls are mates. In order for his to be, it must be connected to its other half—its lifeline. That is the only way his soul can survive," she points out solemnly. "If your soul is not linked with Asher's, his sits dormant. Nonexistent."

"How is that even possible?" I exhale, and study Asher's face. It's tight. His brows are knitted and he looks like he's about to puke.

"The whys are not important, dear. The fact is, you and Asher are the truest form of soul mates. Isn't that romantic?" she coos, her eyes dreamy.

"Lunette, what of the blood link?" Asher questions.

"The blood connection you share with Eve, as protector and charge, is not enough of a lifeline for your soul to awaken. You must become one—body, mind, and spirit. Once that occurs, your soul will thrive in Eve's light." Lunette smiles at us.

I shift my focus to Asher. He's breathing with difficulty. "Ash?"

"It appears, siren, that you are my redemption." He smiles weakly.

13 Chosen Path

I walk into the kitchen, and at the scene in front of me, I'm immediately reminded of how Asher got his piercing. *Damn.* Callan has his apron on and he's pulling blueberry muffins out of the oven. Sensing my presence, he twists his head and offers me his brightest smile.

"Hey, cutie. How was your visit with Lunette?" He grins knowingly.

"Fine."

His eyebrows lift. "Fine? Visits with Lunette are rarely ever just *fine*."

I give him my best-pointed stare. "I know about the nymph and the piercing."

"Don't judge, human. It was a good wager. She was always naked. There was no way he was going to win." He gives me his boyish grin.

"Gross."

"What is?" Abby asks, skipping into the kitchen and planting a peck on Callan.

"Eves knows about the bet." Callan bites back a laugh.

Abby's eyes go wide. "The one we made about the mate mark?" she squeaks.

Callan's expression falters as he shakes his head. "The one about the piercing."

"Wait. What bet about the mate mark?" I ask, narrowing my eyes at Abby.

She flips her red hair over her shoulder and looks everywhere but at me.

I fold my arms and patiently wait her out.

"Gah . . . fine. Callan and I put money on when you'd get Asher's mark," she comes clean.

"What?" I ask in astonishment.

"Again. Another easy way to earn a little cash, cutie," Callan explains, amused.

"I expect this from him," I point to Callan, "but you're supposed to be my friend, Abby."

She sinks into herself. "I am your friend. It's just that I think you and Asher are great together. I know he loves you, and you love him. So it's bound to happen. If it makes you feel better, I was planning to use the winnings to buy you a mate ceremony dress." She bats her lashes at me and goes all Abby-cute.

"I can't believe you two," I admonish.

"What's going on?" Gage questions from behind me.

"Frick and Frack over here are making bets on when I'll get Asher's mate mark."

Gage takes out his wallet and a pack of cigarettes and places them on the island. "I'm in."

My mouth falls open. "Seriously?"

He smirks. "Come on, love. It's the easiest bet I'll make."

"McKenna is right. You are a traitor," I scold.

Gage's lips tilt. "Do I need to remind you, I don't pick sides."

"Odds are now four to one. A hundred bucks gets you into the action," Callan says.

"Who is the one against?" Gage asks, placing a hundred on the granite. *Asshat.*

"Keegan," Abby answers, picking at a muffin top.

"Hello. I'm standing right here," I remind the group.

Callan's face goes soft. "I'm sorry, cutie. It's not really fair but did you want in?"

I girlie growl and stomp out of the kitchen while their laughter follows me. *Damn gargoyles.* When I enter the Tension Room, I come to a complete stop at the sight of Keegan in deep concentration at the pool table. I stand there awkwardly for a moment because, well, it's just Keegan and me, and damn, he's unapproachable.

Just as I'm about to turn and run, he notices me standing quietly, and repositions himself to his full height, then offers an uncomfortable smile.

Yep. No awkwardness here.

"Eve." My name is a curt hello.

"Hey."

"Asher isn't here. He's at a council meeting. Checking in," Keegan offers roughly.

"I know. I was, um . . . just going to relax and watch some TV," I lie.

Keegan's eyes shift to the flat screen and then back to me. "If you'd prefer, you're welcome to join me at pool. I'm not sure if you play or not?"

I chew the inside of my cheek, causing him to pull his full eyebrows together. He is probably realizing we know nothing about one another—at all—and this is a bad idea.

"Um." I fidget. Really, I want to say no and leave. Apparently, my mouth has other plans.

"It's just pool, Eve," Keegan comments.

"I play a little." I shrug and walk over to the wall to pick a stick.

"You aren't going to hustle me, are you?"

"I'm sorry?"

"This isn't one of those instances where you say you can't play, then clear the table?"

I release a scratchy laugh.

The side of his mouth tilts slightly.

I shake my head. "Honestly, no."

He nods. "All right then, ladies choice, stripes or solids?"

"Stripes."

"I'll rack."

"Where's McKenna?" I inquire, leaning on the table and watching him. I really don't want to get into it with her because I'm hanging out with her boyfriend.

Keegan offers me a knowing look. "She accompanied Asher to the meeting. We wanted to be sure there are no additional issues with the council and that they allow his return." His voice is even.

"Smart." I think the last time I was this intimidated was when I first met Asher.

"Ladies first." He places the white cue ball in front of me.

I break. Nothing hits a pocket. We're quiet for the first couple of shots before I speak.

"You like pool?" *Riveting, Eve. Just, amazing dialogue.*

"I enjoy the strategy of it," he answers, while sinking a red ball into the corner pocket.

"Where did you learn to play?" I question, again missing my shot.

"My dad. It was something he and I did, just the two of us. I loved spending time with him without Callan or Asher hovering." His blue eyes shift to the window in longing.

"My aunt and I used to paddleboard together," I offer, unsure of why.

Keegan shifts his focus back to me, then presents a sad smile. "It's nice to have one-on-one time with people you love. It makes those memories of them even more special."

"I might not be the right person to talk to about that. The people I love tend to disappoint."

This time, I sink a striped ball in the side pocket, but forget to call it first.

"It's my opinion, the people we love tend to disappoint us the most in life. It's inevitable."

"Why do you suppose that is?" I exhale.

Keegan contemplates for a moment. "Maybe because we invest so much time into loving them, that when they do let us down, it hurts more."

"Insightful."

He offers me a slight smirk before positioning himself to hit another ball into a pocket.

"Do you miss your dad?" I ask, trying to get to know Keegan more.

The tall gargoyle deadpans, "Every single day, Eve."

I nod. "It must have been hard being so young and having your parents taken from you. I can't imagine raising two brothers, let alone adding McKenna and Abby to the mix."

Keegan gets two more balls in. "Life is hard. You take things as they come and make the best of them. Family is what is important. The rest is just circumstance."

"Do you believe in fate?" I pose quietly, twisting the chalk on the tip of my cue stick.

Keegan looks up before standing tall and placing his stick on the billiard table. He walks over to me, sighs, and crosses his large arms over his taut chest before leaning casually against the table. In this stance, he reminds me so much of Asher.

"Sometimes, Eve, it's hard to see that the path placed in front of us is what we are meant to follow in order to become what we are supposed to be." His tone is sincere.

"Kinda feels like a prison sentence." The statement comes out like a snip.

"It might seem like a sentence, but once embraced, the future can be a wonderful thing," he replies with a stern look.

I close my eyes before reopening them and locking onto his intense ones. "What if someone fails at becoming what they are meant to be?"

Keegan nods in understanding, before moving his hands from his chest and placing them on either side of his body on the pool table. "When we were little, Asher and I were really competitive. I mean, grossly so. We're alpha, so it was easy for us to try to be better than the other. Callan, though, he was the baby. We used to treat him like glass," he snickers. "Asher and I would do everything for him. The kid couldn't even eat a candy bar without one of us breaking pieces off and feeding it to him."

"Sounds like typical older brothers."

"When we came into our gargoyle wings, my dad used to take the three of us out to learn to fly. Asher and I, of course, did it right away, mainly so we could brag about who flew first. Callan, though, he would freak. He would always say, what if I fall? To which our father would always answer, but what if you fly? I think that scared him even more." He chuckles quietly.

I picture a younger, even more adorable Callan. "Eventually though, he did it?"

"He did. One day, Abby was visiting and we were all practicing. Callan was sulking, as per usual. She sat next to him, took his hand, leaned in, and whispered, 'I believe in you.'"

I release a choked laugh. "That's all it took?"

Keegan's eyes twinkle. "It would be a nice story if it were. My baby brother made Abby promise to kiss him if he did it. She promised. He flew. They kissed." The side of his mouth tilts. "There might have even been tongue. I'm not sure."

My smile grows as I lean next to Keegan on the table. "Ew."

Keegan's expression becomes serious. "Sometimes, Eve, it takes only one person to believe in us. Support us.

Stand by us. No matter what, to set us on our chosen path and fulfill what we were born to do."

I nod in understanding. "McKenna is that person for you?"

"She stands beside me and never lets me fall. Whenever I question myself, or my motives, she reminds me that failure is not an option. Kenna's tough, because she has to be. For me."

I inhale and place my stick on the table. "Do you think Asher is that person for me?"

He releases a deep breath. "Asher is a loyal protector, as well as a phenomenal being and brother. He's going to make an excellent king. Our race will be lucky to have him on its side. Anyone, really, is fortunate to have Asher in his or her corner. However, his role in your fate is still up for debate in my book. It would seem that his chosen path and yours are entwined. You're both tethered to this story. He needs you to fulfill his assignment, in order to take his place among our people. You need him to bring redemption to those who need it."

I stare at the wall in front of me. "What about love?" It comes out as a quiet question.

"No, I don't think you have a place in one another's lives. I don't mean to sound cruel, Eve, but love for one another cannot be. This is not a fairy tale. It's real life," he says.

My stomach drops at his words. "Why is it that you are so against Asher and I being together? What have I done to earn your dislike and mistrust?"

Keegan sighs and crosses his ankles. "Eve, it's not that I do not like you. To be honest, you're simply a new toy to Asher. A distraction so he doesn't have to deal with his birthright to be king. He's hid it well over the years, but he's always been hesitant to step into our father's position. You're the perfect excuse for him to not become what he is destined to be. On the flip side of the coin, you're using him to divert you from the ascension, which you are unsure about fulfilling. You're both like scared children, exploiting one another so neither of you has to face what your chosen path is."

I blink the sting in my eyes away. "What makes you think I don't love him, and he me?"

Keegan's expression falters, before he places his stoic mask back on. "Eve, you can't possibly love someone that you don't really know."

"I do know him," I assure.

"You think you're familiar with us, but you've only seen the surface of what this family is and what we do to protect. Those layers run deep, entire life cycles of history and loyalties. You can't begin to understand because you have not been there." His voice is gentle but unwavering.

"That's unfair, Keegan. You can't protect this family from everything," I offer.

"I'm a protector, Eve. Make no mistake. In my world, family comes first. I learned that lesson the hard way when I suddenly became the leader of this clan after my parents' disappearance. I don't have the luxury of brooding about life like Asher, or having a friendly demeanor as Callan does. We all have our roles. Mine is keeping this clan together and everyone on their fated paths." The warning is released with a kind tone.

I straighten my shoulders and lift my chin. "So, I'll always be the outsider to you?"

"Yes."

"Why?"

"You are the only thing I can't protect him from." His voice is so quiet, I barely register it.

"I won't hurt him," I promise weakly.

"You already have."

"How so?"

"Asher's position with the council is in question, he's broken his oaths to his people, and the throne is in jeopardy at the moment because he's too focused on his heart to fulfill his assignment properly and step into his role as king," Keegan lists off.

"What if I'm his fate, and the other pieces you are presenting as his chosen path are false?"

"That line of thought will get him killed, Eve," Keegan warns sternly.

We just stare at one another in understanding before I give up. The sound of the doors opening startles us both as Asher and McKenna walk in. Our focus darts to them. McKenna prowls over and stands between Keegan's legs as he wraps himself around her.

"Thanks for bringing him home, tas ámotas," Keegan mumbles into her neck.

"Always do, ágra-lem," McKenna confirms in Garish, and plants a light kiss on his mouth.

Asher just stands and smiles at me, taking me in. *God, I love his smile.* Keegan's words float through my head, and my eyes drop to the ground before I clear my throat.

"Thanks for the game. Good night." I stand and walk around Asher toward the door.

Just as I reach Asher's side, his hand darts out, grabbing my arm and ending my escape. Not wanting to look him in the eye, I focus on where his hand is touching my arm, burning it. I inhale, trying to ignore the way his touch makes me feel.

After composing myself, I lift my gaze and see his face covered in concern. His eyebrows are pulled together, forming that line in the middle. I offer a weak smile and gently take my arm out of his hold.

"Good night, Eve," Keegan says.

I leave the Tension Room and head up to my room. I walk in and see Gage sitting on my bed. I frown and study him.

"Stalking me?" I question.

He smirks. "We, are going out, love."

"We? As in . . ." I draw out.

"You and me."

"Ah, and where would we be going exactly?"

"To a bar, and before you ask, no, we are not heading to Katana. I'm taking you to a college dive bar, one with peanut shells on the floor and stupid young college students who don't understand the meaning of restraint. It's a rite of passage." His eyes light with excitement.

"And when we get to this rite of passage, what are we going to do there?" I ask.

"Once there, we are going to do shots of tequila until you fall flat on your face and/or puke. Whichever comes first, love."

My eyebrow arches in question. "Why are we doing this?"

"You're in college. You should do normal things like get shit-faced when you need stress relief. Christ, I need stress relief just from hanging out with this clan," he explains.

"I see."

"Should I wait until you change and primp or are you ready?"

"You do realize I am only eighteen?"

He smirks at me like I'm a cute puppy. "Meet me at the car in ten minutes," he orders, walking around me and out the door.

I just stare at the place Gage was sitting, as Keegan's words float through my head. A night of normal college behavior actually sounds really good. I stare at my closet, and ten minutes later, Gage and I are on our way into the city, fake ID in hand.

༄༅

The bad-boy gargoyle was absolutely right. After five tequila shots, I feel amazing. My stress is nowhere in sight. I blink hard. Apparently my vision is nowhere in sight either, because everything is blurring and spinning a bit.

After flirting with girl number four thousand, Gage turns back to me, pushing another lime my way, along with a shot glass filled with liquid bliss.

"Ready? This is the one that will bring you to your happy place," he mutters, and clinks our glasses.

I watch him take his, then follow suit. The burn is no longer present as the alcohol dribbles down my throat, followed by the sour taste of lime.

"You know what I like about you, Gage?" I say, maybe slurring. *Am I slurring?* I giggle at the thought, while pushing my empty shot glass filled with lime peel forward.

"What's that, love?" The right side of his mouth tilts in a seductive smile.

I turn toward him and uncross my jean-covered legs. "You're fun. Asher . . . is no fun. You are like sunshine, and life. He—he is all darkness, and brooding, and blah," I slur again. *Am I drunk?* Why are my lips numb? I pop them together, trying to regain feeling.

Gage just watches me with amusement and lights his cigarette. *Wait, can he do that in here?* His eyes slide down my body, landing on my knee-high, black-leather, five-inch-heeled boots, pulling me out of my thought process.

"Nice shoes," he compliments, rubbing his bottom lip with his thumb.

"See! The way you just said that to me, in a smoldering voice, is so hot!" I exclaim loudly. "Asher would be all, 'Why are you wearing such high heels? You'll kill yourself.'"

He snorts. "Love, I'm sitting right here. No need to raise your voice at me."

"Oops." I cover my mouth and giggle again. *Damn, why am I giggling all the time?*

My laughter trails off as I stare at him. Gage twists on his stool and places his knee between my legs. Wow. He really is panty-dropping gorgeous. I can see why all the girls on campus fall over themselves trying to get him into their beds.

"Thanks," he says with a wicked smile, as his eyes sparkle with humor.

I groan. Shit. Did I say that out loud? *Damn tequila.*

I'm lost in my own thoughts while Gage moves closer toward me. Finally, it dawns on me just how close he is to me.

"What are you doing?" I whisper.

"I'm not sure." Gage's expression is confused.

"You should stop," I warn, in a tone that clearly says I don't mean it.

"You have no idea how illicit you are." He watches my lips.

My heart stops. "So tell me," I challenge, emboldened the tequila running through my veins.

I bite my lip as his lust-filled eyes drop and focus on the movement. I hold my breath and still. When he moves closer, I feel it, crawling up my throat as my stomach bottoms out. The world tilts, and I grip his arms to steady myself. *Oh shit.*

"I think I'm going to be sick," I quickly alert him.

The right side of Gage's mouth tilts before he speaks. "Sounds about right."

I squeeze my eyes closed and proceed to throw up all over him. *Awesome.*

I don't remember how I got back to the manor. I'm sure Gage teleported us as fast as he could. What I do know is that upon our return, Asher had Gage by the throat, and the Angelic Sword pointed at his heart.

At some point during their scuffle, Abby yanked me upstairs, changed me out of my clothing, and is now sitting next to me on the bathroom floor, holding my hair while I vomit up the entire contents of my tequila-soaked stomach.

She sighs. "So let me get this straight, you thought tequila shots would be a good idea?"

I moan. "I just needed to be numb for a while," I answer in a soft voice.

She's quiet while dabbing my face with a wet cloth. "Pretty sure, sweetie, that you're feeling a whole lot of hurt right now, which is the complete opposite of numb. Even with your healing abilities, you're about to have a rough night."

I lay my head against the cool porcelain. "Well, chalk it up to another mistake I made."

She winces and I throw up again. "You've been through a lot lately, Eve. I can certainly understand the need to escape for a few hours. Although I really do wish you would stop trusting Gage so blindly." She hands me water.

"Trust is not something I give freely anymore." I lay my head down on her lap.

"Is that so?" She places the cool rag on my forehead and runs her fingers through my hair.

"Trust is like a mirror—you can fix it if it's broken, but you can still see the crack in that motherfucker's reflection," I say, and close my eyes, willing the room to stop spinning.

Abby laughs. "Did you just quote Lady Gaga?"

"Don't judge me, Abby. I was born this way," I mumble through my drunken stupor.

"Oh my God, I think I love drunk Eve." She giggles.

Randi Cooley Wilson

14 Fragile Heart

I sit back in the lounge chair, wrapping the wool blanket around my shoulders. Even though it's spring, the mornings are still cool. I inhale, watching steam rising off the ground as the sun warms the frost-touched grass.

I've learned to cherish these quiet, peaceful moments, lost in my own head and reevaluating life. They're few and far between. I can't explain it, but I know something is about to shift, and that I won't have these serene moments for long. I can feel it in my soul. War is on the horizon and it will be dark and unsightly.

I'm no longer the ordinary girl I once thought I was. The luxury of ignorance is gone. My eyes are wide open now. Choices have to be made. Who will I become? Can I redeem what needs to be? Am I strong enough to make the sacrifices that are needed to be successful?

A steaming mug is placed in front of my face. My hands wrap around its warmth as Asher sits in front of me, straddling the lounge chair. He's silently watching me. He's always studying me like I'm a chess game and he's planning his next move.

I play with the tiny marshmallows floating on top of the dark chocolate liquid, so I don't have to look him in the eye this morning. My memory of last night is foggy, but I feel like I might have crossed a line with Gage.

The guilt has been eating away at me all morning. I was hoping to find Gage and talk before I saw Asher, but I guess that's not going to happen.

After an awkward amount of time, I break the silence. "Thanks." I lift the mug of hot cocoa. "It's nice to have this back." My eyes meet his. "Gage just kept buying me café mochas, which are chocolatey but super sweet. I missed the simplicity of this," I ramble.

Asher continues to focus on me in silence.

"Not to mention the absurd amount of money he spent buying them," I continue my rant.

Silence.

I exhale, and look up at the brooding gargoyle. "Are you upset with me?"

He shakes his head no. *All righty then.*

"Okay."

His eyes drop and he plays with the leather bands on his wrists.

"Is there a particular reason I'm getting the silent treatment today, or did you forget how to speak?" I take a sip of the warm liquid and squint my eyes at him in a challenging manner.

"I figured your head might be pounding this morning after you drank your weight in tequila shots, siren," he speaks softly. "I wasn't sure if your healing gift covers hangovers."

And there it is—he's pissed. *Way to be passive-aggressive, Asher St. Michael.* "Suckily, no. Hangovers are not covered under supernatural healing powers."

Asher's expression becomes blank, and his eyes dart around before speaking through a tight jaw and rough voice. "After I beat the shit out of Gage last night, he and I talked."

My eyes widen. "You did?" *Oh crap.*

Asher just nods. "Yes. On both counts."

I chew the inside of my cheek. "What did you talk about?"

"You." *Crap. Crap. Crap.*

"What did he have to say?" I ask, trying to be nonchalant, but my voice cracks.

At the change in sound, Asher's gaze lifts to mine. "He revealed the meaning of life."

A small smirk appears on my face. "Wow. Who knew Gage was all-knowing?"

Asher's mouth tilts. "No one ever accused Gage Gallagher of feeblemindedness, siren."

"Where is he this morning?" Asher's brow arches in question. "I mean, I wanted to apologize for last night, but I didn't see him," I fumble.

"For the record, he should be apologizing to you." His tone has a bite to it.

"It wasn't his fault. I agreed to go. He didn't pour the tequila down my throat, Ash."

"No. You did that all on your own," he counters, with a sharp look.

"I thought you weren't mad," I retort, and place the mug on the table next to me.

Asher sighs. "Why did you go with him, siren?"

I play with my fingerless gloves. "I needed space. I just . . . I wanted to feel nothing for a while . . . to be normal. God, Asher, I'm eighteen. Up until a few months ago, my biggest concern was whether I would get into the college of my choice, if I could walk in the heels that Aria picked, or if my summer job would give me enough time off to sunbathe. You'll have to forgive that I misstep a bit. I am human," I state a bit heatedly.

Asher exhales and rubs his face before aiming a dark, irritated glance my way.

"Imagine for a moment that your entire life is turned upside down. You wake up one day to discover that you're not who you thought you were. Your parents are not who they're supposed to be, and suddenly, your friends are supernatural beings you didn't even know existed except in dark fairy tales. That every new breath you take could be the last. Envision walking down the street past innocent people, knowing if you don't accept your ascension, there's no redemption for them. Consider how you would feel if your best friend was killed because of you, or that the person you love most in this life can't be with you because of obligations that are not of your world. So forgive me for having a few shots of tequila last night and trying to just be . . . normal," I spout off, as a tear falls. *God, I'm whining. Shit.*

With lightning speed, Asher moves up on the lounge chair and yanks me onto his lap, his warm lips pressing against my neck. "Fuck. I'm sorry, siren."

I cling to him, because I need to be close to him. "I know," I whisper.

He pulls back and takes my face in his hands. "No, you don't. I know what it's like to need to catch your breath in order to breathe. I get that we live our lives with death hanging over us, but by the grace, I fucking love you, siren. It's you and me. I know I haven't been the best at showing you that, or even being here for you, but give me a chance to prove that to you. If you need something, you come to me, yeah? Not Gage. I am your protector."

"That's just it, Asher. You protect me so tightly that I can't catch my breath," I say quietly.

He releases a deep growl. "Fuck . . . it's just that I'm so fucking afraid that someday this will be over." He motions between us. "I know you're overwhelmed and that I'm adding to it, but it's because you're mine and I will do anything to make sure that you're safe. You get that, yeah?"

"I believe with all my heart that you'll keep me safe, Asher, but what about happy?"

Asher goes still, before swallowing hard. I watch the sexy movement of his Adam's apple as he contemplates what I've said.

"Tell me what to do, and I'll fucking do it. Tell me what you want, and it's yours. You. Come. First. Always," he whispers across my mouth.

"All I want is you," I reply, pressing my lips to his.

"You have me," he responds against my mouth, before kissing me hard.

Breathless, I pull back. "What about the council? Sooner or later, they'll discover you've broken your protector oath. What then?"

"We're forming a strategy to deal with the council. There's an elder in London whom I'm planning to meet with soon. He'll help. It will work itself out. The divination provides extenuating circumstances, and hopefully we can use that to our advantage. For the time being, I don't want you to worry about the council. The clan has the situation under control," he assures.

My eyes shift to the pool, then back to Asher. "You know, if the scrolls are true, there is a way that I can save you. If you have a soul, there's no way you can turn to stone. Even if the council threatens stone petrifaction, it can't happen, Ash," I speak softly.

He shakes his head adamantly. "No. I promised you what we have is real. We're linked by blood, and for now, it will remain that way. In order to link souls, we need to be mated. That's something I want you to do because you want me, forever. Not because you want to save or protect me."

I shift on his lap. "Isn't that what you do to me on a daily basis? Protect me?"

"That's different. It's my job," he barks in aggravation. "Let's keep the soul thing quiet for a bit—I haven't told the clan about it."

I'm still for a moment before I speak. "Keegan seems to think you're not interested in taking control of the throne and I'm simply a distraction. Is that true?"

His grip on my waist tightens as he pulls me closer so our chests touch. "No."

"If we work it out with the council, are you still planning on leading your race?"

"Yes."

"Where do I fall when that occurs?"

"By my side, siren. My mate. My queen."

I scoff. "You think the clans will accept a human? One that you've broken your oaths and laws for?" I ask, as Gage's words come back to me.

"I don't fucking care. I will end anyone's existence who questions it." His voice is hard.

I smirk. "You can't do that, Asher."

"Yes, I can. I am the king." He wiggles his eyebrows playfully. "Or I will be once we get you ascended. Hey, you're going to be late for your first class. Let's get going."

"About that . . . I was thinking of taking a leave of absence from school for a while."

"Eve," he groans in dismay. "It's important that you finish school. You've worked hard to get here. See it through, yeah?"

"Hear me out. I've already missed so much at this point, that if I don't drop, I'll probably fail. Besides, I promise to go back and finish. Right now, if I'm going to focus on the ascension, then I need to—and not on elodea cell labs."

Asher just studies me as I play with the scruff on his jawline. "I'll agree to it, if you promise that when this shitstorm is over, you'll go back."

"If I'm still here, I will." I try to sound strong.

"You will be fucking here and you will be going back, siren," he demands.

I clear my throat. "I promise, then."

"What about your aunt and Michael? Don't you think we should sort this out?" he asks.

I drop my forehead to his. "I can't. It's too raw. I'm not ready."

His hands methodically rub up and down my spine, causing delicious warmth to float through me while he's lost in deep thought.

"All right, siren. We'll go back to London for a bit. We'll work on the ascension and strategize on the council, while figuring out how to prevent—or win—this upcoming war. When all that's done, we'll return, and you and Elizabeth will work this shit out, yeah?"

I try to stand and Asher's hold tightens. "She loves you, Eve, and I know you love her. Life is too short to leave this between you two. She's your mother. She has always been. Don't let a lie that was designed to protect you push her away. Family comes first."

"Okay," I murmur.

"Okay."

"So we're going back to England?"

"I think it's best. We still need to figure out who the traitor working with Deacon is." He runs his fingers gently over my lips.

"Will Gage be coming with us?" I gently kiss his fingers.

"Yeah, siren, he'll be with us. The council's request needs to be upheld, so we'll play nice. I'll call Marcus and have the Manhattan clan meet us over there too, and reach out to Michael and let him know the plan." Asher moves closer and leaves a gentle kiss on my temple.

I groan. "As much as I'm looking forward to seeing Marcus, Morgana is not on my list of favorite gargoyles."

Asher's lips tug into a smirk as he pulls back. "I'm yours, siren. Trust in that."

No longer wanting to discuss Morgana, I change topics. "I haven't seen Michael since the night they dropped the parent bomb. Is he hiding from me?" My index finger runs over his bottom lip. *Good Lord, he has the yummiest mouth ever.*

"As a warrior of Heaven, Michael follows orders. The only way he is allowed to come is if instructed to by the Angelic Council. Otherwise, he isn't permitted," he explains.

"It's so weird to think of him with my aunt." My finger stills, lingering on his mouth.

"Do you want to talk about it, siren?" He playfully bites my hand.

"No." I smirk and pull it away.

"I'm sorry you had to deal with that without me. The council has rules. Once in the meetings, we're not permitted to leave for any reason. I'm glad Gage was there, though."

"We ended up watching *The Smurfs*, so it's all good," I tease.

Asher's face scrunches. "*The Smurfs*?"

"It's a long story," I smile.

"One for another time then?" He moves closer, running his nose along my chin before resting in the crook of my neck. "No more drinking alone with Gage, yeah?"

I nod. "Agreed."

"I'm your safe haven. You need something, you come to me. Only," he orders.

"I love you," I reply.

"Forever, siren."

"Forever," I whisper.

৵৶

"I'm surprised at you, love bug," my Aunt Elizabeth says. "I just need some time to focus on other things," I offer in a weak tone.

She sighs over the phone. "I suppose, technically, you're an adult now. I don't like it."

"One semester. Two tops. Then I'll return and graduate. I promise." I try to ignore the disappointment lining her voice. I recall the difficulty I had getting her to agree to let me go live away at college in the first place.

"Okay," she concedes, before we fall into an odd silence.

"Thanks for understanding. I should get going. Asher wants to be in London by morning."

"Eve, we still need to talk about what happened when you were home last," she reminds.

"I'm not ready. Please respect that." I blink away the sting in my eyes.

Her heartbreak floats over the line. She clears her throat. "I'll respect your need for space, for now. I love you, and when you're ready, I'll be here." Her tone is strong and maternal.

I sniff once. "I'll be in touch." I hang up quickly so I don't fall apart.

"Elizabeth?" Gage's masculine voice drifts into my room.

I throw my iPhone on the bed and turn to face him. "Yep."

"How's the hangover, love?" His gaze collides with mine as his lips tilt in a smirk.

"Let's just say tequila is off the table moving forward," I retort, narrowing my eyes at him.

He chuckles. "Agreed."

"Well, that was easy," I mutter.

"Your gargoyle might actually kill me if I get you inebriated a second time." He winks.

I shift uncomfortably. "Most of the night is fuzzy." I leave the words hanging in the air.

"We talked. You puked on me and I took you home. Abby cleaned you and then your protector proceeded to threaten my existence and blame me for placing you in danger," he lists off casually.

My entire body relaxes. I pinch my brows. "Sorry about the vomit . . . and Asher."

He smiles but it doesn't reach his eyes. "Nothing a dry cleaner and my fist connecting with his jaw couldn't fix."

"Asher mentioned you and he spoke?" I tread lightly.

Gage leans against the doorway. "We did. After he threatened my life, he wanted to know if I had any insight into your mindset. He's concerned with your choices when it comes to me. I simply explained you need a little normalcy in your life, and that not everything has to be about the ascension and protection."

"I'm sure that went over well." I bite my lip.

"My advice earned me a bruised rib," he says sheepishly.

I wince. "Sorry."

"Not your fault, love."

"Actually, it is. Asher tends to be a little overprotective."
Gage feigns shock. "You don't say."

I smile. "He's agreed to work on it."

"I'm sure he has." He laughs, but it's hollow.

I just watch Gage for a moment, remembering how Fiona mentioned he was once part of this family. I'm curious as to why he keeps pushing them away.

"Is it just Camilla that stands between you and Asher becoming close again?" I ask.

Gage's expression drops. "There's a lot of history there, love, that you can't possibly appreciate because you are not from our world. How we relate to one another now won't change overnight. Nor do I think either of us is ready for it to alter. Some things are just supposed to remain what they are."

"I can't help but feel sad for the strain in your relationship with the London clan. Fiona made it sound like you all were close growing up together. Don't you miss that?" I question.

"I miss Camilla," he responds roughly.

"I might not comprehend the full extent of your history with one another, but I certainly can relate to the feeling of loneliness, Gage. Regardless of what you think, this clan did not turn their back on you or Camilla. I know Asher like I know myself. He would never have let her die if he knew what the council and your father were up to," I assure him.

"It's nice to see your undying loyalty to him is back, and intact," Gage muses, and stands straighter, getting ready to flee. "Bad blood is bad blood. It can't be extracted," he ends the conversation.

"When will you be joining us in London?" I change the subject.

"I'll meet you there in a few days. I have some things to attend to first. If you need anything, I'll be staying on the second floor of the flats," he says.

"You run off a lot for someone who doesn't hold appointments with either the Secular or Spiritual Assemblies," I point out, curious as to why he always flees just as we get close.

"I have businesses to run, Eve," he lies.

Just when he starts to get close to us, he runs.

"Family and friends aren't a weakness," I respond.

"In my world, love, alliances and kinships are weaknesses. You'd do well to learn that lesson now, before things get even uglier in yours. Trust me, you've seen how dark my world is firsthand, with Aria. Take your eye off the ball, even for a second, and it's over." Gage's warning is like a punch in the gut. "A fragile heart will get you killed."

At the reminder of Aria, my heart shatters all over again. *God, I miss her so much.* My eyes slide behind him, focusing on the hallway.

"That's an unfair statement," I scold.

Gage's posture becomes rigid as he steps toward me with intent. "Make no mistake, the dark army is lethal. They don't care about love, friendship, or kin. This longstanding war is only about them," he points to the sky, "and them," he redirects his finger to the floor. "You, Eve, are simply a pawn. Mankind is disposable, and the ground you are standing on, it means nothing to either side. Only one side can come out of this the victor, and trust me, it won't be either of us standing at the end."

"That's certainly a pessimistic viewpoint."

"It's reality."

"What if I don't like the reality you're portraying?"

Gage's face softens. "Then you're already dead before you've even begun."

I just hold his stare. "I'll see you soon."

"Until then," he offers, before disappearing.

With my arms crossed, I glance around my room and blow out a strained breath, rubbing my chest at the realization that this path I'm on is about to become even darker. *Can I handle it?* The longer I spend time with this clan, the more they become family. If anything ever happened to even one of them, I wouldn't survive.

Apparently, Gage's heart isn't the only fragile one on this journey.

15 Live for Me

Asher's eyes meet mine, forcing me to suck in a breath at the rawness they're emitting. *Holy shit.* He prowls toward me from the sunken living room in his London flat. I've been standing on the terrace since we arrived an hour ago, admiring the view of Hyde Park. However, his intense presence forces my focus to shift away from the warm sunrise to the beauty that is all Asher St. Michael.

I need a distraction, before I do something embarrassing like jump him and give his neighbors a show with their morning scones and tea. My gaze brushes over the flat. The last time I was here, Deacon had gotten past the protection spell and kidnapped me. As I understand it, Asher went ballistic and destroyed the apartment.

"It's nice to see the flat's put back together." I motion to the living room.

Asher smiles but it doesn't reach his eyes. "I stayed here during my absence from your protection while the council continued their investigation. Fiona and the clowder helped me, ah, reassemble it." His eyes shift, like it hurts him to look at me.

I inch toward him. "I'm happy to be here. It's like returning home."

He knits his brows. "I thought you felt La Gargouille Manor was home?"

I shake my head slowly. "No. This flat is all us. I feel like it's our special place."

His jaw tightens as he moves closer, caging me against the railing with one hand on either side of me. "Do you know why I ripped this place apart when Deacon got you?"

"Tell me," I whisper.

"When you disappeared, siren, I was pissed. Walking around the flat, your presence was everywhere. Your smell, your belongings, everything reminded me of you. Somewhere along the line, you became my home. Don't ever fucking leave me again. I don't think I could handle it, siren. I really don't. I don't ever want to feel that way again," he pleads, dropping his forehead to mine.

I stare at his chest, not wanting to meet his eyes. "To feel what way?"

"Out of control. Lost. Scared. I tried to fight those feelings, because that's what I'm supposed to do as your protector, but when it comes to you, my need to protect you is so fucking overwhelming, it scares the shit out of me," he admits.

My chest heaves at his honesty as he places a knee between my legs and pushes me even farther into the railing. His lips dip toward my neck and he lightly nips at the spot over my pulse.

"You don't have to protect me so closely, Ash. I can handle some things, you know."

He removes his lips from my neck and pulls back, looking me in the eyes before his finger grazes up my throat, then my cheek, and finally tucks a strand of my hair behind my ear. As he removes his hand, he lets it linger on my jawline.

"You're mine to protect. I will protect you, always."

My eyes lift and lock onto his. They're glossed over with such passion that it's hard for me to take in oxygen. Asher covers my body with his and kisses me hard, literally taking my breath away. Finally, when we can't take the lack of air any longer, he moves away.

Panting, he attempts to catch his breath before sniffing me. "You stink." *What the hell?*

Yanked out of my Asher bliss, I narrow my eyes at him. "What?"

His lips tilt in a coy smile. "You smell," he clarifies in a quiet voice.

"What the hell is wrong with you?" I screech. "You know, Asher, sometimes, I wonder if you're lying to me about being in your first life cycle, because no grown, adult male would say something so appallingly childish." I huff angrily.

Asher throws his head back in laughter before pulling my hips firmly to his. "I'm sorry, siren, but if I can't be honest with you, then who will be?"

I try to yank out of his grip, which only challenges him to tighten his hold. "I didn't say you smelled bad." He tries to make it better. "We've been traveling and I think we could both use a shower. What do you say?"

His gaze holds mine.

My brows lift. "Are you asking me to shower with you?"

Asher's face darkens. "That wasn't my plan, but now that you bring it up, that sounds like a brilliant idea. Plus, we'd be saving water. Showering with a friend and all."

My jaw drops at his foolishness.

"Seriously, you're making it hard not to smack the beautiful right off of you," I comment.

He gives me his sexy smirk and leans in closer, so his lips are at my ear. "Eve Marie Collins, would you do me the honor of showering with me?" His voice is velvety.

I bite my lip, considering his question, because honestly, there is nothing I would love more than to soap him up and lick all the water off him. However, I totally need to freshen up before that happens. *Girlie? Yes.*

"No?" It comes out as more of a question than a statement.

"No?" he repeats.

"It's a word used in the English language, to decline requests, such as yours."

"I know what it means. Why not?" He pouts.

"I need some . . . girl time. Not only do I reek, but I could use some private space to, you know . . . take care of some girlie stuff," I stumble, and look everywhere but at him.

Asher contemplates what I've said for a moment.

"Maintenance issues?"

"What?" My eyes widen.

"I'm guessing you need to shave your legs, loofah, and do whatever it is you ladies do. Are you trying to impress and seduce me, siren?" His tone drops to a seductive one.

My face flushes. "This conversation has crossed so many boundaries, I don't even know what to say or how to respond to you."

He cocks his head to the side. "Are you saying we're too close?"

I groan. "Yes. We share way too much."

"Should we discuss this in couples therapy?"

I roll my eyes. "We aren't in couples therapy, Asher."

"I've had my mouth on you. My hands inside you. And I've seen you scarf down two bacon cheeseburgers in, like, ten seconds flat. Pretty sure I understand the need you have to shave your legs."

My face turns bright red. "God, this is mortifying. You really have no boundaries."

Asher loosens his grip and steps back. "There's nothing to be embarrassed about, siren."

I close my eyes. "Oh my God, Asher, seriously. Please just stop talking."

"You want to primp? Be my guest. Shave, scrub, and groom away," he says in a mocking manner, while releasing a light chuckle.

Without a second thought, I walk around him and all but run to the guest room to escape his harassment. The moment I enter the bedroom, I notice none of my things are there. I walk back into the hallway to ask Asher where my bags are, and notice his bedroom door ajar.

Curiosity gets the best of me, and I make my way into his room, and see all of my things laid out for me, causing a smile to form. *Damn gargoyle.*

I approach the bed and observe the shopping bags sitting on top of it. They're from the last time we were in London and I went shopping with Abby. Our outing was cut short by Deacon's mother, Dimia. The stores must have delivered the packages while we were in Wiltshire. But Asher kept them here for me. *Oh my God!* My fingers run over the handles.

Warm arms snake around my waist and Asher's breath is at my ear, causing a surge of desire to hum through me.

"I figured you'd want those when you returned," he murmurs.

I twist in his arms so we're facing one another. "You knew I'd return?" I scan his face.

His eyes bore into mine. "There was never a question, siren. This is your home. Our home. And in our home, you stay in our bedroom. Got it?" he asks, raising an eyebrow.

"Thank you."

Asher's expression turns seductive. "By the way, I like what you bought at La Perla."

I go crimson again. Yeah, that would have been Abby's idea, bra and panty shopping.

"You do?" I reply, studying him.

"I do. Even though I've seen what your tongue can do domestically, I have yet to see it perform internationally," Asher points out, giving me a sexy look.

My face morphs into shock at his forwardness. "Out," I demand.

"You sure I can't wash your back?" he asks in a dark tone while wiggling his eyebrows.

"Out, protector." I step out of his arms and point to the door.

He smiles knowingly and bites his lip. Backing away, he places his hands in the air.

"All right, siren. I'll be in the guest shower, washing every crack and crevice with great care. You know, in the event you change your mind and decide you can't go another second without my body," he teases.

"I'm set." I smirk, and he exits the room. "Damn gargoyle." My murmur is met with hysterical laughter radiating from the hallway. *Gah, he's an ass.* I make my way into the large attached bathroom and smile in delight at the thought of relaxing in the tub.

When the water's temperature is where I want it, I add the coconut-scented bubbles and purr in anticipation. The flight, though on a private jet, from the US to London was long, and I'm looking forward to soaking my aching muscles in the hot gigantic bathtub.

I sniff myself. Asher was right. I am a bid putrid. I let the bubbles hit the top of the tub and turn off the faucet.

Undressing, I sink into bliss and close my eyes, trying not to picture Asher completely naked in the guest shower. It's not working. All I can envision are the droplets of water dripping from his taut chest. I inhale and lay back against the tub, willing myself to calm down and not run into the guest-room shower.

I keep running through the dense forest, trying to ignore the irritating burn in my lungs. My strides are disorderly and choppy as I move over the terrain, knowing I need to get to him. Terrified, I look around in confusion, wondering how I'll know which direction to go in.

I stop, close my eyes, and reach out to his soul. It's easier now that they are connected. I allow mine to guide me to him. Once I've picked up his essence, I continue to move forward.

The sound of my erratic panting momentarily breaks my concentration, and I stumble over sticks and twigs that are sticking out in all directions from the ground. I land on the dirt with a hard thud, skinning my knees and palms. Shit, that hurt. Standing, I see my legs and arms are all scratched and bleeding, but I ignore the stinging and keep going.

The snapping of tree branches under my feet pulls my focus away from my panicked heart. When I come to the wood's edge, I stop. Everything is completely silent. Still. Nothing is moving, not even a bird or cloud. There is no breeze. That's how I know pure evil is on the other side of the trees' borderline.

My heart leaps into my throat, causing a small whimper to release. I can't feel his soul anymore. I push my shoulders back, lift my chin and inhale, preparing myself for whatever I'm about to find. I tread lightly, as my eyes scan the open meadow in front of me. It takes a few moments, but as my eyes drift downward, I see him—lying on the ground, completely encased in stone.

My heart shatters and my throat constricts. At a slow pace, I begin to make my way to his petrified body. Swallowing the bile in my throat, I reach him and kneel down next to his stone body. Rocking myself so I don't break down, I brush my hand over his forehead.

"Damn you, Gage. I told you not to follow me," I whisper, as the tears begin to fall.

My eyes close and I collapse next to him, placing my head between my knees, trying to get control of my breathing before I have an all-out attack. When my vision resumes, I look to my left, and that's when I see the second body. The one I was searching for.

"No. No. No," I scream, and crawl over to Asher's lifeless, blood-covered corpse. All of a sudden, I hear a scream, filled with rage and agony, chilling me to my core. It's then I realize I'm the one screaming. I stand and back away from both gargoyles in shock.

Out of thin air, he appears. Like a mirage, the six-foot-plus half-demon, half-gargoyle stands and watches me. He stretches his tattoo-covered neck as a sinister smile appears on his lips.

"Hello, little girl." His dark voice curls over me, sending shivers down my spine.

"Deacon," I gasp out through my dry throat.

His eyes skim over Gage's and Asher's unmoving bodies before he moves closer to them, kicking at Gage with his black military boot.

Deacon tsks and looks disappointed. "Such a pity. So much potential."

For a moment, the half-demon looks sad, but that expression dissolves immediately as his black eyes lift and capture mine.

With trembling hands, I curl my lip. "I will rip your evil heart out," I seethe.

"Don't make promises you can't keep, little girl," Deacon replies.

"Did you do this?" I ask through clenched teeth, motioning to both gargoyles.

Deacon's lips turn up cruelly. "No. You did."

I awake with a startle from my dream, as dread seeps into my veins. Asher is standing over the tub, wearing only a towel around his lower body. My eyes drift over him, watching the water drip from his hair over the muscles on his naked skin.

He has a crazed look in his eyes. I sit up, a bit disoriented, realizing the bubbles have disappeared. Rubbing my hand over my forehead, I wipe away the lingering images of his and Gage's lifeless bodies.

"The fuck, siren?" His tone is serious and lined with tightness.

I cringe at the sound. "Sorry, I guess I fell asleep."

His jaw drops. "You realize you could have drowned, yeah?" he says in a tense voice.

I don't respond. Instead, I hug my knees and squeeze my eyes shut, trying to remove the image of his cold, dead body. Asher leans over and pulls the drain, removing some of the cold water. After a bit, he returns the stop and runs the hot water, refilling the tub.

He removes his towel and sinks in behind me. Once in position, strong arms wrap around me and pull me to his warmth. Basking in his closeness, I lean into his firm body, twisting my head so my right ear is over his heart. I listen to it pump.

The sound breaks me, and the tears begin to flow.

"Talk to me," he commands in a gentle tone, while stroking my wet hair.

I can't get words to form. Asher just holds me. After a while, I begin to relax enough to share the dream with him. He doesn't say anything. He just listens in the quiet way that he does when he's internally freaking out, but doesn't want me to know.

After I recount what happened, he squeezes my hand and lifts it to his mouth, planting the lightest of kisses on it before lacing and unlacing our fingers together.

"You're pruning. Let's get you out of here." He stands and wraps the towel around himself, then grabs a fresh one off the rack and assists me out of the water, wrapping me like a child.

"Thanks," I whisper.

Asher cups my face and looks into my eyes. "I know you're scared, but I assure you, nothing bad is going to happen to me at Deacon's hands," he vows.

Deacon's statement that it's my fault chokes me. I push it away and allow Asher to lead us into the bedroom. He sits on the edge of the bed and reaches over, pulling me effortlessly onto his lap.

I flick my gaze away from him, not wanting to see the disappointment I can feel bleeding off him because I don't believe his promise.

"You're safe, siren," he breathes against my mouth before crushing his lips to mine.

At his words, something twists in my chest. I'm not really safe, and to be honest, I don't know if I ever will be. My stomach plummets knowing he isn't safe either.

No one is.

I cling to Asher, straddling his hips, clearly aware that all that is between us are the two fluffy white towels.

"I'll protect you with my life," he declares against my lips.

I pull back and inhale. "I know you would die for me, Asher. What I need for you to do is guarantee that you will live for me."

His eyes focus on me for several seconds before he brings his hands up, sliding them through my damp hair. "You are the ONLY thing I live for. You own me," he says firmly.

I inhale a shaky breath and stare at his mouth. "I love you."

Asher's thumbs brush across my cheeks. "Forever."

My eyes flutter closed as he pulls me back to his mouth, seeking entrance. This kiss is the kind that knocks you off your axis. His mouth brands me and his lips move in sync with mine, as we inhale and taste one another in an illicit way.

I moan when his lips graze down my neck, finding the spot that makes every one of my nerves jump to life in anticipation. His large hands slip out of my hair, down my neck, and over my bare shoulders to the top of my towel. With a wicked gleam in his eyes, he deftly unties the knot and opens the towel, exposing my flesh.

At the sight of my chest, Asher releases a throaty, appreciative sound and moves his hands to cup my bare breasts. His touch elicits a small cry from me. My skin is sensitive and crawling with need.

I grip Asher's shoulders tightly when his mouth closes over me. The pleasure he's creating draws my body into him. I gasp at the almost-painful sensation, causing Asher to hold me tighter and closer to him, possessively. Every part of me begins to ache for him as he moves to my other breast, giving it his undivided attention.

I whimper and tilt my head back, rocking my hips into him. At the motion, Asher releases my breast and entangles his hands in my hair, yanking me to him as his mouth scorches mine again. I gasp at his forcefulness, and his tongue slides past my lips, claiming me. His lips move with an obsessive desperation that sends me soaring.

"Fuck, I can't wait to be inside of you," he pants across my bruised lips.

My breath catches and my fingers find their way into his hair. "Now, please."

Asher stills, his lack of movement returning me back to reality.

"There's nothing I'd love more than to throw you down on this bed and slam inside of you, siren. Trust me." He blows out a hungry breath. "Just not like this, okay? Not because you're scared of losing me, yeah?"

"When?" I finally ask, when I find my voice.

He sucks in a sharp breath. "When you're ready to be mine, forever."

"I am," I say, my voice thick with desire.

Asher gives me his boyish grin. "Then soon, siren."

16 The Royal Court

That icky feeling of dread makes its way up my throat, and I attempt to swallow it down. When I awoke this morning, my chest was tight and I felt like I couldn't breathe. I pull the zipper up on my knee-high boots and pull my sleeves over my thumbs before making my way out of the bedroom.

Asher and I spent the night curled up in bed watching cheesy movies and eating takeout, only to wake up this morning to Keegan's authoritative voice letting us know Michael was here and needed to speak with us at once.

The entire clan, including Gage and Michael, are sitting in the sunken living room when I walk out. I squint at the bright sun filtering through the large windows, and curb the desire to crawl back into bed and go to sleep.

Abby offers me a sympathetic smile as I approach the quiet group with a skeptical look. I don't know how I know that something is wrong, but I can feel it. I start to feel more uneasy as I look around at all the grave faces.

Asher moves toward me, and my heart starts to hammer in my chest. His gaze locks with mine, and his blue eyes take my breath with their intensity. For a moment, all I can do is stare at him while all logical thought processes vanish from my mind. He hands me a cup of coffee and pecks me on the cheek.

"What's going on?" I ask no one in particular.

"The Royal Court has requested an audience with us," Asher answers with an edge.

"Why?" I wonder aloud, and sip my coffee.

"War has begun, love," Gage mutters.

That earns him a quick, angry glance from Asher before he turns his focus back to me. "It would seem that the dark army and the Declan clan have set the war in motion."

"I don't understand," I say through a tight throat.

Michael stands and walks toward me with a grace and gait that only an archangel can have. I recoil from him, leaning into Asher. At my reaction, the angel stills.

"Lucifer has grown impatient waiting for the dark army and the Declan clan to turn you over to him. Therefore, he has taken it upon himself to make an even bolder move. In doing so, he's declared war on Heaven." The archangel's voice is solemn.

Asher snags my hand in his, and I know more bad news is about to follow.

"What was the move?" I demand harshly.

A sadness falls over Michael's face before he exhales.

"They have Libby."

"What?" I ask in a hushed tone.

"Deacon handed Libby over to Lucifer," the warrior answers.

Something primal in me tenses and breaks. All of the heartache, rage, and frustration I've felt for the past few months hits me hard and snaps all my defenses. I lunge for Michael, but Asher wraps his arms around my waist, hauling me back to him, as the mug of coffee tumbles to the ground.

"SHE WAS UNDER YOUR PROTECTION!" I shout, pointing at the angel.

"Libby is, was. We had an internal issue. Apparently, the St. Michaels are not the only ones with a traitor that they must deal with," Michael offers, his voice even.

"Lucifer has her? Is she alive?" I ask in a severe tone.

Michael's eyes drop to the floor and skirt around the room, then land on me.

"At the moment, we believe so," he answers flatly.

"You believe so?" I draw out, and narrow my eyes at him, mocking his answer.

Gage stands and faces me. "Lucifer and Deacon are using her, love, to get to you. They'll keep her alive for that reason alone. They've taken her knowing what she means to you. Knowing you would give your soul to save hers. Do you understand?"

My vision flicks to his. I exhale with relief, before it's replaced with fear, and then adrenaline. Asher releases his grip slightly and I turn to face him. He's looking at me with understanding and compassion. He knows what it's like to lose everything in an instant.

I draw in a breath and blink away the tears. "We have to get her."

"We will," he answers through a tight jaw.

"Eves, The Royal Court is aware of the situation. It's why they'd like to meet with you and Asher." Callan's voice drifts over to me, causing me to twist back to the group.

I push my shoulders back and lift my chin, trying to be strong. "Good. Let's go then. The faster we meet with them, the sooner we can get her back."

Callan's expression drops. "You have an appointment with them first thing tomorrow. In the meantime, the Royal Gargoyle Council and the Spiritual Assembly of Protectors will reach out to the Declan clan. Michael's army is amassing and searching for their traitor."

I stare at him in disbelief. "You want me to sit here and do nothing for an entire day?"

"We have our own strategies to devise, love," Gage responds in a gentle manner.

"Michael, is there anything we can do to assist you?" Keegan asks in a militant tone.

"No, thank you. The Angelic Council and my army can handle any internal issues and Libby's return from here. It was simply my request to inform you, Eve, of Libby's situation face-to-face, and personally assure you that I will make sure she is returned, unharmed," he says, before his expression falters. Despair lines his eyes. "Whatever you may think of us, your mother is my world and I will walk through Hell to bring her back."

My heart plummets. "Good," I manage, with a curt nod.

Without warning, his face morphs back into archangel mode. "I'm being called back. I was given a brief reprieve to dispatch the news to you. Let me be clear, Eve: you are not to go after her. Heaven's army will take care of her rescue. In the meantime, I suggest the clan meet with the Royal Court and other protectors to formulate a defense strategy for both the supernatural and human worlds, as well as Eve's safety," Michael orders.

"Of course," Asher responds in an authoritative tone.

"I'll be in touch when I have word of Libby's situation," he says before leaving.

At the warrior of Heaven's exit, my body slumps and goes numb. My eyes cast downward, and I notice the coffee spill on the carpet. *Shit, that's going to stain.*

On autopilot, I move to the kitchen, grab a wet rag, and return to the spill. I wipe at it furiously as Abby bends down so she's at eye level with me. Her hands wrap around my wrists.

"Sweetie, I'll get that," she says, placing her hand over mine.

I ignore her and keep scrubbing the wet spot.

"Eves? Stop," Abby coos in a soft tone.

"It will stain if I don't clean it," I state dully.

"Siren." Asher's voice is gentle from behind me.

"I think she just needs some time," Abby speaks in a soft manner.

"Don't talk about me like I'm not here," I bark.

Startled, Abby's eyes widen and she backs away, and I stand, dropping the cleaning cloth. Asher's strong arms wrap around me, hauling me to him. I sag against him, my body limp. Tears form on the edges of my eyes as a painful lump makes an appearance in my throat.

"Come with me," he whispers in my ear, and leads me into the front sitting room.

He sits on the small sectional and pulls me onto his lap, so I'm straddling him.

"It's okay to be upset by this, Eve," he says, making patterns on my lower back.

"After the way I treated her, I have no right." I choke, unable to say anything else.

Asher doesn't say anything for a moment. "You love her. It's normal to hurt after the news that was just dropped on you. You don't have to be strong. Not with me."

"We need to get her back." I take a serious tone. "It's my fault."

Asher's expression softens. "You are not to blame. Elizabeth knew what she was getting into long before any of this was set in motion. Michael and the warriors of Heaven will get her out of there. You will stay out of it, yeah?"

"How can you ask me to do that, Asher?" I ask.

He wipes away a lone tear with his thumb.

"We have work here to be done. It seems the war has begun, which means we need a defense strategy and to meet with the Royal Court. That is where you are needed at the moment, daughter of Heaven. When Michael has word, he will send it to you," he says.

I shake my head as a wave of panic rolls through me. "How can you be sure that Michael will rescue her?" I ask.

Asher stops his lazy drawing on my back and sits forward. "If he loves her the way I do you, there is no place that he won't go and no lengths he won't reach to get to her."

Sighing, I cup his rough jawline and lean in, placing a chaste kiss on his lips. Pulling back, Asher angles his head, his eyes piercing each of my layers, trying to seek out my soul. Swallowing the tightness in my throat, I stand and help Asher off the couch. Nothing can change the fact that they've taken my family, and despite my promise to Asher, I will try to save her.

"Strategy and the Royal Court," I offer in a neutral tone.

He stands, taking my hand and kissing it lightly. "It's all going to be okay."

I release an emotionless laugh. "Can I get that in writing?"

He drops his jaw so he's at eye level. "I'll sign it in my blood if you want, siren."

❧❧

A light, warm breeze floats through the open walls of the Greek-style hallway that Asher and I are making our way down to meet with The Royal Court. It's ridiculously long.

The large white columns that flank each side must be fifty feet tall. Everything is white marble and smooth, like a Grecian palace. The clicking of my boots echo against the stone as we walk at a leisurely pace.

My gaze lifts, and I notice six arched buttresses covering the ceiling of the long corridor. A single, large black iron lantern hangs from each arch's center. Our path leads to a black lacquer double door, with an arch adorning the entry.

The sculptured stone detailing around the entryway is stunning. I just stand there admiring it for a moment, before Asher turns to me and releases his raven wings. My eyes take in the beautiful sight of him as something flickers in his, before he laces our fingers together and pulls me to his side. *Odd.* He seems nervous.

The gargoyle warrior pushes both doors open, and we enter another all-white, marble room. It's completely empty, though. It looks like one big pallid square. In front of us, there are wall-to-wall deep steps leading to a platform that has five marble thrones. They're larger than life. I'm in awe.

Lady Finella's regal voice pulls me from my state of wonderment. My eyes move to the far left and meet her delighted ones. Seeing the queen of the fae in this location, I'm reminded of just how powerful a supernatural creature she is.

"Daughter of Heaven, it is our great honor to welcome you and your protector into the Hall of The Royal Supernatural Court," she says, and bows. "The court offers our deepest appreciation for your presence on this most sad occasion."

I offer a tight smile. "Your Grace." I return the formal bow.

Asher nods his head in acknowledgment.

"Thank you for your show of respect to the court," Priestess Arabella adds.

"Protector, would you be gracious enough to indulge me as I present the daughter of Heaven to The Royal Court?" the queen of the fae asks.

"We're happy for you to make the introductions," Asher replies formally.

"Lovely, thank you. Eve, I believe you already know Arabella, a member of the Seven High Priestesses, as well as, Lunette, representing the Sorceresses of the Black Circle." At her preface, both ladies bow.

"It's nice to see you again," I reply in a timid tone.

"The two gentlemen before you are Lucian, king of the werewolves, and Valentin, lord of the vampires," she finishes.

For a king, Lucian is certainly rugged and outdoorsy-looking. His hair is sexily shaggy and golden-blond, and his green eyes are soft and warm. He's wearing loose-fitting jeans, hiking boots, and what I would guess is his version of a dress shirt, plaid. To be honest, he looks like he should be leading a mountain-climbing expedition, not a royal seat.

"It's nice to meet you, daughter of Heaven," he offers.

"You too," I respond.

I turn to the lord of the vampires and take him in. He's the complete opposite of the werewolf. Breathtakingly beautiful, he's wearing a tailored suit, and is much more formal in presentation. His black hair is short and perfectly styled, and his slate eyes are assessing. He steps off the last stair to take my hand in his and bring it to his mouth before kissing it.

"Daughter of Heaven, I am most honored," he offers with a Romanian inflection.

Apparently, werewolf and vampire stereotypes are accurate. I laugh internally and take a small step closer to Asher, forcing Valentin to relinquish my hand.

Not only does the lord of the vampires scare me a little, but I could swear he sniffed me when kissing my hand. Maybe I'm overreacting, with him being a vampire and all.

Valentin straightens to his full height and looks at me with mischief in his eyes. *Nope, not overreacting.*

"Eve, dear, might we be so bold as to offer our condolences. It's with heavy hearts that we've been informed that your guardian, Elizabeth, is being held captive by Lucifer and the Declan clan. For this, we are truly sorry," Lunette says, as all five supernatural beings sit.

I swallow the bile rising in my throat at the thought.

"Thank you."

"Fear not, daughter of Heaven. In the end, all will be as it should be," Arabella comments with a sad expression.

I nod at her response. It's all I can bring myself to do, especially since she is a seer, and I'm sure she's seen my aunt's fate.

"Ladies, please. Let's move on to other matters. Perhaps ones that do not make the daughter of Heaven look like we've drained her puppy," Valentin intercedes in a bored manner.

"Yes, of course, dears," Lunette chimes in. "As you may or may not be aware, Lucifer has declared war on Heaven." She exhales. "It's so sad that it's come to this, once again." Her voice trails off and a faraway look crosses her face. "Nevertheless, here we are."

"The dark army has been increasing its presence within the supernatural realms for centuries, in preparation for this very moment," Lucian explains. "Once they discovered your existence, Eve, they began to strategize and amplify their alliances amongst certain sectors of our kind. As you can imagine, there is only so much this court can do as leaders of our kingdoms to ensure your safety and prevent this situation from further escalation. It is this court's belief that Thoren was sent as a final attempt at your retrieval. Since he was unsuccessful, the dark army has been ordered to apprehend Elizabeth."

"Archangel Michael and the Angelic Council are spearheading the efforts to secure Elizabeth's safe return,"

Asher states in an even tone. "The mission is a sensitive one, due to the alleged traitor within the divine realm."

"We are aware of the conspirator within the Heavenly dominion, as well as in the protector sector," Valentin replies. "The Seven High Priestesses have been unsuccessful at utilizing their foreseer gifts to establish who these traitors are. Therefore, we must assume they know black magic."

"Even the sorceresses of the Black Circle are unable to identify the magic source. Whoever they are, they are very powerful," Lunette adds.

"Or they are receiving assistance from a darker force," Lucian offers.

"Lucifer's powers are exceptional. I am positive the dark spirit is the reason for the blockage," Arabella thinks out loud.

"Rest easy, daughter of Heaven, the court will assist your gargoyle protectors in any way we can to discover who these traitorous souls are," Lady Finella addresses me.

"We are grateful for your assistance," Asher replies.

"Keegan has called a summit in London. Each of us on the court will be sending one dignitary whom we trust. They will aid with protection, strategy, and next steps in dealing with the dark army," Lucian states.

"Excellent," Asher responds.

"I will be sending Leo, beta of the Quinnipiac pack of werewolves," Lucian explains.

At Leo's name, my heart squeezes. The last time I saw Aria's boyfriend, he was cradling her lifeless body. Asher's eyes slide to mine in understanding before he returns his attention to the court.

"The Duchess of Sprites, Ainsley, will speak for The Kingdom of the Fae," Lady Finella announces.

"The Seven High Priestesses do not get involved in matters of war; therefore, we will be absent from the summit. I do hope you understand, daughter of Heaven," Arabella says.

"I do," I answer.

"And I will be sending Stephan, my second. He is young and stupid. Perfect for your needs in order to deal with demons and the dark army." Valentin smirks.

For a brief moment, there is silence in the hall. All eyes suddenly turn to Lunette, who is staring into the room with a faraway gleam in her eye.

"Lunette?" Lady Finella prompts.

"Yes?" The sorceress returns her focus to the group.

"If you would be so kind as to announce whom the Black Circle will be sending to the summit," the fae queen urges.

"Oh, dear, I haven't even decided yet. Would it be all right if I got back to you on that one? So sorry, dears." She looks at Asher specifically.

"Of course, Lunette," he replies kindly.

To be honest, I'm surprised she was even lucid for most of the discussions here today.

"I will inform Keegan of the attendance list. Your Highnesses, we thank the court for your assistance in this matter," Asher replies.

"There is no need to thank us, protector. I do believe it is in all of our best interests to assist the daughter of Heaven at this point. If the dark army prevails, I fear it will be detrimental to all of us," Valentin points out.

17 One Perfect Night

I gaze out the window, taking in London and watching the people on the street and in the park. I've been staring at the park since we returned from meeting with the court. A wave of jealousy rolls through me. The random people are going about their lives without a care in the world. I'm actually taken aback by their carefree manner. I miss being normal.

I forgot that there are actually those in the world whose only concern is whether their shoes match their outfit, or if they want to spend money on the pedalos in the park. A pang of sadness runs through me. I miss my life. Just . . . being eighteen.

Strong arms wrap around me from behind. I lift my fingers and trace Asher's reflection in the window. A faint smile touches my mouth at the sight of him.

"What are you thinking about?" Asher asks, his lips brushing the side of my neck, causing a wave of tiny bumps to suddenly appear on my skin. "You look lost and sad."

I sigh and tilt my head to expose more of my throat and lean back into him. "Do you ever feel like the darkness will just eventually take over?"

Asher lifts his head. His gaze collides with mine on the windowpane. "Every single fucking day. I'd never felt the warmth of hope, or light, until the first time I touched you."

I roll my eyes as a burst of laughter falls out of me.

"Don't roll your eyes at me," he jests.

"Sorry, it's just that . . . your answer was extremely . . . cheesy." I twist in his arms.

"Cheesy but true, siren." Those beautiful full lips curve up on one side.

"I could use some hope right about now," I frown.

"Yeah? Then it's a good thing that I'm your boyfriend," Asher says.

My eyebrows shoot up. "Oh?"

"What do you say to a date night? Just you and me?"

"Really?"

"Really," Asher counters with a grin.

"You do realize, this will be our first *actual* date," I point out.

Asher places his hand over his heart dramatically. "I had no idea the daughter of Heaven wished to be wooed. I guess I just assumed that bonding myself to you forever, with blood, and sharing my stone state bed would have been enough to solidify my love for you. It would seem that I was wrong though. My lady wants to be wined and dined. I suppose it's a good thing I have special plans for this evening, or else I'd be fucked," he teases.

"Special plans?" I ask.

"Plans," he confirms, and leans in to kiss me.

"Where is she?" Abby's squeal pulls me out of my Asher stupor.

She breezes over to us with a bright smile and excitement lining her eyes. *This isn't good.*

"Are you ready?" Abby asks impatiently. "You said you'd have her ready, Asher!"

My eyes shift from her to Asher and then back again.

"Ready for what?" I draw out.

"Spa day!" Abby answers as if I should already know this. "We're all set up for a day at the Spa at the Mandarin Oriental. Our first appointment is in about an hour, so . . ."

"I thought maybe you could use a little pampering. With all the training, parental issues, and supernatural crazy, I figure it might be nice for you to have a girls' day before our big date," Asher explains in a shy voice. "If you don't want to go, you don't have to."

I try to hold back the tears. "That was really thoughtful, Ash. Thank you."

"You're welcome. I have to help Keegan prepare for the summit. So you go enjoy your day with the girls and I'll see you this evening, yeah?" He drops his tone to a seductive one.

"This first appointment wouldn't be a Brazilian, would it?" I ask coyly.

Asher's brows rise in humor. "Are you flirting with me, siren?"

"As delicious as Callan's turkey club was going down, I don't want a repeat of it by heaving from your cuteness. So let's go, Eve. Kenna will meet us there." Abby grabs my arm and yanks me out of Asher's hold. I sulk internally at the idea of a spa day with McKenna.

Asher winks at me as Abby practically drags me out of the flat.

❧❦

I can't stop fidgeting. Even after hours of relaxation today at the spa, all I want to do is jump out of this chair. Abby is driving me crazy. She insisted on helping me get ready for my date with Asher tonight. Big mistake. Huge.

At the moment, she's in the process of curling the bottom of my hair in soft waves. Oh, and for the record, my third spa appointment, a Brazilian. I'm still walking favoring my left side. *Damn Asher St. Michael.*

"Do you know where he's taking me on our date?" I ask for the hundredth time.

"By the grace, blood of Eden, if you don't stop asking, I swear I will cut your fucking tongue out," McKenna snips.

Excellent.

"McKenna, I'm shocked that you don't have more girlfriends," I retort.

She huffs and snatches the gloss off the counter, applying it to her taut lips. "Why can't we just tell her?"

"Kenna! Asher wants their first date to be a surprise. It's romantic," Abby admonishes.

"We're preparing for war. Now he wants to date and romance her?" Kenna tosses the gloss on the counter when she's done.

I watch it drop and roll, pushing away the urge to body slam her.

Abby offers me a small smile. "I think Ash just wants you to have a nice evening before the summit tomorrow. He wants to do something special for you. Let him, okay?"

McKenna spins around and narrows her eyes at me. "He's getting soft. Wonder why."

"Kenna, if you're not going to play nice, go home," Abby scolds.

"Fine. Watching you do Eve's hair is about as exciting as watching grass grow. Have a nice evening tonight, blood of Eden. Don't do anything I wouldn't do, and try not to get yourself, or Asher, killed," she throws out.

"Ignore her. You're going to have an amazing time tonight." Abby squeezes my shoulder.

"It's so great that she's so supportive. Truly," I feign sincerity.

Abby giggles and finishes spraying my hair. "Well, what do you think?"

I turn and look in the mirror. I love what I see. My makeup is light and warm, and my light brown hair falls softly around my shoulders and back.

"Thank you, Abby," I whisper.

"That's what family is for," she smiles, watching me.

"Family?"

Abby leans forward and collects my hands in hers. "If you haven't noticed, we think of you as one of our own. You're part of this clan, Eve. You don't need Asher's mate mark for that distinction. You're the missing piece. We've waited a long time for you, and now that you're here, we aren't going to let you go. Not ever."

"I think Keegan and McKenna would differ with you on that," I throw out.

"McKenna and Keegan are hard on you because they consider you family. They tend to allow their fears to drive their behaviors. They both struggle with wanting to protect you and getting close to you."

"Why? It seems more like they despise my very existence."

"You're misinterpreting. They keep you at arm's length because they don't want to get attached, in case you leave. Their love for you runs just as deep as Callan's and mine. Callan and I, we're just more affectionate about it. I guess we're softies." She winks.

I smile and put on the dress we bought today. Abby helps it fall just right. Her eyes catch mine in the mirror. "We'll help you get past all this, and when we do, Eves, you'll see it's just the beginning, not the end."

A knock on the bathroom door pulls us both out of the moment.

"Everyone decent?" Callan asks through a small sliver.

"Yeah, baby, come in," Abby answers.

Callan strolls in and gives me a once-over before releasing a low whistle. "Damn, cutie, you look amazing," he compliments.

"Why, thank you," I answer, doing a little turn.

"Ah. No. Go change. Asher is going to have a heart attack when he sees the back of that dress."

"NO! Eve is not changing. You look stunning. Don't listen to him," Abby freaks.

My eyes flick to the full-length mirror. Black leggings that look like tights are paired with heeled ankle boots. Both look amazing with the Free People Grecian dress that Abby picked out for me to wear. It's off-white and looks almost crocheted. The short sleeves drape down in a lace pattern and the entire dress stops on the top of my thigh, hence the need for the leggings. The back is completely open and drops to the top of my lower back.

"Is Asher waiting on me?" I ask Callan.

"Waiting? More like brooding and pacing nervously. You might want to go out there, cutie, and end the torture. Before he destroys the flat again," he says, with a glint in his eye.

I turn to Abby. "Thanks for all your hard work. I feel so pretty."

Her entire face lights up. "You look beautiful."

Callan turns his attention to Abby and beams. "My girl has talent."

Watching the two of them, I can't help the warm feelings that wrap around my heart. *God, I love these people. My family.*

"Wish me luck," I say, and leave the bathroom.

I find him silently standing on the terrace. His hands are in the front pockets of his black dress pants and his broad back is turned to me. *God, he's beautiful.* The butterflies take flight as the protector energy hums through my veins. With each step closer to him, my throat becomes even drier.

The sleeves of Asher's white button-down dress shirt are sexily rolled up to his elbows. The way he's wearing his shirt shows off his leather-and-stone bracelets and the Celtic cross tattoo. A small shiver runs down my spine as my eyes graze over him.

Sensing my presence, he turns and faces me, halting my steps toward him. The full visual impact of Asher St. Michael is beyond words. He closes his eyes briefly before opening them and stalking toward me with possessive and fluid steps. It's so quiet in the room I swear you can hear my heart pounding.

Asher circles me with a calculated precision. Each movement is filled with control, while his expression is intense and predatory. My stomach drops to my knees with tension.

Stopping in front of me, he releases a quiet rumble. "Fuck, you're stunning, siren."

I can't prevent the small shiver that overtakes me at his words. "Thank you," I manage quietly.

He moves forward, eliminating the sliver of space between us. Strong hands brace my hips as they turn me, so that my bare back is exposed to him. At the sight, he exhales a hiss.

The heat from his body radiates off him, seeping into my skin. Ever so gently, he lifts a finger and traces my spine, starting at the top and working his way down. I suck in a sharp breath when he begins to draw a pattern on my lower back.

Leaning down, his breath fans over my neck.

"What is that you always draw on my lower back?" I ask through erratic pants.

"My mate mark," he replies in a deep sensual tone.

I turn and lock eyes with him. In an instant, I become his all over again.

He holds my gaze, and expels a rough breath.

"We should go. I don't want to be late," he says with lust-filled, glowing eyes.

I nod my agreement. Asher interlaces our hands and tugs me toward the door. We're silent as we ride down the elevator to the garage. He assists me into the Aston Martin before he smoothly folds himself into the driver's seat.

"Where are we going?" I ask, breathing clearly for the first time in ten minutes.

A small smile tugs at his full lips. "It's a surprise."

After a short drive, we approach a tall glass skyscraper that's in the shape of the letter A. It's architecturally striking, with thousands of glass windows. The entire city seems to reflect off their light.

Asher pulls into the valet and hands the gentleman his keys, along with a hundred dollar bill. "Welcome to the Shard, Mr. St. Michael. It's always a pleasure to have you."

"Thank you, Thames. Take good care of my baby. You know you're the only one I let drive her except me," Asher banters.

"Always do, Mr. St. Michael," Thames retorts, taking the car.

I narrow my eyes at Asher. "I do believe we have a deal. I was supposed to work hard, train, and focus on my ascension, and you were supposed to let me drive your car."

Asher's face falters a bit. "I recall. We can discuss it after dinner, yeah?"

I can sense a brush-off a mile away. "Fine."

He walks toward me and places his hand on my lower back, causing my breath to hitch.

"This is the Shard. Are you familiar with it?" he asks, as we walk into the exquisite lobby.

"I'm afraid not."

"This is the best place to watch the sunset in the city. It has the most magnificent views of London, and if you're in the city and looking at the building, you'll be mesmerized by the play of light across the façade."

Asher escorts me to a private elevator, which conveniently he has a key card for. The elevator is filled with sexual tension as we make our way to the thirty-first floor. Asher snatches my hand and tugs me to him, so we're face-to-face.

His hands cup my cheeks as he pulls me closer. "I know tonight is difficult for you, with the circumstances surrounding Elizabeth, siren, but I want this to be special. One perfect night. That's all I'm asking for, yeah?"

"One perfect night."

His indigo gaze stays glued to mine, brushing me like a physical caress. The elevator dings when we reach our floor. Asher doesn't move. He just stands there, frozen.

"We should go," I finally manage.

"Yeah," he agrees with a raspy voice.

We make our way into Aqua Shard, as the hostess ushers us into the contemporary dining room and we pass a three-story-high atrium bar on our way to the private room that I assume Asher reserved for us. Once seated, she hands us the cosmopolitan menu and informs us our server will be with us shortly before taking her leave.

While someone comes in and pops champagne and pours, my eyes flick to the windows that are literally all around us. The sun is setting, and it's truly the most beautiful thing I've ever seen.

"This is amazing, Ash. Thank you," I say sincerely.

He leans closer to me, placing his hand on the back of my chair, since we're sitting side by side instead of across from one another. "It's my pleasure, siren."

The sound of a voice being cleared breaks my Asher focus. I look up to see the server watching us with amusement. Asher doesn't even glance at him. With his eyes fixated on me, he orders.

"Adrian, the lady and I will start with the oysters Rockefeller to share. We'll each have the pea and ham soup, followed by the sirloin accompanied by the Lancashire potatoes and roasted butternut squash. We'll end our courses with a dark chocolate and lavender tart to share."

"Of course, Mr. St. Michael. We also have a few bottles of Krug 1928 for you this evening, per your request," Adrian informs, and then leaves quickly.

"What?" Asher's eyes meet mine with humor.

"You do realize that you could have simply ordered takeout while watching movies in our pajamas, and that would have been just as perfect. I don't need all this, Asher. I just need you."

He leans in, and his lips brush my ear. "You promised. One perfect night, siren."

Damn his seductive tone. I take a sip of my amazing champagne, letting the bubbles tickle my nose while we watch the sun set over London.

"What did you want to be when you grew up?" I ask, slurping my addicting soup. *Seriously, do they put crack in this stuff?* Asher just spent what felt like hours trying to get me to eat raw oysters—I refused. Grateful to be done with his bullying, we're enjoying the second course, our pea soup. It's the most delicious thing I've eaten in my life to date.

"A gargoyle," Asher replies in a serious tone.

I look up and find him grinning at me. "You suck, protector."

He shrugs and takes a spoonful of my soup, and I swat at his hand. He finished his and I don't want to share. It's that good.

"I never really had a say in what I wanted to be. I always knew someday I would become the next king," he responds, as his spoon comes toward my bowl again.

I manage to block it. "You need to back off, protector. If you think I'm one of those girls you take out on a date who doesn't eat, you're dead wrong. The oysters were the exception."

Asher releases a boisterous laugh before surrendering and placing his spoon back into his own empty bowl. "Fair enough, siren."

He sits back and allows his eyes to flick out the window and then back to me. "What about you? What did you want most from life when you were growing up?"

I sit back and play with my napkin. "A family. I used to stay awake at night and wish that my parents would just magically reappear." I snort. "I loved going to my best friend Courtney's house. She has four brothers, all older and fiercely overprotective. I envied her for that. Her home was always so alive. Her mom was always cooking, while their two dogs ran around, and everyone was forever screaming at one another. It was chaotic but full of love."

He watches me for a while. "I like hearing about your childhood. Where is Courtney? You don't talk about her much?"

"Stanford. I guess we've sort of grown apart. It's probably for the best at this point. Everyone around me seems to be in danger. My life makes it difficult to have lasting relationships."

Asher sips his champagne while considering my words. The server replaces our empty soup bowls with our meals. I begin picking at my dinner quietly.

"Your life doesn't define you, siren. You define your life," he says, interlacing our fingers. "Things around you might be complicated, but you have a family. An extremely protective one, that loves you. It might not be ideal, but it's yours if you will have us."

My gaze lifts to his. "Can I ask you something?"

"Anything."

"Why do you always draw your mate mark on my lower back?"

Asher assesses me before speaking. "I guess it's my way of branding you, even if I can't fully make you mine yet."

I clear my throat. "Is that what you want? To make me yours?"

Asher leans forward, locking eyes with me. "In every sense of the fucking word."

Just as I'm about to climb into his lap and accost him, the server comes back to check on us. A short while later we're presented with our dessert, which we eat around lighter conversation.

Once we're done, Asher offers his hand for me to take. Placing mine in his, he pulls us to a standing position. The windows suddenly slide open, revealing a terrace. The warm evening breeze brushes over my exposed skin.

Nervously, I follow Asher out. We're pretty high up.

"Don't worry. I won't let you fall," Asher whispers.

On cue, music starts playing, and I twist in Asher's arms.

"Wow, you've thought of everything," I tease.

"Do you doubt my awesomeness?"

"Never."

"May I have this dance?"

I step into his embrace as we begin to sway.

"Thank you, Asher, for the perfect first date."

"One perfect night."

18 The Summit

All eyes follow me as I walk into the conference room. I push my shoulders back and remind myself that I must appear strong and unafraid, even if I'm not. My gaze roams around the room, taking in each supernatural being that has agreed to join us for this assembly.

"You okay, Eves?" Abby asks, standing next to me.

"No. But I will be." I take in a strong breath, wishing it was last night again. After an amazing dinner, Asher and I walked around London taking in the sights before returning to the flat for an evening of bruising kisses.

When I woke up this morning, he had the coffee brewing, next to a handwritten note that said he needed to greet guests and he would see me at the summit, where I am at the moment.

Judging by the looks I'm receiving from some of the characters in here, it would probably be best if I turned and walked out. Attempting to look unaffected, I walk up to one of the only other allies, besides the London clan, I have here.

"Hi, Marcus," I say politely to the dark-skinned gargoyle standing next to me.

Warm brown eyes catch mine as a smile appears on the leader of the Manhattan clan's lips. "Hi, Eve. It's great to see you again. I'm sorry it's under these circumstances though, baby girl. Don't worry. Michael will take care of Elizabeth."

His words are meant to be reassuring. They're not.

"Where's your sidekick?" I ask, referring to Morgana.

Marcus's eyes twinkle. "My second is most likely stalking your protector."

I internally roll my eyes. Since we haven't discovered the traitor yet, Asher and I are still keeping a low profile on our relationship. Which means, in Morgana's eyes, he's fair game.

Sensing my shift, Marcus snatches my hand and leans in conspiratorially. "Who is the hot guy over there?" he asks, motioning with his eyes to Stephan.

I chew on my lower lip to prevent my smile. "That would be Lord Valentin's second in command, Stephan. He's a vampire."

Marcus's eyes light up with excitement. "Really? Vampires are delicious, don't you think?"

I smile at him. "I'm partial to other supernaturals. But you should definitely go talk to him. Though, he's a bit of a loose cannon, according to Lord Valentin."

"You wouldn't know this, Eve, but I have a thing for loose cannons." Marcus wags his eyebrows at me.

"Want me to introduce you two?"

Marcus stands up straighter and fixes his black Armani shirt. "Nah, I got this, daughter of Heaven. You're supposed to be mingling."

I watch as Marcus heads over to Stephan and flirts shamelessly with him. To be honest, Stephan looks just as enamored with Marcus.

"This is about as lame as it gets." A deep, raspy female voice floats over to me. I turn and am surprised to see a young girl about my height and age. From the sound of her voice, I thought she would be a smoker in her seventies.

She's really pretty and has raven-black hair, matching her black skinny jeans. Her pale arms are folded over a black vintage band T-shirt and she looks extremely bored, kicking her Converses on the ground. I can't explain it but immediately, I'm drawn to her.

"I don't think we've met. I'm Eve," I offer, thinking she's going to ignore me when I see the startled expression in her eyes.

"I know who you are. Pretty sure everyone in this room does," she says.

"Right. And you are?"

"Llughnassad, Sorceress of Prosperity. But everyone calls me Nassa. I'm here on behalf of the sorceresses of the Black Circle. Appointed by my Aunt Lunette."

Stunned, my eyebrows draw together. "Lunette is your aunt?"

"Yep." She rolls her eyes like it's an annoyance to have Lunette as family.

"Did we meet at the circle? I'm sorry if I've forgotten."

"It's cool. We wear robes, so it's hard to make us out. Are we waiting for something?"

I shrug. "I think it just takes time to organize everyone."

"Welcome, everyone. Sorry I'm late." Asher's voice drifts through the room, and I immediately turn and lock eyes with him, wishing I hadn't.

Standing to his left is Leo. The sight of him causes my heart to plummet. To Asher's right is Morgana. *Fan-tab-u-lous.* My eyes zero in on her hand, which is gripping his arm. My arm. I curl my fingers into my hips, so I don't do something stupid, like walk over and rip her face off.

Morgana focuses all her attention on Asher, as if she's meant to be by his side. A quiet growl escapes me, and Nassa turns, her emerald eyes narrowing at me.

"What's wrong with you?" she asks in an accusatory tone.

"Nothing." I attempt to brush off the murderous feelings.

"Yeah, okay. That didn't sound like nothing. It sounded like 'If you don't leave my man alone, I am going to claw your fucking eyes out,'" she whispers.

I ignore the comment. Even though she is right.

"Please, everyone, take a seat," Keegan instructs.

"I'd like to do a quick roll call," Asher requests before taking a seat at the head of the table. I'm on his right and Keegan is to his left.

I watch Morgana pout because she has to walk all the way to the end of the table to the last empty seat next to Marcus. I smile at the small victory.

Asher motions to me with a warm smile. "You all know Eve Collins, daughter of Heaven." I wave shyly before his eyes flick to Nassa.

"Llughnassad, Sorceress of Prosperity, on behalf of the Sorceresses of the Black Circle."

"Thomas, second in command of the Irish clan of gargoyles."

"Sean, second in command of the Scottish clan of gargoyles."

"Marcus, leader of the Manhattan clan of gargoyles."

"Morgana, second in command of the Manhattan clan."

"Stephan, second to Lord Valentin, leader of the Vampire World."

"Leo, beta of the Quinnipiac pack, representing the Werewolf Sovereignty."

"Ainsley, Duchess of Sprites, from the Kingdom of the Fae."

"Gage, leader of the Paris clan of gargoyles."

At Gage's statement, my eyes flick to him in shock that he introduced himself as the leader. I thought he said he didn't want anything to do with that title. He doesn't meet my eyes, because Gage's focus is currently on Nassa. *Interesting.*

"Before we begin, the London clan would like to extend our gratitude that you have joined us today. We understand you're preparing for the upcoming war." Asher's eyes flick to me before readdressing the group. "As you are aware, my family has been charged with protecting the daughter of Heaven." His voice trails off for a moment. "Much to the dismay of the dark army, she is still under our protection. For this reason, they've begun increasing their presence within our realms. Attacking innocents in the hope of breaking our charge. Now, they've declared war on Heaven. I don't need to remind you all of the last time Heaven and Hell battled it out. The human and supernatural casualties were astronomical."

Everyone around the table nods their head in agreement. My eyes float back to Asher. Observing him take command of this group is breathtaking. I've never focused on the royalty aspect of Asher, only the protector one. Watching him in his role within the supernatural world is awe-inspiring. He was meant to be king.

"I understand that recently a higher-level demon paid you all a visit?" Stephan asks.

"Thoren is no longer an issue," Gage answers. "Two members of the Declan clan have also been exterminated. Deacon's mother, Dimia, is one. Her demise is what escalated the dark army's timeline, as well as that of Deacon's brother, Kaiden."

"Your Highness, are you completely certain the Declan clan of gargoyles is working with Lucifer?" Morgana asks. "A protector placing a human such as Eve in danger would be an act of sabotage to our oaths and loyalties. Are you saying Deacon and his clan are no longer following the laws set forth by the council, Spiritual Assembly, or Secular Sector?"

I internally sigh. Morgana knows Deacon's intentions. She was at the last strategy meeting. My nostrils flare at the memory of her standing in the kitchen wearing Asher's shirt.

"There is no doubt that the Declan clan is working with Lucifer. Let me be clear: anyone caught sympathizing with or assisting the Declan clan, Lucifer, or the dark army will be considered a conspirator. There will be no mercy for them. I personally will tear the defector apart with my bare hands. Are we fucking clear?" Asher's voice is menacing.

The room goes silent. Keegan clears his throat and turns the group's attention to him. "All members of the Declan clan are to be considered dark army loyalists. Anyone who associates with them will be treated as having committed treason."

"With stone petrifaction as the punishment," Asher's cool voice adds.

Marcus pins his stare on Asher. "Is that a council directive or royal decree?"

Asher sits back. "Does it matter?"

"What are you in need of, Asher?" Leo asks, avoiding eye contact with me.

"Intel on both the dark army and the Declan clan of gargoyles. It would seem alliances have been made with supernaturals from our realms. We need to find out who these defectors are. In addition, it is essential to continue to amass and train the army. At some point, the demonic legion will come for Eve with reinforcements. We'll protect her, however the destruction they intend to bring to mankind and the realms is unknown, as is the extent of their militia," Asher answers.

"Will the Angelic Council be ally or foe?" Stephan asks, as Marcus's eyes shift to him.

"Ally," Keegan answers with authority.

"We also need an offensive strategy, not just a defensive one. If we're able to attack first, the chances of human and supernatural casualties may be less," Callan offers.

"Ideally, what we need is to prepare within our realms and keep our eyes and ears open. I task each of you today to go back to your dominions and secure them. Be cognizant of the dangers that are lurking. Demons are sly and manipulative. With each kingdom having light and dark for balance, you'll need to secure the dark gateways. Report back if you discover conspirators," Asher adds. "The gargoyles will continue to protect mankind, as if nothing is happening. We don't want to alert and panic the humans," Keegan says militantly.

"What of Eve's guardian?" Ainsley's soft voice travels over me.

"The angelic army is performing an extraction mission for Elizabeth. In the meantime, the London clan will continue to protect Eve," Asher continues.

At Callan's next words, my heart sinks. "Leo, Nassa, and Morgana will remain here in London. They'll be staying in the guest quarters on the second floor with Gage. Nassa will work with Abby in an attempt to expose the magic the dark army is using to block the priestesses from identifying them. Leo and Tadhg will devise a military plan with Keegan. Morgana and Kenna will work on securing the European clans' alliances."

"It's with our deepest gratitude we thank the court-appointed representatives for attending today. We'll be in touch," Keegan says.

"Wait." The intensity covering Asher's face is striking. Our gazes lock, and I swallow hard. He lifts a hand toward me and my eyes widen. *What the hell is he doing?* My eyes shift to Gage, who has gone ashen, before returning to Asher. His hand is waiting for me to place mine into it.

The tension in the room is at an all-time high, with everyone looking around in confused silence. Asher nods once for encouragement, and I gingerly place my hand into his. All at once, everyone begins to murmur. Asher doesn't notice. His eyes soften and a lopsided grin appears as he inclines his head to the group.

"Aside from Eve being under my protection, she is also mine," he declares to the shocked faces in the room. Abby is beaming proudly, while McKenna and Morgana look like they want to decapitate me.

"That explains the growl," Nassa mutters next to me.

"Forgive me, I was under the impression that such relations are against the protector oaths the council has set?" Ainsley breathes out.

"My oaths to my race and to the council have no bearing on my intent to make Eve my mate. The council and I will soon be coming to an understanding as it relates to my relationship with her," Asher answers. "Before we began this summit, you each were sworn to a confidentiality oath. I expect that vow will be upheld until I release you of it."

Keegan's face is pinched in concern. "The St. Michaels have accepted Eve into our clan. She is family—part of the royal family as the king's future mate—and will be treated as such."

Taken aback at Keegan's statement, I just sit there quietly.

"Well then, Asher, congratulations are in order to both you and the daughter of Heaven on behalf of Lucian, king of the werewolves," Leo smirks.

"Thank you," Asher says and kisses my hand. "This meeting is adjourned."

Everyone stands and offers their best wishes as they leave. I just stand by Asher's side, holding his hand in a death grip. Morgana storms out of the room with McKenna in tow. When everyone exits, it's just Keegan, Callan, Gage, Asher, and me left.

"Are you insane?" Keegan spits out at Asher.

"Depends on the day, brother," Asher teases.

"Joke all you want, Asher, but you do realize what you've just done?" Keegan seethes.

Asher watches me with a torn look, before pulling me to his chest in a tight embrace. The desperate need to get out of this room is clawing at me, but I push it down and soak up his closeness and warmth.

"We need to figure out who the traitor is, Keegan. Why not just feed them the information they need? If the council becomes aware that I've declared Eve as my intended mate, we have it narrowed to the beings that were here for the announcement," Asher states, while squeezing my hand. "Besides, I love the speech you gave."

Keegan's face goes red. Literally. Bright. Red. "I did that to show solidarity, not because I agree with you. What if the council decides now they have proof of your disloyalty?"

I pull away to look at Asher, realizing he still hasn't told anyone about the divination. If my soul and his unite, he can't ever be turned into stone.

Asher's eyes narrow dangerously. "I suggest you put that little speech you gave into practice, Keegan."

"Let's go cool off, shall we?" Callan offers, and guides Keegan out of the room.

"I hope you know what you're doing, dark prince. You've just placed yourself, your clan, and Eve in even graver danger," Gage says with a low tone, before offering me a sad smile. "I'll see you later, love."

After a moment, when it's just Asher and me, he turns his blazing gaze toward mine.

"Want to talk about it?" I question in a shallow voice, with my arms crossed, backing away from him.

"No."

I frown. "You haven't told the family about the divination or our souls?"

"No."

"Why?" I ask in a quiet tone.

"That's between you and me. Not the clan, or court, or councils."

"Your family might want to know that you can't physically turn into stone if we're one."

"They'll use it to solidify my position as king. It's between you and me, something we will decide together when the time is right. As a form of commitment, not safety," he fumes.

I lean on the conference table as Asher strides to me.

"Don't you think you should have asked me before you outed us?"

"Why, siren? Are you embarrassed to be my intended mate?" he quips.

"Asher, this is serious," I respond, closing my eyes.

I feel his lips brush mine softly. This kiss is soft and tender. It terrifies and thrills me. His thumbs stroke my cheek. "There is nothing to discuss. You're mine. The end."

I grab his cheeks and force him to look at me. "That's just it, Ash. I'm not yours. Not fully, anyway."

"What are you saying?"

"I'm yours in heart and mind only. We haven't completed the mate mark unification. I want to keep you safe. We should complete it. This way, I'm assured nothing can touch you," I plead.

Asher steps back. His face is marred by sadness and hurt. "This is what I mean. I didn't want anyone to know about our soul connection because I didn't want them to fucking say, mate with her so you won't ever die."

"You didn't even ask me what I thought about that plan," I raise my voice.

"No. I didn't." He exhales and rubs his hands over his face, then through his hair, lacing them behind his head. "When I see you, siren, I see my entire future. There's no existence without you. Don't you see that? Everything that I'm doing now, it's all for you. When I'm not with you, I can taste you on my lips, smell your scent, and see the smile you reserve just for me. The thought of never having that again . . . it's fucking terrifying. I won't survive it." His voice is rough and lifeless.

He turns to walk out, and everything hits me all at once. My eyes sting with a sudden rush of tears. No one will escape this war the same way they went into it, especially Asher and me.

"If something happens to you because of what you just did . . . if you cease to exist, it will destroy me," I state in a hushed tone.

He spins around and takes a step. His fierce, stormy eyes are so protective and focused.

"War is destruction."

"It doesn't have to be."

At my retort his face becomes hard. "Promise me you understand how bad it's going to get." His voice is raw.

I watch him, knowing he needs me to answer. "I promise," I whisper shakily.

He takes another step in my direction.

"Promise you understand there will be death, yeah?"

"I promise." My words are barely audible.

Asher closes the last bit of distance between us and cups my face.

"Promise me you will listen to me. Even if it means the end of my existence."

I close my eyes, relishing his touch. "I can't."

"That's the fucking problem, siren." His voice cracks.

"What is?" I whisper.

"I. Protect. You. Not the other way around."

"Love is a two-way street, Ash."

"I will protect you, always."

Randi Cooley Wilson

19 Turning Page

I stand in the doorway just watching Asher in motion. His commanding presence is breathtaking as he moves around the conference room we've dubbed Base Camp. It's been a few weeks since the summit and so far, not only has the traitor not appeared, but Deacon and Lucifer have not made a move.

Asher's attention is focused on the papers that are laid out in no particular order on the table. He studies them with intense concentration. The muscles in his neck strain as he leans over to hear what Leo and Tadhg are saying.

His jaw ticks in a raw, powerful motion, and his body is tilted at a sensual angle. For a moment, I wonder what it would be like to be laying on the table with him leaning over me, giving me the same expression. I shiver at the thought.

With the agility of a cat, Asher takes a seat. A frown mars his face. My heartbeat drums loudly. Whatever they've shared, it doesn't look like good news. I exhale a breath and approach him from behind, wrapping my arms around his chest.

"Tell me what's going on," I murmur in his ear.

"Siren, you're barely holding it together with what you do know. There are some things that you're just not ready to handle yet." His tone is soft.

Anger flares in me. "Stop protecting me from the truth, Asher. We're supposed to be in this together."

An array of emotions flashes across his features.

"I'm sorry."

Before I can respond, Nassa approaches us. "Sorry for interrupting, but Lunette sent word that Lady Finella wishes to meet with you, Eve."

Asher's head turns and scans my face, before he addresses Nassa. "When?"

"In about ten minutes," she answers.

I raise my hands to gently caress the worry line between his brows. At my touch, it softens, but doesn't disappear.

"She knows I'm here at the summit. I won't be able to escort Eve," he points out, confused.

"It's fine. I'll go meet with her, and you can finish your meeting," I whisper in his ear.

"No. You're not going unaccompanied."

I roll my eyes. "You're being overprotective again. I've met with her by myself a thousand times before. I'll be fine," I murmur against his mouth.

He moves his beautiful lips out of my reach. "It's my job to protect you, siren."

My lips pull into a small smile. "I thought your job was to be king of the gargoyles." I wiggle my eyebrows. When I don't get a response, my expression falls.

"I won't be long," I try to soothe his worry. "I'll realm jump and be back before you know it."

"Actually, she's coming here," Nassa adds.

I almost forgot she was here.

"She's coming to the earth realm?" Asher clarifies.

I move around him and straddle his lap at the inflection in his tone.

"She thinks it's safer than in the supernatural realms. It's her opinion that the dark army has eyes and ears everywhere now. Including here at the summit," Nassa explains.

"Interesting," he comments, and stares off into space.

I rock my hips once in an attempt to gain his attention. "Hey, stop worrying about everything." I lift my hands and cup his face. His five o'clock shadow scratches my palm.

"I'm sending a protector to go with you," he states in a firm voice.

"Ash—" He cuts me off.

"Do not fucking argue with me about this, siren. Your safety is my main concern."

"Okay," I give in, knowing it's more for him than me.

"I'll go with her." Morgana's ridiculous voice filters over my shoulder, causing me to still on Asher's lap. His hands tighten on my hips in reassurance.

259

"You want to go as Eve's protector?" Asher questions in surprise.

Can't say I blame him. Nassa offers me a sympathetic look.

Morgana shrugs. "She needs a babysitter. You and Gage can't leave the summit. McKenna, Keegan, Callan and Abby are reaching out to the other clans. Looks like I'm all you've got, Eve," she says snidely.

"I'm not sure Eve wants that, Morgana," Asher offers.

God, I love him.

The female gargoyle sneers. "I'll protect your precious Eve. Besides, I only charge fifteen dollars an hour when I babysit. Can't beat the rate," she quips lightheartedly, but there is an underlying tone in her statement.

"It's fine." I exhale in annoyance. It's not, but Asher has bigger things to worry about.

"Are you sure?" He lifts his brows in disbelief.

"It's Lady Finella." I stare him. "Nothing is going to happen."

"That's not what I am concerned about," he deadpans.

"You think we're going to catfight over you?"

"Are you, siren?"

"I make no promises, Ash."

He takes my lips domineeringly while his hands move my hips in a rocking motion. "It's so fucking hot when you get all possessive of me," he growls into my mouth.

"Asher, if you'd be kind enough to pry yourself away from your human pet, we should probably get going," Morgana interjects, annoyed.

"I don't like it." He exhales near my ear, causing me to tremble.

"I'll be fine," I reply against his cheek.

His head tilts back as he scans my face. "I'm going with you two."

"Asher, you're needed here," I say, fixated on how sensual his mouth is.

"End of discussion, siren. I'm going."

I nod my agreement, knowing there is no way I can win this argument.

"She would like to meet in the park by the statue of Achilles," Nassa says.

"Okay. How far is that?" I question Asher.

"It's located near the Queen Elizabeth Gate, so not too far," Asher replies, grabbing the Angelic Sword.

I stand and step away from the warmth of Asher's body, to be met by Morgana's cold eyes.

That's right, bitch. He's mine. I smile brightly at her as I walk toward the door, but not before she steps into my path and brushes shoulders with me. A clear warning that suggests I'm anything but safe with her.

She's lucky I don't grab my sheathed daggers because I would love nothing more than to stab her. I sigh. It's going to be a long afternoon.

෧෧

"Did you know, siren, that Achilles's mother was a nymph? Thetis, I believe was her name," Asher offers. "I think she was the goddess of water or something, if memory serves me."

"You have an unhealthy fascination with water nymphs."

Asher gives me a half-grin.

"Hesperia is a celestial nymph. Totally different creature," he corrects, while his lips twitch with amusement. "I'll go check the wooded area in the back. Usually Lady Finella likes to keep out of sight when in the earth realm."

"Asher has a fixation with the opposite sex in general. A little friendly advice," Morgana chimes in, as we approach the massive monument.

"I'll keep that in mind." I grin stupidly at her.

Morgana just huffs and throws her glossy black hair over her shoulder. "Sad, isn't it?"

"What is?" I ask, my eyes fixed on Asher's retreating back.

Brown eyes flick to me. "Even Achilles had a weakness that eventually got him killed."

"If I recall my Greek tragedy correctly, he died avenging his love," I retort.

"Yes. But the question is, which of his loves did he die to save?" she challenges.

Just as I'm about to respond, Asher and Lady Finella approach. Grateful to be sidetracked from Morgana, I step forward to embrace the fae queen. Asher's standing slightly behind her and he shakes his head to stop my movement. Sudden unease trickles down my spine.

His eyes flick to Morgana, who stiffens next to me. Something isn't right.

"POSEUR!" Asher shouts.

In a split second, Morgana pulls out throwing stars from her belt and flicks them at Lady Finella without hesitation. To my shock and complete dismay. *What the fuck?*

At the sight, I step forward. "Stop!"

The small blades hit their target, and the image of Lady Finella begins to flicker in and out, like an old television transmission, before she bursts into blue flames.

"What the hell?" I ask.

Asher steps to me and grips my upper arms to get my attention. "It was a poseur. A demon that takes on the appearance of someone or something."

"They can also turn into bats," Morgana adds casually.

My eyes widen. "So that wasn't Lady Finella?"

"No, siren, it was a demon pretending to be her." He leans in and kisses me on the cheek.

"Holy shit. If it took on her form, it had to have known I was meeting her, right? I mean, Asher, she could be in danger," I say, trying to mask the panic in my tone.

"Lucifer could have instructed the demon to look like her, knowing your fondness for the queen," he responds. "As a trap to lure you to him." His eyes dart around, seeking additional danger.

"I don't see or sense another demon," Morgana responds. "Looks like it was a one-off."

"Regardless, we should get Eve back. Something doesn't feel right. I knew it," he retorts.

"Agreed. Would you hand me my shuriken?" Morgana coos, and bats her eyes at him.

The urge to kill her increases with each breath she takes.

"You okay?" he asks, ignoring her.

I simply nod. This shit keeps getting stranger. I brush it off and offer a reassuring smile.

Sensing Asher isn't going to help her, Morgana sighs and bends to retrieve her weapons. At the last minute, Asher rolls his eyes and moves to help her.

Damn adorable gargoyle.

Suddenly, my head is wrenched backwards, and panic floods me. On instinct, I reach for my daggers, but they aren't there. *What in the world? I sheathed them myself.* With lightning speed, the female that has my hair in her grasp teleports us to the other side of the monument.

My head is jerked up so I'm forced to look at Achilles. "See something you like, daughter of Heaven?" Jade's voice hisses at my ear. "He is rather well-endowed, wouldn't you agree?"

Asher and Morgana approach us in an instant, with their wings released. I'm surprised to see Morgana's are raven black, like Asher's.

Crap. Not the time for jealousy Eve. Focus.

I run through all my training with Callan, in my head, trying to figure out how I'm going to break free from the hold Deacon's mate has on me.

Just when I decide my plan of action, she places a knife at my neck that begins searing my skin. *Fuck, that hurts.* Tears sting my eyes from the pain, and my stomach rolls at the smell of my flesh burning.

"Do not think about coming closer, protectors," Jade warns.

My eyes dart around, and I notice that she's alone, without assistance. *Interesting.*

"I'll only warn you once, Jade. Release her," Asher's deadly voice advises.

"This must be a familiar sight to you, Asher. Only this time, instead of my neck burning from the touch of the Angelic Sword, its Eve's from the Angel Blade," she spits out.

Asher's eyes flick to the blade. Morgana pales. *Well, shit. That can't be good.*

"Eve isn't an angel. She can't be killed with the Angel Blade," Asher informs.

"How quickly you forget, though, dark prince. Eve may not be an angel, but she carries a soul touched by an archangel. That means the blade will end her all the same," she leers.

"Asher," I whisper his name, because seriously this fucking blade burns.

"Release her now!" Asher demands in a raw, primal growl.

"You must love her with all your heart," Jade snipes at Asher.

"I do," he answers, not breaking eye contact with me.

Morgana tenses. Her jaw tightens at his admission. Other than that, she's focused.

"Then you'll do anything to ensure her protection?" Deacon's mate asks.

"Without question." Asher's voice is menacing.

"Let's play a little game then, shall we?" The evil gargoyle grins. "To save your love."

"What kind of game, Jade?" he asks with irritation.

"What if. What if we all get what we want, dark prince? You see, you have a traitor in your midst and I have a mate who's neglecting me. Deacon has become slightly obsessed with your love and the upcoming war. That makes for an unhappy mate," she purrs.

Asher throws a cold, calculating stare her way before returning his eyes to me. I have to fight hard to stay alert, because the pain from the knife is beyond words. My legs begin to wobble, and Jade tightens her hold so I won't collapse.

"I'm listening," Asher says.

"What if I give you the name of your traitor, and what if you allow me to take your love to Deacon. You'll have peace since there will be no war and your precious humans will be safe. Deacon can finally relax and refocus his attentions on me," she negotiates. "It's a win-win."

I notice Morgana's eye twitch, before I'm pulled away from the sight when my neck pulsates in pain, causing me to release a small whimper.

Asher's eyes flick to the blade and then back to my eyes. "No."

Jade exhales her disappointment. "I was afraid you would say that."

With his protector speed, Asher lunges for Jade. Surprised by his sudden motion, she flinches, releasing me. As she does, the knife slides across my throat. I fall to the ground writhing in pain, my neck bleeding and burning. For some reason, my entire body is paralyzed, causing me to watch the scene play out helplessly from the ground.

"Let's get something clear before I send you back to your mate with a message," Asher seethes. "Do not touch her ever again," he spits. "Tell Deacon I look forward to seeing him, and that every time he looks at this scar on your body, it should remind him of me."

Asher lifts the Angelic Sword, moving toward Jade. Morgana finally pulls herself out of her shocked state and grabs her throwing stars.

Jade stands strong, with a tight grip on the Angel Blade. My vision begins to blur as I move in and out of consciousness. I attempt to focus on my blood dripping off the blade, so I don't pass out.

"Harm me and Deacon will end you," Jade warns.

"Threat or promise?" Asher asks. He lunges for her again, but she's faster and vanishes.

"FUCK!" Asher shouts, looking around at the empty area.

I produce an odd gurgling noise from my throat, catching Asher's attention. He prowls to me and kneels.

"Fuck. Siren, hold on, yeah?"

I can't answer him, but I blink a few times, hoping he understands. Asher takes off his shirt and gently wraps it around my neck to soak up the blood. Within moments, I feel his healing energies being pushed into me, and the pain begins to subside.

My vision starts to focus and I see Morgana's face over Asher's shoulder. *This would have been a good time to pass out.*

"She's lost too much blood, Asher. We need to get her back and into stone state."

Lovely. Now she cares about my wellbeing. I inhale and my eyes shift behind Asher, then widen in fright. Jade's face suddenly reappears behind him. She has the Angel Blade lifted so she can pierce him through his back, into his heart. My heart is erratic and sinks in despair. I try to speak, but the injury to my neck won't allow me to, so instead I thrash around.

"Easy, siren. You're going to be okay," Asher soothes.

Morgana sees my expression and follows my eyes behind her, now seeing Jade. Instantly, she jumps in front of the blade, shielding Asher and pushing his body into me.

"Get down, Asher," she shouts, before screaming in pain.

It all happens so fast my mind almost doesn't process it. Asher rolls off me and twists, now aware of what's happening. Jade is sneering at Morgana with the Angel Blade buried in her heart. Crimson liquid flows out of the deep wound.

Asher stands. Angelic Sword in hand, he charges at Jade while she yanks the weapon out of Morgana's heart. The beautiful gargoyle's body crumples to the ground next to me, limply.

In an instant, Jade vanishes, teleporting again. Asher scans the area, but she's gone. He spins back around, and his eyes roam over Morgana's body, which is now turning into stone. His face falls in pain as he crouches next to her. With soft eyes, he brushes the hair off her face in an intimate way. He turns her head so she's facing me as Asher strokes her hair.

"Fuck. I'm sorry, sweetheart," he says sadly in her ear.

When the granite is halfway up her body, my daggers fall out of her belt. My eyes lock onto hers in understanding.

She took them.

She set me up.

She's the traitor.

Her eyes meet mine in apology. Once the stone reaches her neck, she mouths a name to me before her face morphs into granite. Seconds later, her stone body crumbles and is nonexistent. I close my eyes because it's not Deacon's name she mouthed. It turns out our traitor is bigger than all of us, and when Asher finds out, it will destroy him.

When I reopen them, the dust of what is left of Morgana blows in the light spring breeze. At the sight, my body succumbs to my wounds, and I slip into unconsciousness.

❧

I struggle to open my eyes. The light is dim in the room, but it still causes searing pain when I attempt to see. Finally, after several tries, my eyes flutter open. I gaze around Asher's bedroom. All the curtains are pulled. The sound of faint beeping draws my eyes to the left.

A heart monitor stands next to his bed. Lifting my arm, I see an IV attached to it. *What the hell? I thought I healed myself in stone state.*

Asher's face comes into view. "There you are, siren." His voice is raw. He looks exhausted, like he hasn't showered or slept in days. He leans over me. A tight, grim smile forms at the corners of his mouth and he brushes the hair off my face.

"Hi."

"Hi," I croak out.

My neck is throbbing. Automatically, my hand lifts to touch it. Asher quickly takes the hand and interlaces our fingers, pulling them away from my injury.

"You're still healing. Don't touch it, okay?" he says in a hushed tone.

I attempt to nod, but can't. My throat is dry and I need some water. "Water?" I rasp.

"Here ye are, lad." Fiona's voice wafts over me as she hands a small glass to Asher.

He brings a straw to my mouth, encouraging me to sip. The cool liquid feels amazing. When he thinks I've had enough, the cup is pulled away and handed back to Fiona.

"Better?"

I smile my response. "Why have I not healed?" I ask with great effort.

"Jade was using an Angel Blade. It's the only demon weapon that can actually kill an angel." He winces. "That's why it burned. It's going to take a little longer for you to recover from the wound. It wasn't deep, and when you are fully healed, it won't scar. The burn caused the most damage. It's why you're having difficulty speaking, and why you were paralyzed, which has already worn off. The pain should subside shortly, and you will be fully recovered in a day or so. We have an IV for fluids, and the heart monitor is because your heart gave out twice." His pained voice trails off.

My eyes widen. "It did?"

Asher's eyes close and then reopen. "A side effect of being paralyzed. Your heart went into shock, though we didn't know that at the time. Fiona's been here taking care of you."

"You look exhausted. Are you okay?" I lift my hand and place it on his cheek.

Asher nods at my question before turning and kissing the inside of my palm. "I am now." He looks sad. Memories begin to flood me as I recall what happened.

"I'm sorry about Morgana," I say with sincerity.

"Me too, siren. Me too."

"She was the traitor, Ash. She set me up and took my weapons."

"Yes." Asher inhales deeply, closing his eyes tightly. "Jade tricked Lunette. She sent the poseur demon as Lady Finella to get word of the meeting through Nassa," he explains. "We think Morgana knew all along. Marcus, as you can imagine, was devastated to find out. He also feels extremely guilty. As do I."

"Come here." I motion for him to get on the bed. Careful not to move me, he slides in, gently lifting my body so I can lean on him. He strokes my hair in a soothing manner. I squeeze my eyes shut. I know Asher didn't see Morgana mouth the name of the one she was working with. I need to figure out how to tell him, because when I do divulge who it is, Asher's world will shatter into a million pieces.

Randi Cooley Wilson

20 Redemption

I awaken to the smell of cigarettes and spice. I've never really been comforted by Gage Gallagher's scent, but it's beginning to feel a lot like home. I look over to see him sleeping in a chair in the corner of the room. *That can't be comfortable.*

I scan the room, but Asher and Fiona are nowhere in sight. Frowning, I sit up. The IV is gone and so is the heart monitor. My neck feels a thousand times better, and I can actually swallow. I lean over to collect the water next to my bed, waking Gage up in the process.

"Hey," he says in a groggily sexy voice.

"Hey, yourself," I answer, glad that my throat isn't rasping.

"Need help, love?" He points to the glass and moves to the side table to pour me some water. When it's full, he hands it to me and sits on the side of the bed.

I sip the liquid slowly and watch him. Like Asher, he looks tired.

"Thanks." I offer a small smile.

"How are you feeling?" he asks with soft eyes.

"Better." I sit up taller, feeling less weak. "I didn't mean to wake you. Have you been sleeping well?"

"That's a loaded question." He winks. "I've been having . . . nightmares."

I peer down at my hand. "What kind of nightmares?"

His eyes slide to the left as he focuses outside. "Your injury was similar to Camilla's. It forced old wounds and feelings to the surface." *Oh shit. I forgot Camilla's throat was slit.*

My eyes squeeze tight and I snag his hand. "I'm sorry, Gage."

"It's okay. You're still with us." His voice is tense.

"Did Asher tell you all about Morgana?" I question, and take another sip.

Gage's eyes meet mine. "He did. What I can't figure out, though, is whom she was revealing the information to. Morgana didn't have a direct line to Deacon. I know this because for a while, I was his right hand. So that tells me she was working with someone else. Any ideas on who that could be?"

I swallow a mouthful of water and shake my head. "Nope."

Gage just scans my face. "You're a terrible liar, love."

My face pales. "Am not." *Brilliant, Eve.*

Gage concedes, dropping the topic. "I am truly happy that you are okay, Eve. I know we've had our differences, but you've sort of grown on me, and I would hate to see something happen to you." He squeezes my hand before letting it go.

"Thanks for staying last night." I point to the chair. "That couldn't have been comfortable."

Gage lets out a small laugh. "Don't get any ideas. I have a job to do, just as you have. I was on protection duty last night."

For some reason, that stings. I thought we were getting closer. "Okay," I draw out and stare at his heartbreaking expression. The thing about Gage—his pain runs deep.

An unpleasant frown forms on his lips. "I couldn't save her. It nearly killed me. I don't plan on living through a repeat of history with you."

"Gage—"

He cuts me off.

"Camilla's the reason I agreed to protect you. No matter what the bad blood is between Asher and me, no one should ever suffer the loss of the love of his life. No one stepped in and prevented Camilla's death. I can. I will. I'm going to see this through." His vow is sincere. "You're protected with me."

"I'm not Camilla," I counter in a quiet tone.

"That is true, you are not her. Though, there are similarities. You are a stubborn human female who fell in love with her protector, and I do believe that you just had your throat sliced," he deadpans. "So forgive my need to shield you from her end result."

I absorb what he's said. "I don't sculpt and I'm not from Spain. So there's that."

His lips twitch. "I've seen your sketches, and an artist you are not, love."

We just hold one another's gaze and smile, trying to lighten the mood.

"You're my redemption," he says in a distressed tone.

Confused, I pull my brows together. "I don't understand."

"Aye, da lass 'tis awake." Fiona's warm voice slithers through the room. "Mornin', luv. 'Tis good ta see ye." She pats my face before narrowing her eyes at Gage. "Da lads are lookin' fer ye, boy. Ye best be gettin' down da stairs."

He stands, letting go of my hand. "Yes, ma'am."

My brows rise. "Wow. You'll have to show me how to do that, Fi."

"It's best not to give Fiona lip. Her swats hurt." He winks and leaves.

"Let's get ye up, lass, and bathed. 'Tis time fer ye ta rejoin da world."

I place my cup down. "Yes, ma'am."

That earned me a swat. Gage is right. It does hurt.

"Don't ye be fresh, lass," she scolds and helps me to the bathroom.

࿇

While I am thrilled to see Fiona again, enduring her overbearing mothering is starting to grate on my dignity. After bathing, and I mean *she bathed me*, followed by a session of force-feeding me soup, I finally escape to venture down to the second floor and find Asher.

I'm just about to enter the conference room when I hear Keegan's angry voice.

"Every moment you spend with her, Asher, you strengthen the bond. I suggest you break it before it destroys you both when you each need to fulfill your destinies."

"Did you fucking misunderstand what I said at the summit? Eve is my intended and she should be treated as such. Regardless of your wants in this matter, it is not up for discussion," Asher responds coolly.

"I can't stand behind this, Ash," Keegan answers in a quiet tone.

"Then don't," Asher states.

"What happened to clan first?" Keegan asks in annoyance.

"EVE IS MY FUCKING FAMILY," Asher shouts. "She's just as much a part of this clan as anyone else. Your continued disapproval of us is going to force my hand, brother. I suggest you take a different approach," Asher warns.

Keegan lets out a cold laugh. "What are you going to do, Asher? Finally step into your royal role and have me sentenced for disloyalty?"

Silence.

"Well, at least you'll be living up to your bloodline," Keegan spits and storms out.

Hearing Keegan's exit, I quickly jump into another hallway so he doesn't see me, before I make my way into the quiet room. My vision lands on Asher, who is sitting in a chair with his head in his hands.

I walk over to where he's hunched over, and kneel down in front of him. Wordlessly, I wrap my fingers around the

Randi Cooley Wilson

leather bands on his wrists and gently pull his hands out of his hair, away from his face, then place them securely around my waist.

I cup his face and force him to look at me. His eyes are red and watery. The idea of him breaking down like this rips my soul in half. I lean in so my mouth is within a breath of his.

"I love you," I whisper across his lips, before placing a light kiss on him.

When I pull back, a single tear falls down his face. With my thumb, I wipe it away. At my movement, he tightens his hold around my waist and pulls me into a firm embrace. All I want to do is rescue him from all of this.

"Forever," he finally whispers in my hair.

"I could kill Keegan for making you feel this way."

"You heard?" he whispers.

"Every word. I'm sorry that I'm coming between you and your brother."

Asher pulls back so he can look at me. "You're not, siren. Don't ever think that. Keegan is just being stubborn. I would think if anyone can appreciate that quality, it would be you." He smirks.

I offer a sad smile. "I don't want you to hurt. When you do, so do I."

He exhales and rubs his hands over his face and through his hair, as I sit back. "Then stop getting injured, because I swear to fucking God I'm not sure how many more times I can see you lying helplessly. When your heart stopped, so did mine. You understand?"

I scan his eyes, and after a while, I nod. "Okay."

"The thought of an existence without you—" He stops and just pins me with his eyes.

"Now you know how scared I am of losing you, Ash." My voice is a quiet hush. "If there was something you could do to ensure my existence, would you do it?"

"In a fucking heartbeat." His tone is serious.

"Then allow me the same opportunity. I can guarantee your existence." He shakes his head.

I grab the sides of his face, forcing eye contact. "The divination states that if our souls become one, my light will breathe life into yours. Don't you see? You can't cease to exist at someone else's hands that way. We'd be liberated from the fear of stone petrifaction."

"You haven't even finished your ascension, siren. We don't know what a soul bonding will do to that. I don't want you to mate me for the sole reason of redemption."

Aggravated with him, I growl and take another approach. I stand, push my shoulders back, and tilt my chin before crossing my arms over my chest and lowering my voice.

"Do you doubt my love for you, gargoyle?" I challenge.

"What?"

"Do. You. Doubt. My. Love. For. You? It's a simple question."

Asher takes in my stance. "No."

"Do you doubt my loyalty to you?"

"No."

"Do you doubt that I want to spend the rest of my existence by your side?"

The sides of his mouth turn up. "No, siren. I don't."

"Good." I nod my head once. "Then Asher St. Michael, will you do me the honor of being my mate?"

Asher just gives me his sexy smirk, sits back in the chair, and folds his arms. "Are you seducing me, siren?"

I can't help my smile. "I'm asking you to spend forever with me."

"So you're proposing bondage then?" *Damn gargoyle.*

"Asher," I sigh in exhaustion.

"Siren," he retorts wickedly.

"Stop being an ass," I reprimand.

"I'm just saying, a gargoyle—" He pauses. "Correction, a royal gargoyle, likes to be romanced. I mean, if you're going to ask me to bond my soul to yours forever, I expect a proposal on one knee, maybe a ring to solidify our union. For sure sexy lingerie."

"You know what, I've changed my mind. I hope that you enjoy a long life as a stone statue. I mean, you are, after all, a gargoyle. It would seem the only '*royal*' thing about you, Asher St. Michael, is that you're a royal pain in the ass." I spin to leave, but not before Asher's up in the blink of an eye. He twists me so I face him.

"Don't you want my answer?" he asks, then presses his lips to my neck.

"Nope. I'm all set," I reply with defiance.

His eyes widen in surprise. "Really?"

"Really," I confirm.

"You sure?" he teases, stepping into my space so our hips and chests touch. *Damn him.*

"Positive. I can't think of anything worse than being stuck with you for eternity."

"Is that so?" He arches a brow as his gaze flicks to my mouth.

"That's so." My lips part on an inhale.

"Too bad."

"Why?"

"Because I would love to be mated to you, siren." His voice is deep and sexy.

"You would?" I breathe.

"If you truly want me forever, I'm yours," Asher says with a grin.

"I do. I want you. Forever," I answer in a low voice.

He watches me for a moment before his eyes warm.

"Then it's settled."

"It is?" I question in a breathy manner.

"We leave for Wiltshire this evening."

"Wiltshire?"

"I want you in my stone state bed when I take your virtue and make you mine forever."

My heart slams against my chest. "Oh," I manage lamely.

"Oh?" His lips curve.

I bite my lip and smile. "I mean, that sounds amazing. You're so awesome, Asher St. Michael. I can't wait to be bonded to you for eternity. I'm the luckiest girl alive," I tease.

He growls and yanks me forward. "Fuck, that's what I wanted to hear, siren."

"I do hope I am not interrupting." Michael's voice booms. *Damn his timing.*

"Not at all. Eve and I were just discussing divine intervention and how it affects modern society," Asher says with a serious face.

"I see. Eve, if you would like clarification on divine intervention perhaps I could be of assistance. I am, after all, an archangel. A protector is not a being I would take advice from on that matter," Michael clips.

I step in between them.

Asher comes up behind me, wrapping his arms around my waist and pulling me to him tightly. His chin drops and rests on my shoulder. *Clearly, he's marking his territory.*

"Any word on Elizabeth?" I ask.

Michael ignores Asher's stance as his face falls. "Not yet. We are working on a plan of extraction. However, we're awaiting orders from the Angelic Council before we can proceed."

I pull my brows together. "So you're telling me you can't go save her without approval?"

The archangel sighs and leans against the conference table, crossing his arms. "It's not that simple, Eve. There are rules and protocols that need to be followed."

"The same rules and protocols that were followed to keep her safe?" I bark.

"Settle down, siren," Asher whispers in my ear.

"Eve, I understand you are still getting used to our ways, however, this is not a game. I am a warrior of Heaven. Therefore, I need to abide by the Angelic Council's rules and wishes. When I am called back, I go. When I am sent down to the earth realm, I come. My missions are granted by Heaven," he explains.

"I see. So you're saying your life is not your own. You have no choice in the decisions that are made for you. Well, that, angel of Heaven, is something I can relate to." I level him with my stare.

Michael's eyes twinkle with something that looks like pride. "Mr. St. Michael, would you be kind enough to give Eve and me a private moment, please?"

"You okay with that?" Asher's breath tickles my ear.

"Yep." I pop my *p* for effect.

"I'll go make plans for Wiltshire." His voice is filled with promise.

I turn my head and meet his eyes. "Okay," I whisper.

He kisses my temple and lets me go. My gaze follows his retreat until he's left the room, then it swings back to the angel in front of me.

"You really do love him?" Michael says in a soft manner.

"Yes," I blush.

Michael sighs before standing tall. "Though I've made my opinion on the matter clear as the warrior of Heaven . . ." He swallows and trails off. Michael's eyes shift to the right and then back to me. "As your father, I am very pleased with your choice, Eve."

My gut clenches as if I've been punched. I'm not sure how to process the statement. So, I just sit down in a chair and stare at him. "I don't know how to respond to that."

"Which part? That I approve of your boyfriend or that I am your father?" he asks.

"Both." I exhale. "For the record, I think dads aren't supposed to approve of the boyfriend."

This earns me a light chuckle. "Then it would appear I have some research to do on being a father."

"Um . . ." I draw out.

Michael grabs a chair and places it directly in front of me before taking a seat.

"I do not desire to cause you pain, Eve, but I wish you to know that you are so much like Libby. I had not realized it until now. You are strong, beautiful, and full of life and spunk. She has done a wonderful job raising you."

I remain silent while the heat seeps across my face. I focus on fiddling with my nail polish. It's chipping. I really should get it fixed.

"I was there, you know."

"Where?" I ask.

"Throughout your life, though you may not remember, for protection purposes. Many times I had to watch from afar, but I was there, Eve. I held Libby's hand through your birth. I watched you blow every single birthday candle out from age one to eighteen. Each first day of school, I looked over you to make sure you were all right. I experienced every recital, game, and accomplishment you've had over the years. I held myself back from killing the human you picked for your first date. I was present for each and every holiday. I was part of it all."

My eyes begin to sting with tears from the pain of his words. All I ever wanted was a mother and father, and it turns out both were there, all along.

"I realize your path is not easy but you are strong, brave and intelligent. Thanks to Libby. If anyone can fulfill this destiny, daughter of Heaven, it is you. I will still be here, by your side, every step of the way. You can count on me. Libby and I love you very much. We are both extremely proud of the woman you have become. Though we might not have handled our roles in your life very well, know this: we are proud to be your parents," he chokes. "I will bring your mother back to you. Rest assured."

I swallow the painful lump my tears are causing. Wiping them away with the backs of my hands, I nod. "Thank you." It's all I can manage. I'm tired of fighting.

"It truly is my pleasure," he responds.

"Why didn't you both just tell me from the beginning? Why all the lies and the human parents? What was your reasoning?" I question.

Michael rubs his face before his hands clasp in front of him. "In my world, Eve, there are rules. If they are not followed, an angel is sentenced to fall. Do you know what that means? It means that the angel is cast out of Heaven. For some, the punishment is Hell, and for others, it's to live a mundane life on earth. We are bound to Heaven, created to serve and protect. If we break that oath, we are exiled."

"How does that relate to lying to me?" I ask tersely.

"Angels are not allowed to fall in love with humans, let alone mate with them. The moment I saw Libby, though, I was spellbound and charmed by her. Instantly, we fell into sort of a passionate madness, if you will, one that neither of us wanted to end. I told her I would fall for her, in more ways than one." His lips twitch into a sad smile. "However, being the fiercely stubborn woman she is, she would hear none of it." His voice is wistful.

"Angels and humans can obviously have children," I state in irritation.

Michael pauses a moment. "Technically, no, Eve. Only a fallen angel can mate with a human. When they fall, even though they are not granted a soul, they become human. Their offspring are called nephilim. It is, however, uncommon for an archangel and human to produce a child."

"Why?" I ask with a sinking feeling.

"We are created of fire, not human DNA. Therefore, it is normally impossible. This was an exception. The ONLY exception," he reminds.

"So you just left? I guess in this instance, love was sacrificed for duty?" I throw out.

"I'm afraid that even the beauty of love cannot override destiny and responsibilities, Eve. That is the lesson I have been trying to teach you." He smiles to himself. "Although, like Libby, I see that your love for him is endless."

"I will not disregard the sacrifices he has made for me, for destiny," I state.

"It was Libby's desire I keep my position as a warrior of Heaven. It was her wish that I stay in Heaven while she remained here on earth with our daughter. We, too, made sacrifices on your behalf, Eve. When we discovered Libby was with child, our first thought was your protection. You are the only one of your kind. You are the wonderful creation of love between an archangel and human. If discovered, your existence would be ended. The divine would see you as a betrayal of my service. The dark army would see you as a threat. Unlike the nephilim, your bloodline is pure. You have the blood of Heaven like an angel, yet a human soul, which makes you dangerous to everyone."

"So you changed my bloodline?"

"In an attempt to hide you, I had Everley, the cherub, touch your bloodline, altering it. I went to the council and made sure they understood how important your existence is to them, so they would protect you. I knew Lucifer would want you destroyed no matter what. The divine, though—if I positioned you as a weapon to use to tip the balance in the war—I knew they'd protect you with all of the offerings of Heaven. Which they did, until your eighteenth birthday."

I just sit back and attempt to wrap my head around this.

"And Asher's bloodline?"

"I am not at liberty to divulge that information."

"Your plan is flawed because I am human. With emotions and feelings. I was a child, abandoned by her parents. Only to find out it was all a lie." My tone is curt.

"We were protecting you," he says.

"By lying," I retort. "You both should have told me."

"You are correct. For that, I am sorry. We only did what we felt was best at the time."

We sit in silence for a while, both just taking in all the pieces of this fucked-up tale.

"I hope, in time, you will begin to accept and lean on me when you need to," he poses.

"How much longer do we have to wait to get Elizabeth?" I question nervously.

He shrugs. "I'm not sure, Eve. When the council approves the mission, I will go."

I chew on the inside of my cheek. All the scenarios of what Deacon and Lucifer could be doing to her run through my mind.

"How much longer until I finish the ascension?"

"Again, I am unsure. You are the only one in existence. Only time will continue to reveal your abilities and what that means." He stands and his face softens. "I am proud of you, Eve."

When my decision is made, my eyes meet his. I walk to the conference table, and grab a pen and piece of paper. Folding it, I turn and hand it to Michael.

"What is this?" He watches me, expressionless while he reads what I wrote. "Why are you not giving this to your protector?"

"I need your help to confirm the name and their part in this betrayal before I bring it to Asher, because when I do, his world will implode. I will protect him, always."

Michael nods once and morphs into warrior stance. "I will do as you ask, daughter of Heaven. Thank you for allowing me redemption."

21 Surrender

I try not to fidget too much in the passenger seat of Asher's Aston Martin. My stomach has been in knots since my earlier discussion with Michael. I know the archangel is doing his best, but I can't let my aunt—um, mother—continue to be held captive by Lucifer. Nor can I wait any longer for Michael's heavenly army to extract her.

As pathetic as it is, I'm suddenly nervous to be alone with Asher. He glances over to me. My eyes meet his, and his lips tilt in a reassuring smile before returning his focus to the road. I clasp my hands together tightly, going over the plan in my head one last time before I execute it. Asher was right, war is ugly. I sigh.

Twenty minutes later, he turns onto the road leading to La Gargouille Manor in Wiltshire. At the gate, Asher enters the code. The gates creak open, and we continue up the long, birch-lined driveway to the empty estate. Fiona, Gage, and the other members of the London clan are still in London, allowing Asher and I our privacy this evening, which is perfect. I can put my plan into action without their knowledge. By the time they figure out what I've done, I'll be gone.

I exhale, trying to calm my nerves, which are stretched and frayed around the edges. Asher pulls into a parking spot and kills the engine, before his indigo eyes meet mine again.

"You ready, siren?"

I smile. "More than you will ever know, gargoyle."

Asher smiles slightly as he picks up a strand of my hair, playing with it. "Are you sure?"

I take a deep breath and let it out slowly. "You and I, we're forever, Asher."

He nods, releases my hair and exits the car, moving around to my side to open the door and extend his hand. Without hesitation, I place my clammy palm into his and allow him to guide me into the manor.

Once inside, Asher turns and lifts my hand to his lips, planting the softest kiss onto it. "I'll meet you in the chamber in a bit. Go on and relax, and I'll see you shortly."

I nod, knowing that in a few hours, my time with him will be over, forever. "Okay," I whisper, reminding myself that I made my decision.

She needs me.

Asher studies me for a moment, before releasing my hand and walking backwards toward the stairs. His eyes never leave mine. He knows. He has to.

A little while later, I close my eyes and take in a deep, calming breath. I exhale and tell myself to leave all my fears behind as I make my way to the chamber, toward my forever.

કૃ-ૐ

At the top of the stairway, Asher secures the chamber door. The sound of the entrance being sealed causes my heart rate to spike. *Shit. I need to calm down.* I go back to focusing on my breathing.

My skin is burning. Heat crawls all over me. I can't decide if it is warm because of the three oversized, blazing fireplaces or Asher's intense presence.

Slowly, I open my eyes and witness him taking the last stone step before he comes to a standstill a few feet in front of me. His eyes pierce through me, penetrating each layer, ending on my soul. I wet my lips, and his eyes darken with hunger.

The glow from the hundreds of lit candles flickers, casting shadows over my protector's striking features. His focus intensifies. Infatuation-filled eyes move down my body at a leisurely pace, caressing me.

Goosebumps appear on my skin at each place he's branded me with a simple look. My stomach takes a dive at the way he is studying me, like he can read me from the inside out.

Standing in front of the stone state bed, I shiver in anticipation. In this moment, I compel myself to forget the outside world. I push away all thoughts of leaving. I know it will crush him, so this is my final gift. I remind myself that this is how I want him to remember me. Us.

Realization hits me that I'll need to hold onto this memory when it becomes too much—because I know it will. This recollection will become my happy place. The place I'll float to when I need to escape, to feel love and happiness.

Asher's softly glowing eyes lock onto mine, searing me. I savor the effect his gaze leaves on my body. The need to know how it feels to be his rises with each passing second. Heat spreads through me as my body craves him. My love for him is purely dangerous.

Asher takes a step toward me. His movements are slow and calculated. My body hums with exhilaration. When he's within three steps of reaching me, he stops. I close my eyes and completely stop breathing, while talking myself down.

Relax.

Step.

Take a deep breath.

Step.

Not working. I think I made it worse.

Step.

"Open your eyes, siren," he demands.

And that's it. With those four words, I surrender to him. My eyes flutter open and he lifts his hand toward me. My body automatically moves into him. Asher's right hand turns so the back of his knuckles brush down my cheek, over the blush that surfaces. My stomach muscles tighten at the delicate way he's caressing me. I tilt into his touch, needing more.

When his hand hits my jawline, he turns it again, taking my chin between his fingers and lifting my head. He moves closer into my space, still leaving a breath of air between our lips.

"Don't be afraid. I take care of what's mine." His voice is rough.

My throat goes dry, while his fingers drag lazily in a downward motion over my neck, pausing at the base. Holding eye contact, he gently wraps his hand around the lower portion of my throat.

Bending forward slightly, his mouth moves to the side of mine, almost kissing me, but not. He applies enough pressure to walk us two steps back, in the direction of his stone state bed. My pulse beats wildly under the touch of his fingers, his chokehold intimate and powerful.

"You're trembling. Are you sure?" he whispers across my lips.

"Yes," I breathe out.

He releases a rough breath before allowing his lips to lightly rub across mine in a left to right motion, a promise of safety and security. The sensation of his lips and his hand wrapped around my throat, along with his intense stare, are my undoing. I swear to God I almost combust right there and he hasn't even fully touched me yet.

Holy shit.

Asher releases the pressure on my throat and runs his hand down the front of my shirt. Crowding into my space so that our hips touch, he roughly fists the bottom of my shirt then gently drags it up until he's removed it and I'm standing in my white lace bra and matching boy shorts. Both of us are breathing deeply.

His eyes cast downward, releasing my hazel ones as he takes me in.

"Fuck," he exhales, and swallows hard as he admires me like a piece of artwork.

I chew on the inside of my cheek. He's seen me before, but this time is so much more intense.

"I'm so fucking grateful that you're mine," he grits out through a tight jaw.

I don't flinch under his powerful stare or the weight of his words. I hold myself steady, allowing him to absorb me. So that he'll remember . . .

Asher leans over and presses a kiss to my forehead. I close my eyes, absorbing the touch, as he brings both hands up and cups my cheeks. My hands automatically splay across his chest as he bends and takes my mouth, gently at first, stoking the flames as our tongues dance in the familiar way only intimate friends would know, then rough and commanding.

My hands lower to the base of Asher's shirt and without breaking the kiss, he reaches behind his neck and pulls it up. Releasing my lips for only a second, he tugs it over his head before returning to devour me. I open my mouth and dip my head back to grant him access.

My hands roam over him, committing to memory every indentation and muscle. When the sensations become too much, Asher pulls back. With ragged breaths, he slides his hands from my cheeks into my hair as he releases a deep, throaty growl.

Slowly, I move my lips forward to the protector tattoo, letting my tongue dart out and run along the artwork until I reach the scar from my dagger. Once there, I press my lips to it and linger with my eyes closed because it's too much. *God, I love this man with everything I am.*

"Shit," he pants, and fists my hair harder.

Forcefully, he tugs my hair once so my head drops back and I catch his gaze. His tongue darts out and runs across his lips before raking his top teeth over his lip and biting down.

With a wicked expression, he untangles his hands from my hair and slides them down each side of my neck, over my shoulders, taking the straps of my bra with them.

Each band droops on my arm. Asher reaches around my back to undo the clasp. He tilts his head into my neck and begins to suck on the spot under my right ear. I let out a pathetic whimper filled with need, and he steps back.

Our eyes lock and I slowly release the lacey material, so I'm bare to him from the waist up, standing only in my white lace boy short panties.

"Christ, you're beautiful," he rumbles in appreciation.

The intimidating gargoyle moves forward, pressing his hand to the middle of my chest, the pressure a request that I lay down on his stone state bed, and I do, without thought and without removing my gaze from his.

Asher smirks, clearly pleased with my position. His hands move to the button on his jeans as he drags both his pants and boxers over his hips and down his legs, and then steps out of them, at the same time removing his motorcycle boots.

I swallow and arch an eyebrow at the impressiveness of him, again. The apadravya piercing glints in the flickering flames, causing my mouth to water. *I try not to think of all the crazy ways this is actually going to work and just focus on Asher. Clearly, this is my first time.*

His lips tilt into a smoldering grin that pushes all thoughts of logistics away. I watch him with fascination as his vision methodically travels up and down my body before he kneels on the bed and crawls over me. The feel of his weight clouds all common sense, and I revel in all the places we meet.

Asher's hands move to each side of my face as his lips drop, meeting mine in a delicious rhythm. I sigh and lose myself in him completely. Every stroke and caress brings new sensations. One of his hands trails down my body, over every curve. I quiver at his touch. A strong, controlled hand slips inside my panties, his fingers dipping inside me. I gasp as he takes me higher and catches me each time I fall.

He takes his time, with a painstaking amount of teasing. Asher's nose runs over my jawline, up my neck, and toward my ear. All the while, his fingers keep working their magic, sliding in and out of my body while his thumb rubs my nerves in circles. I begin to see stars.

The proof of his excitement rubs against my leg. The smooth silver ball of the piercing rolls over my skin, cooling the heat. My hand caresses his body, causing a deep, vibrating moan to fall out of him.

"Do you like my hands on you, siren?" he whispers quietly into my ear.

"Yes."

"Do you like my fingers on you?"

"Yes."

"Do you want my mouth on you?"

Asher takes my heavy panting and gasping as a yes, and trails kisses down my neck. He shows meticulous care to each of my breasts before continuing his unwavering descent.

Looking up through his sooty lashes, Asher shows me his panty-dropping smirk before looping his fingers into each side of my panties, slowly sliding them down. Once they are off, he sits back on his heels and locks onto my eyes before lifting the lace to his nose. He inhales deeply and groans in ecstasy. *Holy. Fucking. Shit.* I might have come at the sight of that. I can't be sure because I also think I just blacked out.

He gently places the delicate material next to my head instead of throwing them to the side. Holding my eye contact, he brings his fingers to my mouth and waits for entrance.

"Taste yourself, siren," he orders, as his fingers enter my mouth.

I begin to suck as he leaves light kisses down my stomach. Asher removes his fingers and drapes my lower legs over each of his shoulders. At the first stroke of his tongue, my entire body tenses with desire. It's like he flipped a switch and I can't seem to stop it.

He continues with his merciless assault until I've panted, screamed, and come down twice from his mouth alone. While I attempt to catch my breath, Asher plants a gentle kiss onto me, as if apologizing to the spot for the assault of his fingers and tongue. Then he slides his body over mine so we're back at eye level.

Again, his hands come to each side of my head, holding me still so he can search my face and eyes. My hands move to the leather bands on each wrist, wrapping my fingers around them and bracing myself for the final step that makes us one.

He bites his lip as his piercing strokes my entrance. My eyes flutter rapidly in pleasure as my head falls back. *Oh. My. God. I may not survive this.*

"Look at me, Eve," he commands.

I have no choice but to obey. Our eyes connect and his desire-filled face softens.

"Thank you for giving me this." He sighs as he pushes in the tiniest bit, causing my body to arch toward him. "Ilem jur pri tú-tim, ew tú-tim pri pos-tim ali ide in-zen, máni, vas-wís, ew ter-ort. Esta-de ai esta Ilem de, Ilem pos-tim in-saengkt pri, tú-tim," he vows in his Garish tongue.

At his words, my soul lifts to meet his and my heart clenches with absolute love.

"I am forever yours, in darkness and light, tas ámo," he promises.

"I am forever yours, in darkness and light, my love," I repeat in a whisper.

My eyes shift to his protector tattoo. The black lines have turned red. Reaching up, I trace my finger over the design that is now in motion.

"Your blood rose to the top of the mark. It recognizes you as my mate now, not just my charge," he explains. "It will return to black once our souls have united."

"I love you." My declaration is barely audible.

"Forever," he vows firmly, and drops his lips to mine in a searing kiss as he slides into me completely. A sharp, stinging pain shoots through me as I whimper, forcing back the tears. *Holy shit that hurts.* Asher stills, allowing me time to adjust to the sensation of being filled by him.

He keeps my head in place, his thumbs coming to my bottom lip and gently rubbing against it, as he holds my eyes and pushes healing energies into me.

After a brief moment, the pain subsides and makes way for something much more intoxicating. My entire body begins to shake with a deep and intense need. Feeling him inside of me is like coming home. He grins and leans forward, nuzzling my neck. At his movement, the ball on top of the piercing hits the perfect spot, and stronger sensations pulse through me. My head falls back in pleasure and I release a whimper.

"You okay?" he asks in a gentle tone.

"Yes." I exhale a needy breath.

"You feel like pure fucking heaven," he grits out, before lifting his head and locking our eyes as he begins to move slowly at first, and then in a rhythm that causes my body to sing.

Asher's hands roam over me as I arch into his touch. I bask in his scent, the feel of his strong hands on me, and the beautiful way he looks, as if he wants to consume me from the inside out.

I'll etch each of these into my memory and keep them with me, always. Asher lowers his mouth to mine, kissing me so deeply I actually feel our souls swirl and morph into one, uniting us forever.

→←

Wrapped in black sheets and protective arms, I lean up on my elbow. My eyes roam over the beautiful gargoyle next to me. I can't help but smile. The past few hours have been amazing. My cheeks flush as I remember all the incredible things Asher did to make my body hum multiple times before we fell asleep entwined around one another. God, I love this man with everything that I am. He owns me, completely.

I move slightly and wince. Not only are my muscles sore, but my lower back still stings from the angry protector mark that now adorns it. Asher's mark. I frown as a wave of happiness and bitterness crashes through me. All I want is to snuggle into him and fall back to sleep in his protective arms.

Asher's long, dark lashes jolt while his sleeping eyelids hide his indigo eyes. I brush my fingertips over his stubble-dusted jawline. I memorize each line and curve of his striking face. I swallow the painful lump forming in my throat.

"You're about to hate me," I whisper.

22 Dark Fairytale

When I was a little girl, Elizabeth would read me fairytales. They were stunning stories of love, courage and triumph. And in the end, the beautiful princess would always be saved by the handsome prince and live happily ever after.

In truth, fairytales are dark. They're about sacrifice, lost love, and worlds where pure evil exists only to torture innocent souls. The storyteller simply leaves out the suffering, anguish, and loss that the prince and princess experience along the way in order to achieve a happily ever after.

My story is a dark fairytale. Filled with evil, loss, suffering, and loneliness. There is no happy ending for me. Even in the happiest of fairytales, someone must die, be defeated, or suffer in order for the prince and princess to succeed and be allowed to love.

War has begun. Love can no longer be. It's time to make my sacrifice so that this dark fairytale can have its happy ending. Even if that means I no longer exist in the story.

Asher's and my story doesn't end with a happily ever after. What I'm about to do isn't the stuff romance novels are made of. I lean over Asher's sleeping form and place a final kiss to his full lips, carefully so I don't wake him.

"I love you," I murmur against them, fighting back the tears. "If you take nothing else from tonight, remember this . . . I'm yours, forever."

I close my eyes for a moment, begging for strength. Once I'm centered, I open them, lean down, and pull the numbing serum out from under the mattress. I inhale while the tears fall.

As instructed, I let the smallest drop fall into the seam of his mouth, along with my deceit, forcing him to lick them and swallow. Asher does, and my heart breaks into a million pieces.

After he ingests the liquid, I move toward the protector tattoo and work fast, dripping almost all of the remaining serum onto it. My matching mark pulsates in anger at what I'm doing to Asher's. I grit my teeth and force all thoughts of pain away.

I wait nervously for a few moments, knowing that it worked and his body is numb enough because my mark has lost all feeling, matching his.

Once I think an adequate amount of time has passed, I unsheathe my dagger and dip the tip into the last drop of the liquid before throwing the vial onto the floor. *Oh God, I can't.*

The clanking sound stirs Asher. His eyes open slowly as he smiles lovingly at me before his vision slides to the dagger. That I'm holding over his heart. His brows pull together in confusion before he attempts to move.

I watch his eyes widen at the realization that he can't. The serum paralyzed and anesthetized his body. *Crap, I'm so sorry.* I remind myself it's temporary. He'll be fine.

"Siren?" he whispers, as I lift my dagger and let it fall into his heart.

Asher exhales sharply but not in pain, in disappointment. I watch the crimson liquid leak out onto the bed that we just shared. Through our completed bond, I know he's not in pain. He'll heal within an hour. I scream I'm sorry over and over again in my head because I am.

As I was told, the potion works. Asher doesn't turn to stone. After a few moments, he just drifts into a healing stone sleep. Relief floods me that his soul has been ignited. I've breathed life into him and he can't cease to exist. My respite is brief. I remind myself he'll never forgive me for the betrayal.

That's it. My tears descend and mix into the blood staining his naked chest. The combination trickles over and seeps into the protector tattoo maze. At the sight, I let the bloody dagger slip, and it crashes on the floor next to the empty tube.

My heart hurts as I remove his shirt from the floor and clean him up before I pull myself together. I grab the bag that was left for me from under the bed. Quickly, I pull out the dress, wondering why on earth this was chosen. I look around for my shoes and realize not only are there not any in the bag, but I also didn't wear any down to the chamber. *Shit. Stupid, Eve.*

Asher's healing sleep should give me enough time to escape. The rest of the gargoyles have also been immobilized in London, thanks to some internal assistance. I'm unsure if I have enough time to run and grab something for my feet, so barefoot it is.

Once dressed and ready to leave, I turn to Asher once more and remind myself that when it's all too much, and Deacon and Lucifer torture and hurt me, I'll allow my mind to return to the memory of Asher sliding into me for the first time. I'll picture his beautiful face as we came together, united as one. I lean over and kiss his lips one last time, choking on a sob.

I begin my ascent up the stairs, away from the chamber, knowing I have only a few hours before all the gargoyles in the world discover what I've done. This time, they won't come for me. That is exactly how I want it, to protect them.

߬߬

I'm standing on the jagged wall of rocks. My white dress flows around my body like cascading water. My bare feet are sore from the sharp edges of the rock formation, as I curse myself for not stopping to grab shoes.

I look around in bewilderment. *Crap. It's just like my previous visions.* The unmoving trees project their anger at the approach of a stranger. I inhale slowly, needing to move through my fear.

The forest's eyes watch me. The dark spirits scrutinize, waiting in anticipation of my arrival. I sense their excitement. It's unnerving, as their Welsh murmurs drift through my ears.

"Cartref merch Croeso duw," they speak softly.

Welcoming me home. This time, I know better. I'm not home.

The gloomy and lifeless castle appears behind a light layer of fog. I stare at it in apprehension. My heart pounds with each movement forward.

I know what Lucifer wants. He wants me. Without me, all is lost for him and his dark army. I scan the forest, aware this time of who he is and the danger I'm in.

I take a step toward the fortress, then another, and another. Each footstep takes me farther and farther away from Asher, and toward Deacon and the Declan clan.

My eyes close in silent prayer that I'm not too late to save my mother.

I try to focus on Elizabeth as I begin my descent down the uneven path. Faintly, I hear Asher's voice drifting to me, floating like a feather on the air that caresses my soul.

It can't be. He's in stone state healing, I chastise myself, and move forward.

"Come back to me, siren," he whispers on the wind.

"I can't," I answer in a quiet voice, placing my hand over my heart to ease the ache of not being with him.

Fuck, this is too hard.

This is my fate and he can't be part of it. I have to protect him and the London clan at all costs. That's what tonight was about—making them hate me so much, they won't come. I won't survive if they do.

Focused, I keep moving toward the castle.

The voice on the wind reaches me again.

"I will protect you, always," he promises.
I believe him—until he wakes and remembers what I did.
I pray he won't come for me.
Taking in a deep breath, I reach out my hand, and Gage takes it.
"It's time, love. You've chosen."
And so it begins.

EXCERPT FROM REVOLUTION

From darkness comes light. I whisper the assertion in my head, over and over again, as a form of reassurance. Distracted eyes take in my surroundings, seeking out a focal point of luminosity. Nightfall shrouds the ill-omened forest I'm standing barefoot in.

My gaze lifts toward the heavens, searching for light. There is nothing. No stars shining brightly to guide me. No flush of the moon's silver rays caressing the ominous tree-lined confinement I find myself in. Panic begins to claw at my throat.

Everything is unnaturally still. The trees are motionless. There's no breeze to embrace me. No woodland creatures at home to calm me. Only silence. It's eerie and yet oddly familiar.

"Hidden within the darkness, the unseen will eventually be divulged, revealing the true purpose of your existence." Gage's deep, masculine voice penetrates my trepidation.

I shift my body and tilt my head, meeting a pair of sea-green irises. The gargoyle clasps his warm fingers over mine in a soothing gesture, while the scent of cigarettes and spice drifts over me. His presence rescues me from the shadowed corners my mind finds itself in.

I inhale, for what feels like the first time tonight. A small smile appears on my lips at the sight of the good-looking protector. Gratitude washes over me, because I'm not alone on this self-imposed journey.

The moment of reprieve passes quickly when I remember who I am and what I've done. At the thought, a sharp, unyielding pain presents itself deep within my heart. The sting causes my breath to hitch as my hand moves to cover the twinge.

In the distance, a faint, familiar sound floats over me. "Come back to me, siren," it whispers. The memory of how much hurt I've caused seeps in. "I will protect you, always," the voice, belonging to Asher St. Michael, my gargoyle protector, and now my mate, promises. My stomach lurches at the recollection of my actions this evening. My treachery.

Instantly, I fold at the waist and vomit into the plant life lining the forest's floor. Gage steps closer to my uncontrollably trembling body. Releasing my hand, he gently holds my hair back, allowing me to empty the contents of my stomach into the undergrowth. *Shit.*

"You're okay, love. It's just the adrenaline wearing off. Take deep breaths," he soothes.

I close my eyes, trying to block it all out, as my body hums from the protector blood bond. In rapid fire, images of this evening flash through my mind, each one cutting my soul like the dagger I used in my deception. All I can see is Asher. My dark prince. My everything.

Asher's gentle hand wrapped around the lower portion of my throat, showing dominance. The feel of my gargoyle's body pressed against mine, pushing me into his stone state bed. The stunning and blissful expression he had as he slid into me for the first time. His scent. His touch. His declarations of forever, all marred by my deceit.

I've ended us by showing my disloyalty. When his indigo eyes met mine, my dagger fell into his heart, forcing him into a healing sleep. Protecting him. Then, I walked away from my love to save another whom I hold dear to me. My sacrifice.

A shiver passes over me and my breathing becomes ragged. My stomach churns again and my knees buckle. If it weren't for Gage's large hands wrapped around my waist, I would collapse in despair on the dirt-covered pathway.

Crap. Pull yourself together, Eve.

"Are you all right, love?" Gage questions quietly into my ear, holding me close.

Once the visions dissolve, so does the nausea. I open my eyes to meet Gage's troubled ones. Taking a step back, I allow for some distance from his protective arms. Then I center myself before pushing back my shoulders and lifting my chin.

"Yes," I say firmly.

He knits his brows together, while running a hand through his golden-blond hair. "Are you sure, Eve?" he questions, with worry lining his voice.

I'm actually taken aback by his apprehension. Normally, Gage doesn't show signs of unease. It's unnerving, and making me question my resolve. I straighten and nod once.

"I said I am." My voice is strong, even though inside, I'm terrified.

The unreadable gargoyle's gaze searches mine. His features are strained, and marred with disbelief.

"I really am," I assure him and attempt to turn my attention to the mist-covered fortress in front of us. I don't want to see his troubled expression.

Gage doesn't let me twist though. Instead, he snatches my chin roughly and tips my head back. His gaze roams over my face before locking onto my eyes with a raw intensity. "With every moment that goes by, they turn a deeper shade of indigo, love," he whispers.

My breath hitches and I slam my lids down, hiding the irises. Asher and I triggered our mate bond and fulfilled the divination of redemption. My light ignited and awakened his soul, protecting him from stone petrifaction. I was so concerned with his safety that I failed to remember his mate mark wouldn't be the only change to my body. My eye color changed from hazel to blue, the clan's hue. *I really should have read more paranormal books. Crap.*

Opening my eyes, I take in a deep breath through my nose. The memory of my intimate night with Asher disappears. His mate mark angrily pulses on my lower back, alerting me to Asher's emotional state. He's pissed. *Of course he is. Why wouldn't he be?*

Gage sighs in annoyance. "One look at you, and the Declan clan will not be able to overlook the fact that you are the dark prince's mate."

My eyes narrow in response. "Not fully. Abby told me that the mark and eye color are temporary until my new mark is infused with Asher's blood. If that doesn't happen, with time, both will disappear and release him of our soul connection. That's what needs to happen, Gage. I only did this to protect him from the council and dark army."

Gage releases a hollow laugh that sounds more like a bark. "You're naïve, daughter of Heaven, to think you gave yourself to him in the name of protection only."

My teeth clench in aggravation. "You said you would help me. I need to extract my aunt Elizabeth from Lucifer before he kills her. I'm the one he wants. It's my role to save her. By any means necessary. Asher wouldn't have let me do this, you know that."

He holds my gaze for a moment in contemplation.

"Don't you mean your mother?"

"What?"

"Ever since finding out that Elizabeth and Michael are your biological parents, you continue to refer to her as your aunt. She's your mother, Eve. You are her flesh and blood."

I pull my chin out of his grasp. "Fine. I need to save . . . my mother." As the words tumble from my lips, my stomach sinks at the recollection that both the archangel and my guardian, whom I've known since birth as my aunt Elizabeth, lied to me for years before recently revealing my biological lineage.

"Are you going to help me or not?" I snip impatiently.

Gage's focus shifts from me down the haze-filled path, toward the ominous castle that belongs to Deacon, the leader of the Declan clan. Since Gage was the half-demon, half-gargoyle's right-hand man for a short time, he is the only one who knows of its location, which is why I entrusted him to assist me with this plan.

My eyes follow his line of sight, landing on the stone fortress, and unease trickles down my spine. The last time I was here, Deacon was holding me hostage. Despite the bad blood between the two, Gage had helped Asher and his family, the London clan, with my rescue.

Deacon's entire focus has been to hand me over to Lucifer and the dark army. He killed Aria, my best friend and college roommate, while she was protecting me—after which both Deacon's brother Kaiden and his mother Dimia died doing his bidding.

I shudder at the thought of what he'll do to me this time, knowing that Asher and the St. Michaels won't save me. Stabbing Asher, the future king of the gargoyle race, in the heart with my daggers was the ultimate betrayal. I've ended the protection the clan offered.

Releasing a slow breath, I remind myself that I'm the weapon created by Heaven to tip the scales in their favor and bring redemption to the world, ending this centuries-old war.

Heaven sees me as a pawn, but for Hell, I'm a threat to their very existence. It's why they're hunting me. If not restrained, I have the power to destroy the dark army. This time, though, I'm going to make it easy and surrender, exchanging my life for Elizabeth's.

Chewing on the inside of my cheek, I wait for his answer, deciding then and there, with or without his help, I'm still doing this. It's my fault that Deacon and the demonic legion kidnapped my mother to get to me. Gage faces me with a soft look. I can tell he's made his decision.

Silently, he extends his hand for me to take, and I do, causing relief to flood through me. The grip he has on me tightens, almost painfully, as he yanks me harshly to his chest. Without warning, his gray wings snap out from his back. Gage's face morphs into one of regret.

My expression turns to one of confusion at his sudden coldness, wordlessly questioning him.

"Sorry, love." Gage whispers in my ear before disappearing with me in his possession.

GLOSSARY

Tas ámotas: My love (Garish)

ágra-lem: warrior (Garish)

DIALECT TRANSLATIONS

Aperi, ex imperio auguratricis Lunette: Open at the command of Sorceress Lunette. (Latin)

Ego praecipio tibi, ut liberare custodia clausum invernerunt: As the guardian of the scroll, I command you to release the lock. (Latin)

Venit hora, et filius hominis, ut ostendat divination Evae filia redemptionis: The time has come to show the daughter of Eve and the son of Adam the divination of redemption. (Latin)

Ilem jur pri tú-tim, ew tú-tim pri pos-tim ali ide in-zen, mání, vas-wís, ew ter-ort. Esta-de ai esta Ilem de, Ilem pos-tim in-saengkt pri, tú-tim: I promise you forever, and forever you shall have my heart, soul, mind, and body. With everything that I am, I will protect you, always. (Garish)

Cartref merch Croeso duw: Welcome home Daughter of God. (Welsh)

ACKNOWLEDGMENTS

Many thanks to my husband and daughter for enduring my deadlines, crazy conversations with my characters, and endless ramblings about plot and character lines. Thank you for your support and love.

My girlie Kris Kendall. You're the only one who I will allow to touch these damn gargoyles because I know you love them as much as I do. Even though, at times, I do catch you playing favorites to Gage. Best. Editor. Ever! Kristin with Indie Solutions by Murphy Rae and Liz Ferry Editing, thank you both for polishing the storyline so that it shines.

A big thanks to the team at Bravebird Publishing for, once again, producing the most amazing cover an author could ask for. A huge hug to Hang Le for all the branding she's designed and I've drooled over. Jeff Senter with Indie Formatting Services, the interior looks beautiful.

As always, a special thank you to the beta readers: Sara Dustin, Maureen Switalski, Terri Thomas, Theresa Hernandez, Heather White, Meghan Tate, Kayla Clinton, and others, for your continued dedication toward this series and these characters.

I'm neither going to confirm nor deny that the contest sayings from *Pick Callan's Next Apron Saying*, were created after a few rounds of margaritas during a day of tailgating at Jimmy Buffet. That said, thank you to all the fans for voting.

I'm humbled by your love and support for these characters and this series.

A big shout-out to Kelly Tannacore, who won the opportunity to name a character in *Redemption*; Everley the cherub is forever in your debt.

Nichole and the team at *YA Reads* and all the amazing bloggers, who ALWAYS host my books with enthusiasm and love, there are not enough words to show my appreciation. Thank you all for being warm and accepting of this series. You have been so kind, and supportive of these books and me, I can't thank you enough. Please be sure to support book bloggers because it is truly something they do out of love for the written word.

Randi's Rebels, you all ROCK! Thanks for supporting the Revolution.

As always, my deepest gratitude to the readers, thank you for taking a chance on this series. I'm humbled that you've embraced it as you have. It's been a journey of self-discovery, love and sacrifice for not only these characters, but me as well. Thank you for allowing me to be a part of your reading library and literary world!

ABOUT THE AUTHOR

Randi Cooley Wilson is an author of paranormal, urban fantasy, and contemporary romance books. Randi was born and raised in Massachusetts where she attended Bridgewater State University and graduated with a degree in Communication Studies. After graduation she moved to California where she lived happily bathed in sunshine and warm weather for fifteen years.

Randi makes stuff up, devours romance books, drinks lots of wine and coffee, and has a slight addiction to bracelets. She currently resides in Massachusetts with her daughter and husband.

She loves to hear from readers, please reach out to her at: **randicooleywilson.com** or via social media outlets:

Twitter: @R_CooleyWilson

Facebook: www.facebook.com/authorrandicooleywilson

Goodreads: www.goodreads.com/RCooleyWilson

Randi's Rebels: www.facebook.com/groups/randisrebels

46188041R20184

Made in the USA
Middletown, DE
25 July 2017